THAT GUY

A SWEET AND SEXY ROMANTIC COMEDY

KIM JONES

This book is dedicated to all the ladies out there looking for their That Guy.
And to all the ladies who have already found him.

CHAPTER ONE

Never in a million years did I think I'd be running down a sidewalk, bag of steaming dog shit in my hand with one pissed off owner and one really fast Golden Retriever on my heels.

People in Chicago take shit way too seriously.

What kind of person decided it was a good idea for everyone to make a habit out of picking up a hot dog turd? The park here even provides these little complimentary bags in a dispenser that has a picture of a dog holding a plastic bag in his mouth filled with his own shit.

In my small hometown of Mt. Olive, Mississippi, nobody cares where your dog craps. If you happen to step in some, you just scrape your foot on the grass until you get most of it off. If you walk in a store and see people sniffing the air, saying, "I smell dog shit" it's a natural reaction for everyone to check their shoes. Then it's a courtesy for the victim to say, "It's me." And everyone else nods in acknowledgment and points to the nearest grassy spot around.

Right now, home feels like a million miles away.

I dodge a parking meter and nearly mow down a woman with a stroller. "Sorry!" I hold my hands up and jog backwards as I continue to apologize to the woman. She glares back at me as she squats down by the stroller and unzips the screen to check on her baby. I feel ten kinds of terrible. Until the little Chihuahua cranes it's tiny, scarf swaddled neck toward me.

For fuck's sake...

Stupid Chicago.

Stupid dog.

Stupid shit.

Stupid Luke Duchanan.

It's been years since I acted a fool in Target and had to take an anger management course. But I can still hear the voice of my coach in my head every time I get pissed.

"Now Penelope, it's not anyone's fault but your own that you're in this situation. Let's reflect on your actions that got you here."

Yeah. Let's do that.

Luke Duchanan stole my best friend's heart while she attended a summer internship program here in Chicago. Six months later he crushed it when she caught him with his dick in another woman's asshole. She moved back to Mississippi. In with me. And I've had to hear her cry and sniffle and sob and watch her drink all of my damn wine for the past two weeks.

So when she told me Luke had a dog shit phobia, I knew what I had to do. I had to max out my credit card. Fly to Chicago on the eve of the biggest damn blizzard the state of Illinois has ever seen. Put some dog shit in a bag, set it on fire on Luke's porch and video him stomping it out.

I upload the video. It goes viral. I ruin Luke's life. Make my best friend, Emily, smile. We go to a bar. She retells the story to a guy who's hotter than Luke. They bang in the parking lot. Emily gets over her broken heart. And then she moves the fuck out of my apartment.

Simple, right?

Wrong.

Why?

Because it's a struggle to find dog shit in Chicago, Illinois.

When I closed in on the huge pile of crap, my arm rolling six complimentary plastic bags deep, the owner asked me what I was doing. So I told him.

"Look man, I just really need this dog shit, okay?" I didn't think he would chase me through the city, yet here we are. And there's no damn way any of that is my fault.

Stupid anger management.

The dog's bark becomes louder. I chance a look over my shoulder and they're close. Too close. I take a quick left at the corner onto an even busier street lined with cars. The direction of the wind hits me head on and I'm blasted with arctic gusts of air so damn cold I swear I can feel pneumonia in my lungs.

Out of breath, cold, legs burning, chest hurting, I make a bad decision. I yank open the back door of a black limo and dive onto the back seat. No sooner than the door closes behind me, the owner and dog pass the car. I breathe out a sigh of relief.

That lasts all of two seconds.

I'm in someone's car.

It's all rich black leather and soft seats. Clean carpet and blacked out windows. Fancy decanter filled with amber liquid. Tinted partition. *Is the driver on the other side?* Of course he is.

"Miss Sims?" The voice booms through the speakers and I freeze. "Mr. Swagger asks that I drive you back to his apartment once you've finished shopping. Would you like to go there now?"

Swagger? *Mr. Swagger?*

My eyes move to the intercom. To the door. Back. "Yes, please."

Why did I say that? In that accent? I am not British. Or Australian. And I'm not sure which of the two I replied with. I always get them confused...

"Very well, Miss. We'll be there soon."

The car pulls into traffic and I have a three-second freak out.

What have I done?

I'm so stupid.

This car is so warm.

I could use a drink.

Fuck it.

The bag of dog shit hits the floor and I squat-wobble to the bench seat across from me. The decanter is heavy and hard to manage. I wrangle it between my legs and pull hard on the cork. When the suction gives way, my hand flies back and smacks me in the face.

"Son of a bitch!" I clear my throat. "Son of a bitch!" I repeat, in accent.

The whiskey is so strong it singes my nose hairs when I take a big sniff. I'm not sure if that's a good thing or a bad thing but I pour a glass anyway. Or a finger. Whatever they call it. I contemplate adding ice, unsure of how this is supposed to be served.

I wish they had beer.

This gasoline they call liquor burns all the way to my toes. But it has a nice, smoky flavor that lingers on my tongue. Anxious for the next sip, I finish off the glass and by the time it's empty, I feel warm all over. And a little more confident in the bad decisions that placed me here.

I mean, what's the worst that can happen? I rode in a car. There's no law against catching a ride to escape the blistering cold. If I get caught, I'll just frown and tell them I'm poor.

That's not a lie.

I am poor.

Which is another reason I made this trip—though I'll never admit that to Emily.

In addition to my seek-and-destroy plan, I'm hoping to find my perfect muse so I can finally write that sexy, cliché romance I've been attempting for months. The kind of romance with the hero who I refer to as *That Guy*.

You know, the super-rich, powerful CEO who is beyond sexy. Lives in a penthouse. Is wicked in bed. Has a driver. A big cock. Is kind of an asshole, but really he's not because he harbors some major secret that you find out at sixty-five percent, which explains all his past demons that reveal why he is the way he is—therefore completely redeeming himself and making all the readers who hated to love him swoon.

The car stops.

"Miss Sims?" It's the intercom voice again. "Would you like me to walk you up?"

"N-no. That won't be necessary."

Why do I keep using that accent?

"If you don't feel comfortable with the concierge—"

"The concierge is fine. Thank you."

On cue, the door opens and a gloved hand reaches inside. I take the offered hand, grab my bag of shit and exit the car.

The sudden blast of strong winds causes my eyes to water. My fingers squeeze and I cast a side glance to the man next to me. He offers me a polite smile and a nod. I look up, up, up at the massive building, then back at him.

"What kind of apartment has a concierge?" My voice carries away in the wind as he pulls me into the lobby. I stop just inside the door and stare. The snow and ice on my ruined Uggs melts into the dark rug as I take in everything. Mouth hung open like an idiot, I scan the entry and all its opulence.

Soft, cream-colored furniture arranged in a semi-circle faces a gray stone fireplace that stretches all the way to the top of the high ceilings. The orange and red flames inside the hearth dance and sway to the faint sounds of classical music that plays throughout the room. I want to stick my hands and frozen ass to the fire, then sprawl out like a cat on the thick rug in front of it.

"This way, Miss Sims."

I follow the man through the room. My boots squeak against the marble floors and leave a trail of dirty water in their wake. I twist my head up and around. Everything is gold and glass. Accented with hints of yellows and grays. From vases to hanging lights, sculptures and paintings, the place radiates a magnificence far fancier than anything this small-town girl has ever seen.

"If you need anything at all, don't hesitate to ring me." Alfred—I shit you not that's what his name tag reads—comes to a stop in front of a massive elevator door. The solid, flat black color is a stark contrast to the other four elevator doors that are mirrored glass tinted in gold. As he slides a card through the little back box next to the door with a big "P" over it, I chance a look into one of the mirrors.

My curly brown hair sticks out all over my head like broken twigs and falls over my shoulders to the middle of my back. My "all weather" jacket that's appropriate in Mississippi is nothing more than a raincoat in Chicago. And my once fashionable skinny jeans, are now soggy and sag heavily on my hips. Stretched out from being worn so long, one might think a covey of quails just flew out of the ass of my pants.

The elevator door glides open and Alfred gestures with his hand for me to enter. I snap back to reality.

"Alfred..." I reach out and grab his arm.

The corners of his mouth dip to a frown and his eyes widen.

"I have a confession to make."

He pats my hand and his anxiety disappears, replaced with a warm smile. "Say no more. I already know."

"You do?"

"Of course. And don't worry...*Miss Sims.*" He leans in and drops his voice to a whisper. "Your secret is safe with me." He straightens and winks at me. "Mr. Swagger won't be back until noon tomorrow. You'll have the place to yourself. Enjoy it."

Is it possible that this man knows I'm not Miss Sims?

Does he often let strangers invade this man's home without question?

What kind of person is this Alfred?

I step inside the elevator. The doors close and I skyrocket to the top of the building so fast, I have to reach out and hold onto the railing for support.

I hate elevators. There's something terrifying about being in an enclosed space, dangling above the ground in a heavy metal box suspended in the air by nothing but wires and pulleys and...*what if the power goes out?*

My nose finds the wall. I close my eyes and hold on tight, humming my favorite song to keep from passing out. Finally, there's the telltale ding and the doors are opened. I step out into a small hall with a table decorated with the biggest damn vase of flowers I've ever seen. A solid wood door with a sleek, golden handle stands beyond the table.

Without the pressure of a driver or a concierge or a man and his dog, I have the time to stop and think about this shit.

If I open that door, I could go to jail. And though I know jail is a possibility in the event Luke Duchanan catches me on his property, trespassing won't be near as serious of an offense as breaking and entering.

I call Emily.

"Yeah?"

Damn. She sounds awful.

"Hey Em. How you holding up?"

She sniffs a couple times and I hear what might be a laptop closing. "Luke just posted a picture of him and his new slut on Facebook."

"Yeah? Well, she's ugly."

"No she's not."

"Want me to punch her in the face? Make her ugly?"

Emily sighs then blows her nose. "No. They're on a date. Looks like our prank isn't going to work. They'll probably be out all night." Her voice cracks on the last word.

"I can still do it tomorrow." The hopeful hint in my tone does nothing to ease her. She wants me to abort. To come home so we can drink wine and eat chocolate. But I can't leave. My curiosity demands I find out what's on the other side of the door. Research demands it. The good Lord does too.

My eyes zone in on the golden handle of the door. It shimmers like an angel's halo.

Things like this don't happen without help from a man like God. Maybe this is His plan for me. Maybe that dog was in that park for a reason. Maybe the owner was an angel who chased me to the very place I needed to be. That car? It wasn't waiting for Miss Sims. It was waiting for me. Alfred? He may be an angel too. What if Mr. Swagger is my *That Guy?*

Now, I understand.

I've been divinely favored.

I'd explain this to Emily, but she just wouldn't get it. She'd tell me I needed to stop allowing my imagination to take over. *Why did I even call her?* She's way too emotional to be of any help.

My mind is made up.

"I gotta go, Em. I'm at my room."

"You have a room? When did you do that? Why? How?"

I roll my eyes at her questions.

Emily likes to stick to a plan. She's one of those people who keep a calendar. She never strays from it. If Jesus shows up on the same Thursday as her dentist appointment, I have no doubt she'll tell him he has to wait. *"Sorry, Jesus. You're not on the calendar."*

I don't own a calendar. My plans change depending on the conditions. I'm supposed to wait out my flight in a crowded airport. Fate has decided that I stay in a luxurious apartment instead. The circumstances have been altered in my favor and I refuse to ignore them and deny myself this opportunity.

"Penelope..."

"What?"

"You can't afford a room."

"Sure I can."

"How?"

"I called and got a credit increase on my card." A lie. But the truth will bring questions I don't want to answer. Which will turn into more lies.

"But...how?"

"Don't question the unexplainable, Em. Just go with it, okay? I have to check-in now. I'll call you tomorrow. Fuck Luke Duchanan."

There's a pause before she releases a breath. "Fuck Luke Duchanan."

I end the call.

Put my hand on the door.

Offer up a quick prayer of thank you, an apology for all the bad things I've done and a promise to not curse as much in the future to show my appreciation for what I'm about to receive.

Then I turn the handle and walk inside...

"Holy-motherfucking-shit."

CHAPTER TWO

I 'd like to go on record and say that I lied.

But really...what did God expect?

I'm standing inside the minds of millions of readers. This place is the penthouse of every rich hero in every romance novel. Open floor plan. Floor to ceiling windows overlooking downtown Chicago. Hardwood floors. Spiraling staircase with glass rails. Artsy shit hanging from the ceiling that I'm pretty sure is just a fire hose that's been sprayed with gold paint.

I toss my jacket to the floor and kick off my boots and pants. Wearing nothing but a sweater, I pad further into the room. My hand slides along the back of the white, leather couch, dips to touch the mahogany table beside it. Then flattens against the curved glass that stretches the length and width of the entire wall. It's warm to touch. Not cold, as I thought it would be.

The view.

OMG the view.

Lights twinkle and blaze against the backdrop of a clear, black sky. Buildings staggered in height and lit in an array of colors loom high over the streets dotted with the smaller lights of moving cars. It's almost overwhelming. The idea of waking up to this in the morning—watching as the sun rises behind the buildings...

This is so worth going to jail for.

If the rest of this place is as miraculous as the view, I might have to stay until Mr. Swagger gets home. Then I'll make him fall in love with me. Shouldn't take long. I'm a good catch.

I toss my bag of shit on the bar and open the massive, stainless steel refrigerator. It's stocked with the type of groceries that can only come from one of those fancy whole food stores.

Both doors opened wide, I snap a picture. I close them and get a few more pictures of the kitchen and all its state of the art appliance glory. Then I take a picture of the view. The living room. Long, glass dining table.

"Yeah, baby." I drop to one knee for a different angle. "That's the one. Smile for the camera."

To the right of the kitchen, there's a small bathroom that really could be a little more elaborate, but it's nice enough. Another door off the living room leads to an office. I recognize the aroma of spice and the hint of eucalyptus. Mr. Swagger smokes cigars.

Visions of my *That Guy* sitting behind his desk wearing nothing but a cigar and a smile causes desire to pulse through me. I want to dry hump his chair and rub my vagina on the walls to mark my territory.

Chill, pervert.

My eyes drift to the tall shelves lined with endless books that stand on either side of the door. A massive, wooden desk sits across on the other side of the room facing the entrance. I take a seat in the thick, leather chair. I spin until I'm dizzy, then check all the drawers. They're locked.

No computer. No stationary. No personalized pens. I lift the big, gray rock on the corner of the desk that I guess is a paper weight. I touch the lamp and it lights up. I touch it again and it brightens. Six touches later, it starts to dim. Then I have to touch it eight more times just to turn the damn thing off. The only other item on the desk is a sleek, black phone with no cords that must be from the future.

I take a picture.

Upstairs, there's a guest room with more of the same fancy décor shit. I roll across the bed that's probably never been slept in—messing up the pillows as I do. My elbow bangs on the light gray nightstand that matches the other furniture in the room. It hurts like a bitch.

I trail my finger across the soft, white curtains on the wall opposite the bed. Behind them is another view of downtown. It's a different part of the city but is still just as pretty as the view from the living room.

Back in the hall, I pass a door bigger than the rest with a small keypad next to it. I squeal when I try the handle and find it locked.

OMG...

It's a sex room.

I just know it.

Filled with all sorts of torture devices and spanking benches. Walls the color of red. Shackles and crosses and nipple clamps, oh my!

I skip to the last door and nearly piss myself. It's the master bedroom. Or suite. Whatever. It's the epitome of a CEO's bedroom. King sized bed. Navy, silver and wood accents. Another view. An oversized chair and ottoman where *That Guy* sits and reads the paper. Puts his shoes on. Or cradles a sub after he spanks the shit out of her.

There's a walk-in closet lined with CEO suits. I sniff them. Drawers of ties and watches and folded socks and white button downs and boxer briefs. I touch them all. Shoes that I can see my reflection in. I smudge them with my fingers.

"Ray Donavan, meet Christian Gray."

I take a selfie with all the cool shit in the background. I'll put it on Instagram later.

#guesswhereIam

Nothing can compare to the master bath. Of course there's a shower that will easily accommodate twenty people. A massive Jacuzzi tub. A towel warmer. Double vanity. Linen closet big enough to sleep in. But no one ever talks about the toilet.

Ever.

And this toilet?

It's a toilet fit for a king.

Not only does it sit at just the perfect height, but it's in a small nook all to itself with a door for privacy. There's a magazine rack. An iPad. The fanciest damn toilet paper holder I've ever seen. And if you close the door, there's a T.V. behind it.

A T.V.

A damn T.V.

In the bathroom.

The damn bathroom.

I spend the next two hours of my life in the bathroom. First, on the awesome toilet that comes equipped with a censored courtesy flush. Then in the shower. Then a long, hot soak in the Jacuzzi.

Every once in a while, my nerves get the better of me and reality infiltrates my mind with stupid questions.

What if the real Miss Sims shows up?

What if Mr. Swagger comes home early?

With each worrisome thought I find something new to distract me. Like the button on the side of the tub that illuminates a touch screen which allows me to control the temperature of the water, the lighting, the music and the pulse of the jets.

I let the sweet, instrumental music take me away and the jets lull me nearly to sleep until I'm like a raisin. Then I get out. Put on a little *Maroon 5*. Grab a towel from the warming rack. Almost die from a heat stroke. Lie down on the floor in the hallway to cool off because the tile in the bathroom is heated. And then I saunter naked into the closet and pick out one of the white, button down shirts that is a million percent cotton and feels like clouds on my skin.

"Sugar" plays—my jam.

I jump on the bed like it's a trampoline. Fall flat on my back and look up. I wonder if this is what Miss Sims would do. She obviously doesn't live here. Or if she does, she doesn't dress here. Unless her room is the locked room. What if she comes home?

Don't think like that.

She will not come home.

This is God's plan.

He will not let her come home.

But what if Mr. Swagger isn't the Mr. Swagger whose babies I want to have? He might be ninety. Batshit crazy. And smell like mothballs—which I highly doubt considering his clothes smell like the richest, most wonderful scent of clean with just a hint of the kind of cologne you can't even get at Macy's.

He's not old.

He can't be.

Remember....

This is God's plan.

I trust God. Really, I do. But I search the apartment for a picture of Mr. Swagger anyway. Just to be sure. After digging through every drawer and looking in every room, minus the locked one, I come up empty handed.

In the office, I use the phone and hit the button labeled, *concierge,* and Alfred picks up on the second ring.

"How can I help you, Miss Sims?"

"Y'all got a restaurant here that's open?"

"No, Miss. We don't have a restaurant on site. But I can certainly refer you to one in the area."

"Well, I don't really feel like going out. And it seems the only restaurants in this part of town are really expensive..." *What kind of apartment has a concierge but not a restaurant?*

I flip my hair over my shoulder. *This place is so cheap.*

"No worries there, Miss Sims. I can assure you there's not a place in the city that I can't order from. Whatever you want is available."

Wow. Mr. Swagger has the hook-up. Which means as his guest, I do too.

"Might I suggest Alinea? They have the finest salmon and terrine Chicago has to offer."

What the fuck is terrine?

"Um...well I had that at lunch. You know any good pizza places?"

"Of course, Miss Sims." I can hear his smile. "Tell me what type of pizza you prefer and I'll give you my opinion of the best."

"Yeah, I just like pepperoni with lots of cheese. And lots of pepperoni. And Dr. Pepper."

"Very well, Miss. I'll put the order in right away and will ring you before I come up."

I hang up with Alfred, take a spin in the chair, stumble into the living room and curl up on the couch with the big fluffy blanket that's draped across the ottoman. A scary movie seems fitting. But I can't figure out how to turn this damn T.V. on. I'm still struggling with it when Alfred arrives with my pizza.

He turns on the T.V., shows me how to dim the lights and even offers to get me a glass from the kitchen for my drink. Then he leaves with his signature instruction for me to call him if I need anything.

That damn Alfred...such a nice guy.

If I ever decide to write one of those age-play stories with the hot, older man who plays "Daddy" to the chick in her twenties, I'll use him for my muse.

It only takes me an hour to figure out it is not a good idea to watch a scary movie in a place that has floor to ceiling windows with no blinds or curtains.

Every few minutes, I look over my shoulder and have a mini freak out thinking the creepy bitch from the movie is staring back at me. Then I realize it's only my reflection—not some grotesque woman who could use a shower and some leave in conditioner.

I settle back into the couch that looks like something from the Star Trek Enterprise but is actually quite comfy. I throw my leg over the back of it and pull the blanket up to my chin—ready to cover my eyes the next time something or someone in the movie jumps out of a dark hallway.

I'm fully prepared to have the shit scared out of me. But I'm not at all prepared for the voice I hear on the other side of the door, or the soft click of the lock as it opens.

You know that moment when terror seizes you? When your stomach drops and your heart stops and you hear a faint whistling deep in your ear because you're straining so hard to figure out just what the noise that has you so terrorized actually is?

That's where I am.

"What the..."

I can't be any more afraid than I am in this moment. Perhaps because of that, my brain takes on survival mode and focuses on something other than my fear—like the deep tenor of the booming voice radiating around me. Then a light comes on, temporarily blinding me, and after I blink through the shock, my brain begins to process the person that voice belongs to.

And holy mother of fuck.

It's him.

That Guy.

CHAPTER THREE

I could tell you the sight of him has my nipples tightening.
Thighs clenching.
Heart shattering.
Pussy watering...

But there's no need. Because when you see this guy, you're going to experience all of that shit yourself.

Cue walk out music. Maybe something by *The Weekend*. Or the theme song from *Jaws*.

Standing 6'2, weighing in at two hundred and thirty pounds, wearing an Armani suit and a look that would kill me dead if it was lethal, I give you...

Shit.

"Are you Mr. Swagger?"

His hands move to his hips. "Yes. I'm Jake Swagger. Who the fuck are you? And what the hell are you doing in my house?"

"One sec." I hold my finger up and fall back against the couch, breathless.

Jake...Jake Swagger.

It just doesn't get much sexier than that.

"What?" *Oh man, he's even sexy when he's confused.*

"I just, I just need a minute for my head. It's a writer thing. You wouldn't understand."

I disregard his incredulity. I overlook his anger. I completely ignore reason. How can I not in a moment like this?

Before me stands a man with messy, charcoal colored hair. You know, the kind he runs his fingers through. The kind you fist your hands in when he has his mouth suctioned to your vagina.

His jaw has all those masculine features that authors use words like chiseled, strong, square, dusted-in-hair-as-if-he-hasn't-shaved-in-a-day, to describe.

Lips ripped straight from Tom Hardy's mouth.

A nose that can't be defined because, who the fuck knows how to describe a sexy nose.

And those eyes? Blue like the ocean—maybe. I can't see them from here. And they're narrowed in curiosity? Lust? Probably anger...

My gaze moves south. Over the small dimple in the center of his chin. Down his Adam's apple that bulges slightly when he swallows. Lower to the little bit of chest visible from the opening at the collar of his white shirt.

The dark suit jacket hugs his long arms. I follow it from his shoulder to his wrists. *Son of a bitch he's wearing cufflinks.* And a belt. Hard, flat stomach above it. Outline of a big cock below it.

Long legs.

Hard thighs.

Shiny shoes.

You get the picture. But in case you didn't, Jake Swagger is really fucking hot.

And super fucking pissed.

"Who the fuck are you?!"

I shake away my stupidity and scramble to get up. The half empty pizza box slides from my lap to the floor. It lands right side up—next to my dirty napkins and the two-liter Dr. Pepper bottle.

I stand in front of him and a shiver of fear snakes up my spine from the silent anger he emits. I want to disappear back into my writer brain. Run away from reality and build a perfect, fictional world where he is my *That Guy* and I am his heroine. But there is no escape from his scrutiny.

Dressed in nothing but his shirt, he has a full view of my legs. My collar bone. The top swell of my breasts. And Jake Swagger doesn't just flick his eyes over my body. He drags them heatedly over every inch bared to him. He might be angry, but there is no mistaking that he is a man who likes what he sees.

As he should.

I've been killing myself at the gym. It's about damn time somebody notices. And who better to notice than my That Guy?

His attention settles on my face. "Do I know you?" He tries to place me. Like maybe he's seen me before. *There's only one reasonable explanation to that...*

"You probably know me from *Saving Forever.* It's a book I wrote years ago. I'm kind of a big deal author. I mean, I haven't written anything in a while, but I still have fans and a bunch of followers on social media. I did a podcast once. Back in like, 2014."

"No. I don't know you. Is that my shirt?"

I frown down at the pizza sauce on his shirt. I lick my finger then scrub at the stain. *Damn scary movie...making me drop shit.*

While I'm scrubbing away, *That Guy* turns on his heels and disappears up the stairs without a word.

I glance at the wide open front door. It would be a good time for me to bolt. But I really want to sniff him and see if I can put a name to his scent. I've come this far in my research. No point in quitting now. Besides, if he really is *That Guy,* he'll feel sorry for me and we'll fall madly in love before he has a chance to know everything I've done.

I'm folding the blanket and throwing it over the back of the couch when he comes back down the stairs.

"You went through my house?"

"What?" I snort laugh—something I always do when I need to kill time to try and think of an answer. "Um. No." I twist my fingers in the hem of my shirt and avoid eye contact. "I mean. Not really. Hey..." I tilt my head to the side and meet his gaze. "What's really behind that locked door? Are you a dominant?"

He doesn't admit it, but when he straightens to full height and his hands fall from his hips and fist at his side, I know.

And I swoon.

"How did you get in here?" He doesn't ask. He says it in a way that lets me know that he'll strangle me to death if I don't tell him.

"Well, it started when I accidentally got into the wrong car."

"MotherFUCKER!"

He explodes and I stand in silence as he picks up his phone. He shouts to someone to get up here now, hangs up and dials someone else. It must go to voicemail because he tells that person to call him back.

He places his phone in his pocket and his eyes land on the bag. The one I left on the counter.

He starts to pick it up.

"I wouldn't—"

He gives me that "shut the hell up" glance. I think his eyes are more of a dark gray. Or green. I should get closer. Or keep my distance considering he's holding the bag now.

Putting it close to his face.

Sniffing it...

"Is this..."

"It's dog shit."

He drops the bag as if it's poison. He composes himself, clears his throat and wipes his hands on a towel he retrieves from a drawer. "Is there a reason you have a bag of dog shit on my bar? The bar where I fucking eat?"

"Wow," I breathe, shaking my head back and forth in awe. "You have a really nice voice. So controlled and deep. You should be a narrator."

"Why the fuck would you put a bag of shit on my bar? Are you out of your goddamn head?" *So much for controlled...*

"Dude." I hold my hands up. "It's just dog shit. You don't have to be such an asshole. Some people would run through the streets of Chicago during a blizzard for that very bag of dog shit."

He might explode again.

You know how in romance novels the heroine always just "knows" the hero would never hurt her? Like she can sense it about him or something? I'm looking for that in him. Not real sure I'm finding it.

The door opens and we both turn to find a middle aged man dressed in a suit and a hat like those limo drivers wear.

"You wanted to see me, Mr. Swagger?"

Mr. Swagger. That name really does fit him.

He points a long, manicured, possibly skilled, finger at me. "Ross, who the fuck is she?"

Ross looks at me, then back at Mr. Swagger. "Miss Sims, sir?"

"Do you really think this *country bumpkin, hillbilly hick* could be Miss Sims? She doesn't look like Miss Sims. She doesn't sound like Miss Sims."

I might take offense at his attempt to sound like a country bumpkin, hillbilly hick, if it wasn't so damn funny. Or if I didn't have the pressing need to defend Ross—who I now know is the driver.

"He didn't see me. And I used an accent." They both look at me. "I mean, the chances of that actually being *her* accent are like, crazy. I'm not even that good at it. I don't know if I'm Australian or English...By the way, who is Miss Sims? Do y'all really call her *Miss Sims?* Like, she doesn't have another name?"

They're staring at me like *I'm* crazy when Alfred walks in.

"Mr. Swagger, I can assure you this was just a terrible mix-up." Alfred cuts his eyes at me. The disappointment there has me feeling real guilt for the first time since I got here. "I've never seen Miss Sims." *What the hell? Does nobody know what this lady looks like?* "When the car arrived, I just assumed the lady inside was her. And she tried to—"

"I tried to get him to give me the key, but he wouldn't," I cut in. If my assumptions about Jake being *That Guy* are accurate, then he's the kind of asshole who will fire Alfred. Of course he'll rehire him once he discovers he was wrong and Alfred was just doing his job. But I'd hate for the old man to be out of work while Jake comes to his senses.

"Get out of my house. Both of you."

The men shoot me a cold look. Like they're mad. At me. The one who just saved their asses.

I should leave too. But I need that bag of dog shit lying at Jake's feet. I move to get it and he halts me with a lift of his finger.

"Not you. You're not leaving until I know exactly what happened."

"Okay first, you have *got* to stop talking in that tone. I mean it really just—"

"*Talk,*" he barks.

I viscerally jerk at his tone. "Fine! Okay...so my best friend was doing a summer internship here. She met this guy and they dated all summer and when the internship was over, she moved back home but they did that long distance thing. But we both know that never works out." I pause for him to maybe agree or something. He doesn't.

I clear my throat. "She came to visit him and found out he was cheating on her with a chick he'd had here in Chicago the whole time they were dating. So, because I'm a good friend, I came here to avenge her broken heart."

I point at the bag on the floor.

"I stole that dog shit so I could light it on fire on his doorstep. See, he has this really weird dog shit phobia. Anyway, I was chased through the city by the dog and his owner. And when I rounded a corner and saw a car sitting there waiting, I jumped in to hide. I was going to get out but then Ross offered a ride to this mysterious Miss Sims that no one has ever seen, and I accepted, needing to get as far away from the deranged man and his dog as possible.

"When I got here, I was going to leave. But I'm writing a book about a millionaire CEO who has an apartment like this. I've been dying to find my muse and just—*look* at this place! I mean have you seen these windows?"

I point at the windows, and Jake Swagger just stares at me with *the* look—you know the one.

"Uh, okay, yeah so you've seen them. Anyway can you blame a girl for staying here to do research? Didn't think so. Especially since I was going to be gone before you got home, which was supposed to be tomorrow at noon. But you came home early. So I feel like if all of this is anyone's fault, it's yours, Mr. Swagger."

He stares at me. A little dumbfounded, I think. I'm not good at reading emotions. But his jaw twitches. And his neck is red. This little vein in his forehead appears above his right eye.

Okay. Maybe that's not surprise. Maybe that's rage.

"Get out."

How strange is it that his voice is so very calm when he is literally shaking with anger?

Or lust.

Nope. It's anger.

"You know, I'd be happy to stay for dinner," I offer, even though it's three in the morning.

His body stiffens. He gapes at me as if I'm mad. I'm not, really. I'm just an opportunist. Speaking of opportunity, I've managed to casually take a few steps closer to him in hopes of catching the color of his eyes. Now that I'm only a few feet away, I can see that his eyes are a gray/blue/green.

"You're lucky I'm not calling the police."

I quietly listen to his rant while I breathe deep to catch his scent. They make it sound so easy in the books. They lie. From two feet away, I can't smell a damn thing.

I take a step closer. He takes a step back.

"What are you doing?"

"I kinda want to tell you, but sorta don't. I'm pretty sure you'll freak out. But I'm only doing it because you're that guy, you know?"

"What guy?"

"THAT guy!" I point at him. All gorgeous. Just like the books say. Intimidating as shit too. He's even got the hair right. The stance. The height. Width. Breath of shoulders. So perfect. Like he just stepped out of one of those—

"Get out of my house. And make damn sure I never see your face again."

I jerk at his angry growl and quickly nod. "I completely understand. How about a hug?" *Surefire way to smell him*...you know? For research. Only chance I might ever have.

Holding open my arms, I take another step forward. He takes another step back.

"Get the fuck out of my house!" *So explosive!*

"Geeze. Okay." *Panty-melting, too. Ugh. Why do I like the difficult ones?*

"And take your dog shit with you!"

"I am!" I shoot him a really nasty look and grab my bag of dog shit.

I stomp away. Barefoot. Half naked. Horny...

My face morphs from a scowl to a frown. Eyes wide, lip trembling, I give him my best poor face. "Mr. Swagger?" *Wow. There's even a quiver in my voice. I'm so good...* "Do you mind if I use your dryer? My jeans got wet and—"

He stalks toward me on a mission. *To kill me?* I refuse to risk my life just for a sniff, so I jump over the couch and sprint to the door—grabbing my clothes in my haste.

For a moment, I contemplate faking a fall just to see if he'll help me up. That fades when he gets within reaching distance of me.

"Wait! My phone!" I yell before he can slam the door. He snatches my phone off the table and tosses it to me. I fumble with my boots and jacket and lunge for the damn thing. I catch it, because I'm a Ninja, but it still pisses me off.

"You're a real asshole!"

He slams the door—not even bothering to make eye contact as he looks down at his own phone. I throw my shoes at the door, feeling a little bit of satisfaction at the dried mud that scatters as I do.

I glance at the door as I shuffle into my damp jeans and pull on my wet sneakers. It should only take seconds, but I drag it out longer. Part of me hopes he'll open the to see if I'm still here. Even if he only does it to yell at me, I wouldn't mind seeing his face once more before I leave. Maybe I could even snap a picture.

The door never opens. Disappointed, yet not at all surprised, I step into the elevator and place my nose in the corner. I try not to dwell on what will happen if the brakes on this bastard fail, and instead think about how lucky I am.

He didn't call the police.

He let me walk away.

What would have happened had I came home and someone was in my apartment? I would have freaked. Unless of course my intruder looked like Jake Swagger. Then I would have forced him to have sex with me in exchange for me not dialing 9-1-1.

The instant I clamber out of the death trap, I'm met with a still-pissed Alfred. He sneers and I have to bite my cheek so I don't tell him how unattractive it is.

"Mr. Swagger wants you off the premises immediately. So instead of waiting for a cab, he's instructed Ross to drive you to your hotel."

Alfred's anger makes me feel like shit. I could've cost him his job. My actions might still result in consequence for him.

"I'm sorry, Alfred. Truly. I never meant to get anyone in trouble."

His hard gaze softens the tiniest bit. It's not much, but at least it's something. He nods once and turns on his heel. I follow him into the lobby. On the other side of the glass that stretches the front of the building, everything is white. Snow continues to fall in slanted, thick sheets.

So this is what a blizzard looks like.

A lesser woman might cry if she found herself in my situation.

But I don't cry.

Ever.

Am I disheartened? Feeling a little defeated?

Yes.

But it's going to take more than a lot of snow and a really hot dickhead to make me cry.

Alfred looks down at me. His disapproval evident. He disappears through a door then returns with a hat and coat. "It's not the most fashionable, but it's better than what you have." I take the offered clothes without looking at them as he picks up the phone next to the podium. "What is the name of your hotel?"

"I don't have a hotel. My plane leaves in three hours."

He nods. "Ross, would you mind driving...*the young lady* to the airport, please? Yes. Okay. Thank you."

"I'm not going to the airport, Alfred."

Once again, his look is disapproving. But his anger has dissipated. "You're not? You don't have very much time to do anything else."

"Don't care. I came here to Chicago to do something and I aim to do it."

"Really? And what is that?"

I lift the bag in my hand. "Set some shit on fire."

CHAPTER FOUR

I'm grateful for the hat and jacket Alfred gave me.
Really. I am.
But I look like an idiot.

The "jacket" isn't a jacket at all. It's one of those floor length trench coats that has as many pockets as it does buttons. And the "hat" isn't a beanie or a ball cap. It's a top hat. With fuzzy little ear muff things. Add that to my ruined boots, wet pants and Mr. Swagger's white button down, and I look like a damn hobo.

I apologized to Ross the moment I got in the car. He responded by asking for the address to where I was going. I gave it to him, then halfway there, I realized I didn't have a lighter. Or a paper bag. When I asked Ross to stop at a 7-11 first, he shot me an angry glare through the rearview mirror. Still, he pulled into a convenience store without a word. I didn't expect him to be there when I got out, but he was.

Maybe that was his way of accepting my apology.

I peel away the paper bag from the forty and shove it in the pocket of my coat to keep it dry. When I do, something sharp stabs at my finger. It's the corner of a business card. I pull it out and study it as I chug my beer.

Jake Swagger.

The name looks even hotter than it sounds embossed in silver lettering on the black card. The only other thing on the card is a number.

Like the bag of shit sitting beside me, I want to set the card on fire.

Instead, I bury it back in the front pocket of my coat. Not because I want to remember my time with Jake Swagger, but because I can use it for my research. I'll design my *That Guy's* business card to look as sleek and sexy as this one.

The car rolls to a stop outside Luke Duchanan's house. Ross stares straight ahead without as much as a glance in my direction. His lips pressed into a thin line.

"Ross, I really am sorry. I didn't mean to get anyone in trouble. You seem like a nice dude." After a moment, he clears his throat and gives a tight nod—still not meeting my eyes.

I step out and close the door. The car disappears and I'm left standing in the snow, at three in the morning, buzzed and all alone in a big city by myself. The dark street intimidates me. But the nightlight on Luke's porch shines like a beacon—reminding me that all the shit I've been through on this trip will be worth it just to see Emily smile.

And retell the story to a stranger.

Fuck him in a parking lot.

Fall in love.

Move the hell out of my apartment.

I'm such a good friend.

I slip and slide and almost break my neck on the icy steps. Before I make it to the top, the rest of my forty ends up down the front of my jacket. At last on the porch, I toss the bottle over the railing, pull the paper bag out of my pocket, untie the plastic one, transfer the dog shit and grab my lighter.

The small awning over the door provides no shelter from the sheets of ice and snow that blow in sideways. So I kneel down and use my trench coat to block the wind while I set the bag on fire.

The shit really catches fire. Blazing scary hot and flaming like nobody's business. I grab my phone and hit record. Then I ring the bell and bang on the door over and over and over until I hear footsteps inside and the voice of Luke Duchanan demanding that I "hold the fuck on."

My plan goes off without a hitch.

Luke opens the door. Sees the fire. Stomps the bag in his fancy ass house shoes. Then the vile fumes of the warm and toasty dog shit wafts into the air and hits the back of Luke Duchanan's throat just as he pulls in a deep breath of shock.

Initiate gagging.

Witnessing this grown man scream like a girl in between dry heaves and tears is greater than I imagined it would be.

And I've got it all on video.

And it's epic.

Even I, future bestselling author extraordinaire, couldn't just make this up.

I'm so entertained by the scene before me, I don't even notice the two approaching officers until they're next to me. Stuffing my phone in my pocket, I try to maneuver around them, but it's a small porch. And they're pretty big guys.

"Okay, lady. Come on. We've warned your kind about snooping around down here," the cop grabbing my left arm says.

Another cop grabs my right arm. "I can smell the alcohol on her. How much you had to drink tonight? You high?" He shines a light in my eyes.

"Do you know this lady, Ma'am?"

I blink past the spots in my vision and look at the woman in the doorway. She must be the new bitch. Emily was right. *She's not ugly at all*. She's actually really pretty. All sweet and rich looking in her satin robe with her perky nips trying to bust through the fabric.

"No. I've never seen her before. I don't think my fiancé knows her either." *Fiancé?* "I'll ask him, but I'm pretty sure she's just another bum."

"May we speak to him, ma'am?"

"He's...indisposed at the moment." Somewhere in the house, I hear Luke retching and can't help but hide my smile. She narrows her eyes at me. Damn. She has some really great lashes.

I drop my head. If she's done as much research on Emily as Emily has on her, she might recognize me from Emily's Facebook pictures. As much as I want to take credit for pulling off the oldest prank in the book and for Luke to know it was me who caused his great freak out, I'm smart enough to know that everyone assuming I'm just some drunk bum is probably for the best. Besides, he'll know it was me when I upload the video.

"We've been seeing this a lot in the neighborhood. The cold weather always brings the stragglers out of hiding. So we were patrolling the area when we saw the fire. Glad it wasn't any worse."

"Yeah, me too," the *fiancé* says, stretching her neck like a damn giraffe to try and get a better look at me. Leaning heavily against the cop on my right, I dip my head even lower.

"We'll take her downtown and let her sober up. If you want to press charges, you need to do it before nine tomorrow morning."

"I don't think we'll be doing that."

I should be thankful, but I'm kind of pissed at her indignant tone—like I'm not worth her time. Fuck her. I'm good enough to press charges against...

"Have a good day, Ma'am." I catch the officer ogling her tits and roll my eyes. He stares longer than any gentlemen would then leads me down the steps. I glance back at the pile of ash and unburned dog turds and feel a strange sadness.

We'd bonded...me and that bag of shit. I'd miss it.

I'm forced to look away when the officer places handcuffs on my wrists. Then, with his hand on my head, lowers me into the back of the car.

As the adrenaline wears off and the numbness fades, I realize how damn cold I actually am. I shiver and shake. My teeth chatter and my head twitches. This only adds to my alcoholic bum façade and even earns me a sympathetic look from the officers who talk as if I'm not in the car.

"Was that dog shit or human shit?"

"Never can tell with these people."

"Did you see how that Duchanan prick freaked out? Funniest thing I've seen in a while."

"Who the hell falls for that, anyway? It's the oldest trick in the book."

"Hey sweetheart..." I don't acknowledge the cop. "I'll buy you a week's worth of liquor if you can pull off your little stunt at 2189 West Beutreau Street. Hell it'd be worth two weeks' worth of liquor to see my ex-wife stomp out a flaming bag of shit."

They laugh, but they don't know how hard dog shit is to come by around these parts.

Just as I start to get warm, they drag me back out into the cold and inside the police station. I've been to jail a couple of times. Nothing serious, but I've spent a few nights in county for some unpaid tickets. Been arrested once or twice for disorderly conduct. So I'm surprised when they don't take any of my personals. Or take my picture. Or my name.

They simply lead me to a big cell that faces the front offices. Bunk beds line the wall, but only one is occupied. I'm given a pillow, sheet and blanket, gently pushed inside and then the door slams shut behind me—waking the only other person in the cell.

She's as big as a damn house. Looks as mean as a rattle snake. When I try to take the bunk across from her—so I can keep one eye on her at all times—she shakes her head. I move to the next bunk. She shakes her head again. It continues like this—me stopping at a bunk, looking to her for permission, her shaking her head, me moving along to keep from having my face bashed in.

At the last bed in the back of the room, she lets out a grunt and rolls over. I make the top bunk the best I can and climb in fully dressed. It doesn't take me long to figure out why she forced me to sleep back here. It's colder than a damn witch's tit.

I pull out my phone and I have one percent battery life left. So I watch the video of Luke Duchanan freaking out until my phone dies.

And it's the best damn thirty-seven seconds of my life.

CHAPTER FIVE

I wake up to my cell mate staring at me.

Her feet are flat on the floor and we're eye to eye.

This woman scares the shit out of me.

"You're snoring."

I hate when people snore. I know how annoying it can be. So I apologize. "I'm sorry. I'll roll on my side." I start to roll away from her, but she shakes her head.

"I got a better idea."

"Really? Rolling on my side usually works. My grandma used to make my grandpa—"

"Stop breathing."

I stare at her in confusion. Her stare tells me if I can't stop breathing on my own, she can make it happen.

I draw in a breath and fill my cheeks with air. She nods in satisfaction and stomps back to her bunk. The springs groan beneath her weight when she shifts on her side so she can watch me.

Just before I lose consciousness, the door to our cell opens.

"You." The cop points at me. "Let's go."

I untangle myself from the blanket and jump down. As I pass my cell mate who growls at me, probably because she can hear me breathing, I do something really stupid.

"Your breath smells like a fart," I hiss, shooting her the finger. Before she can get out of her bunk, I'm safely out of the cell and the door is closed—trapping her inside. I smile because I'm a free woman and she can't kill me.

"Sit." The officer points to a metal folding chair that sits in the aisle next to his cubicle. I sit down as he pours a cup of coffee and hands it to me. He tosses a plastic spoon, a couple packets of sugar and some powdered creamer beside it.

I fix my coffee while he takes a seat and starts punching the keys on his keyboard with only two fingers. He looks bored. His suit is too small. Glasses smudged. Hair combed over a bald spot.

Leaning back in the chair, he crosses his arms behind his head and stares at me. "The guys who picked you up said you started a fire on someone's porch."

I nod and take a sip of my coffee.

"Wanna tell me about it?"

I give him an edited version of the truth—starting at the part where I arrived at Luke's home. It takes me a while to tell the story because he can't stop laughing. And he keeps interrupting me by repeating everything I tell him in the form of a question. By the time I'm finished, he's fighting to hold in his laughter and I have the urge to punch him in the face.

"Look," he says, once he can speak without smiling. "Since you were only picked up on a minor infraction, I'm gonna let you walk...if you can find someone to come pick you up."

"Can't I just leave on my own?"

He shakes his head and gives me a hard look. "I'm doing you a favor. Don't push it."

"What if I don't have anyone to come get me?"

"Then I'm gonna have to book you. And feed you. And it'll cost money. And I don't want to do that."

I wouldn't mind being booked. I could serve my sentence, have some breakfast and use the time in solitary to figure out how in the hell I'm going to get home, since my flight left three hours ago. Problem is, I pissed off my cell mate. So now, either I find someone to come get me, or I die.

My eyes move to the front pocket of my coat. Part of my brain screams at me that it's a bad idea. The other says this is better than death.

The officer drags his phone across the desk and sets it in front of me, then leaves—telling me he'll be back in a few.

I pick up the receiver and punch the numbers in quickly while I still have the nerve. Someone answers on the first ring.

"Mr. Swagger's office." The lady speaks in one of those annoying high pitch tones only pretty people have.

"Hello, this is Penelope Hart. I'm a friend of Mr. Swaggers." It just came out. I couldn't stop it.

"How can I help you Miss Hart?" The woman sounds bored. I feel stupid. I'm probably not the first person to call his office and say I'm his "friend."

"Um...Well..."

I can't do this.

My shaky hands fumble with the receiver until I get it back in the cradle.

How could I be so stupid?

So reckless?

So...just...stupid?

Jake Swagger wouldn't come get me. He hates me.

His loss.

If he had invited me to stay for dinner, he could've gotten to know the real me. I could've charmed him. Made him love me. The he would've forced me to get a restraining order against him, because men tend to cling to a woman like myself.

But he missed out on all of my fabulousness and chose to only acknowledge the bad things—like me breaking into his apartment and putting a bag of dog shit on his counter. So the only thing Jake Swagger might do for me is send his lawyer down here to press charges. He'd make sure I lived out my final moments with Big Bertha who will no doubt sit on me and breathe in my face until I die a slow, agonizing death.

I'm on my third cup of coffee. I have no clue where in the hell the cop is. The clock on the wall says he's been gone for over half an hour. I could probably just sneak out the door without anyone noticing—if I wasn't wearing a ridiculous top hat that has earned me a bunch of funny looks from everyone in the office.

Thanks a lot, Alfred.

I stare at the card in my hand, contemplating calling the cell number listed on the back. Jake's cell number. I could hear his voice. Maybe apologize. Or I could just wait until I get home and drunk dial him. If I make it home.

Think Penelope!

Emily.

Emily knows people in Chicago. Right? She interned here. Surely she made a friend or three other than Luke Duchanan. Perhaps she could call one of them and get them to come pick me up. Then I could get my mom to wire me some cash to get home. I know she doesn't have it to spare, but she'll no doubt make it happen. And I can sell body to some desperate man to pay her back. Or my soul to the Devil. Or my imminent fame to the Illuminati.

"Penelope?"

I look up at the man standing over me. And just...stare. He's like, That Guy's hot best friend. The one who wears the smirk. Has the playful attitude. The sexy look. The one you're hoping the heroine's best friend will hook up with so there will be a book two.

My eyes roll at my stupid writer brain. "Yes?"

He scans me from my top hat to my dirty boots, studies the card in my hand a moment and then meets my gaze. He lifts a brow. "You're Penelope?" I'm not sure if that's amusement or skepticism. I get them confused.

"Yep. And you must be Captain Obvious."

He laughs and reaches for a bottle of water next to the coffee pot. With his back to me, I give him a full body scan.

Nice ass. Nice build. Big feet. Friendly. Charming. Seems like the kind of guy you could have a good time with. Yet there's something off about him. He wears a gun but not a badge. A suit and not a uniform. *A detective?* But his suit is really nice. Fitted. Not the cheap twill that most detectives wear. And he doesn't have a gut. Or tired, worried lines around his face.

"I can pull it out and let you look at it." I jerk my eyes from his crotch to his smiling face. I was looking at his ass. He turned around. Not my fault.

"Sorry, I don't have my reading glasses."

I'm treated to another throaty, sexy laugh of his. If I wasn't so hooked on the vision of my *That Guy*, I'd use this hunk for my muse.

"Touché, Miss Hart. You ready to get out of here?"

"Who are you?"

He grins and sticks his hand out. I shake it. Of course it's warm and strong and all the wonderful things masculine hands are supposed to be. "Cam Favre."

"Detective? Officer? Lieutenant?"

"Just Cam. But you can call me *sir* if you want to."

I ignore his waggling eyebrows. "So if you're not a cop, what are you?"

"I'm a real boy," he says, in this really impressive Pinocchio voice that has me smiling. "Come on. Jake cooked breakfast."

Oh shit.

"J-Jake sent you to get me?"

"Yeah." He points to the card in my hand. "Said you called the office. Line got disconnected. Must be the storm. But we traced the number back to here."

"You *traced* the number?" *Oh my God. What kind of guy is this Jake Swagger that he can trace a number and have someone here to get me in less than an hour?*

"Caller ID, babe. Ever heard of it?"

I'm so stupid.

I should probably ask more questions. Like who is this guy really? Who is he to Jake? His lawyer? Brother? Friend? Lover? And why in the hell would Jake want me to come to his house? Why is he cooking breakfast? He should have a cook that does that. A middle aged woman who is having a secret affair with Ross. Or Alfred.

"So you coming or you want to stay here?"

"I'm coming. I'm coming."

He shoots me a sexy grin as he scans me from head to toe. "Even through all those clothes, I can tell you have a wicked little body to go with that pretty face and sassy mouth. Now I see why Jake is so anxious to have you."

Have me?

What does that mean?

I can't think because Cam is walking and I'm struggling to not look at his ass.

I lose the battle.

But I only look for a second. •

An SUV with the engine still running sits parked next to the building. Not your normal cop SUV. A damn Range Rover with blacked out rims, windows and a bumper that could take out a tank.

He opens the passenger door and I'm assaulted with the scent of cologne and leather. So intoxicating. So erotic. So...panty melting that I glance in the back seat wondering if I stripped naked and laid down across it, would it be enough to convince Cam to handcuff me to the door and have his way with me.

I really need to stop reading them damn dirty books....

I stare out the window at the white scenery to avoid looking at Cam.

We're not even out of the parking lot though when his voice has me turning in my seat to face him.

"You're...different."

"What do you mean?"

His eyes flit from the road to my top hat.

I pull it off and try to smooth my hair. "It's a long story."

"I bet you have a lot of good stories considering your line of work." He winks, like he knows some big secret.

I'm sure Jake told him I was a writer. No doubt he Googled the title of my book the moment I left. Which is probably how he figured out my name. I want to tell Cam that there's nothing very suggestive about a writer having a lot of good "stories." But I don't want to sound like an asshole.

"Yeah. I guess I do." I shrug my shoulders and look back out at the passing city.

Cam's phone rings and as much as I want to eavesdrop on his conversation, I can't get the idea that something isn't quite right about all of this out of my head. Why would Jake save me? Why is he anxious to have me? Why would he allow me back into his house after so rudely kicking me out? Is he cooking breakfast because he feels guilty for denying me dinner?

"Jake's going to be pissed about this, Lance," Cam says on a laugh. As if Jake's anger brings him joy. Since Jake's anger has a similar effect on me, I tune in to the conversation. Of course, it ends the moment I do.

"What's Jake going to be pissed about?"

"The FAA has grounded *all* flights out of Chicago."

Good. Maybe I'll be able to reschedule my flight without having to pay for it. Which means I won't have to rob a liquor store on my way out of town.

"Was Jake going somewhere?" I feign nonchalance.

Cam shoots me a disbelieving look and an eye-roll. "Nah. He rented donkeys for the two of you." *What?* "We expected cancellations with commercial flights, but they just announced that no plane would be cleared for departure. Which means even the almighty Jake Swagger can't get permission to put his bird in the air."

"He has a plane?"

He gives me another sideways glance. "You feeling okay?"

Am I?

I'm a little cold. A lot of tired. And I'm starting to get the sniffles. "I'm fine." He doesn't need all of that other information.

Cam's on the phone again. Something about a generator that needs to be replaced ASAP. *Boring.* But I listen. Did you know backup generators can have backup generators? *Wonder what happens when the backup to the backup goes out?*

We pull up at Jake's apartment building and Alfred is all smiles. Until he opens the door and sees me. Undeterred by his scowl, I'm give him my best pageant grin as I slide out of the car.

"Good morning, Alfred. So great to see you again. By the way, this hat is bitchin'. I've gotten so many compliments on it."

Cam laughs as he steps beside me, twirling his key ring on his finger as he pulls open the door. Alfred just grunts a response and begrudgingly holds open the door to the building for us. He doesn't follow us to the elevator this time. Instead, he moves behind the podium and snatches up the phone. As Cam and I continue down the hall, I hear him say, "They're on their way up now, sir."

"Never known Alfred to frown at anybody." Cam lifts a brow at me as we step into the elevator. Then, as if he just thought of something, he gives me a wolfish grin. "You two got history or something?"

"Or something."

In the elevator, I press my nose to the wall and hum as we shoot like a rocket to the thirtieth floor. Cam says nothing, but I see him smile as we step into the foyer.

My gut churns and twists. I think I may vomit. Not from fear like a normal person. From excitement. Like the crazy person I am. Okay, and maybe a little bit of fear.

Is Jake going to tell me he's sorry for being a jerk?

Or demand I pay for his shirt?

Take me in his arms and hold me?

Or sell me as some sex slave?

Kiss me on my head and tell me I'm pretty?

Or blame me for some shit that's missing? Some secret shit. That he lost. And his plan is to set me up to take the fall...

Cam opens the door and...bacon.

I smell bacon.

All the bacon.

My mouth waters and I moan. Then I moan for a completely different reason.

Before me stands Jake Swagger. At a stove. Dressed in nothing but a pair of low-slung flannel pants, spatula in hand. His back ripples in muscles and tanned flesh. His shoulders are wide. Hips narrow. Everything cut and sculpted, yet soft and smooth. The pop of bacon grease and the low voice of the news anchorman are the only sounds in the room.

I instantly picture this moment as a real-life, cheesy Hallmark movie—snow falling outside the window. Everything warm and homey. I'm fresh out of bed, sleepily admiring my prince who got up early just to cook me breakfast.

Of course I can only imagine this because I've already scanned the room for mafia and shady looking people who might want to kill me for stealing something I really didn't steal. There's no one. Just me. Jake. Third wheel Cam. Air. Opportunity...

My mind goes from a PG rating to triple-X rating in a matter of seconds when Jake's muscles contract as he slings a dish towel over his shoulder. I imagine me over his shoulder. Legs around his neck. Vagina in his face.

He pivots to face me. I smile. My cheeks flushed from my dirty thoughts. Eyes half-mast from lust. But I can play it off. Like maybe I just woke from a nap. Like in my Hallmark fairytale. He'll say, "Good morning, beautiful." I'll be all shy and sweet. He'll say my blush is pretty. Then kiss me breathless...

Sigh.

I can't believe I'm really here—me. Penelope Hart. Author in progress. Standing in the kitchen of a luxurious sky-rise penthouse apartment, with my very own, half naked *That Guy*.

And who could be his hot best friend.

And no mafia.

And bacon.

And not even divine intervention could ruin this moment.

CHAPTER SIX

J ake Swagger is *not* God.

But damn can he ruin a moment.

He faces me with no smile. Instead, I'm met with a look of utter horror and disgust. No, *good morning, beautiful,* either. Only a, "What the fuck is she doing here?"

"What?" Cam asks. Jake and I stare back at one another as he continues to speak. Jake looks like he might detonate. I study the two little red dots on his second and sixth ab. *Bacon grease splatters?* Probably. *Who the hell fries bacon shirtless?*

"You said pick her up and bring her home. I assumed home was here. Did you want me to take her to the other apartment?"

Squee! He has two apartments.

Jake sobers. Grows an inch or two in height. His muscles tense. Forehead vein protrudes. Fists clench. *He's such a dominant.* "You're Penelope Hart."

I refrain from using my Captain Obvious joke again. And from asking him if I can touch his chest. Or to abandon his calm, deep tone and say my name again like he might if he was coming.

"I am."

"You called my office."

"I did."

"You told them you were a friend of mine."

"People really toss that word around too much. I blame Facebook. I mean, how many of your *Facebook friends* are truly your *friends?*"

"We're not Facebook friends."

"No, we're not."

"We're not real life friends. We're not acquaintances. You're not even a friend of a friend."

I tilt my head and narrow my eyes at him. "You sure about that? I bet I'm a Facebook friend of a Facebook friend. You'd be surprised how small this world really is. Especially when you have a social media presence like I do. I have like, four thousand likes on my page. And I've hit my five thousand max friends limit."

Several moments of intense silence pass. Then Jake points a spatula toward the door. "Get out."

"No...I'm not going to...*get out.*" I cross my arms over my chest to hide my trembling fingers. "Not until I know what's going on. You're the one who had me picked up. I want to know why."

"Because I thought you were someone else."

"Wait...you know another girl named Penelope Hart?"

"I thought you were Miss Sims."

Now I'm really confused. "But I told them my name was Penelope. You just asked me if I was Penelope so you knew my name wasn't Miss Sims."

"For fuck's sake." He runs his hand through his hair and huffs out an exasperated breath. "It was a misunderstanding on my part, okay?"

"How the hell did you mistake Pah-nell-ah-pee Harr-ttt for Miss Sims?"

"It's an alias! The name Miss Sims is an alias!" he shouts to the ceiling. "Mother of fuck, woman. You're like a goddamn fungus!"

I smile. I can't help it. "Because I'm growing on you?"

Jake's eyes close. He's trying to control his temper. Doing a damn good job of it too. The silence is intense. Cam's laughter breaks it.

"Wait," he says, in between bites of bacon and sexy chuckles. "She's not Miss Sims?" He points at me and looks at Jake who just glares at him. He's probably thinking what I'm thinking. *You're just now figuring that out, genius?* "Well who is she? How do you know her?" His hand pauses halfway to his mouth and his eyes roam over me from head to toe.

"You're fake Miss Sims." His attention shifts to a silent, brooding Jake for confirmation. "She's the one who faked everybody out? Who broke in here last night? This girl? This one? This is the one you claim is batshit crazy?" He wiggles his finger toward me again.

"Okay, now just hold on a damn minute." I hold a palm up toward each of them. "Let me get this straight. You sent a car to pick up a woman whose name you don't know and whose face you've never seen. Gave her full access to your *penthouse* apartment. Told your staff to cater to her every need. Was willing to bail her out of jail...cook her bacon, and you think *I'm* crazy?"

"That was Jake that called you crazy, babe. Not me."

"Enough!" Jake snaps with enough malice in his tone to wipe the grin off my face and send a shiver of fear down my spine. "Get this woman out of my house, Cam. And find Miss Sims." He tosses the spatula in the sink and with an eerie calm, walks out of the kitchen and into his office. I tense, waiting for the door to slam, but it simply clicks shut.

"Well that was anti-climactic," I mutter, a little annoyed that he didn't act a fool. Or hug me...

Cam's low laugh draws my attention. I find him leaning against the counter. Shaking his head as he digs his phone from his pocket. "You're nuts, you know that?"

I shrug because...I am a little nuts. "So now what?"

"Now, I find the real Miss Sims." He moves across the floor to tower over me. "And you, Penelope Hart, get to walk away from this knowing that you are the only woman in history to breach Jake Swagger's mighty fortress and leave unscathed."

Unscathed.

Does that mean other woman who have been here before me have been tied to a spanking bench and tasted his leather belt, then fucked into another dimension? Did they leave here in an orgasm induced, foggy state with nothing but the stripes on their asses and the soreness between their legs to remember him by?

"Yo...crazy girl...You get that?"

"Huh?"

He rolls his eyes. "I have to make a few calls then we'll figure out the fastest way to get you back home, okay?"

I nod.

His face sobers and his tone is no nonsense. "Don't touch anything. Understood?"

"Fine. Can I at least use the bathroom?"

"Sure." He points to the one off the kitchen. "Make it quick. I'll be back shortly."

"You're leaving?"

"No...I'm stepping out of the room to make some calls."

"Yeah. Uh. Okay. And what do I do when Jake comes out and kills me because I'm still in his apartment?"

"He'll be in there a while." Cam pats the top of my hat, pushing it down over my eyes. "He has more bark than bite. Don't worry, he won't kill you."

I smile and lift my hat to look at him. "Because he secretly likes me?"

"No, babe. Because it won't read well in the papers."

Oh...

"Jeff? It's Cam Favre. I need a favor..." Cam's voice drifts as he walks out of the kitchen.

I snag the rest of the bacon and pour myself a glass of juice. I glance at the table then back at Jake's office door. Breakfast in the bathroom seems like the safest option, so I lock myself inside and eat with my back against the door.

I try to figure out the deal behind this mysterious Miss Sims. Why would she use an alias? Who is she to Jake? Obviously nobody important. I mean he hasn't even seen her damn face. Yet he's gone to great lengths for her. Is she a client of his? What does he even do?

Stupid phone.

If it wasn't dead, I could Google him.

Finished eating and tired of thinking, I peel off my soiled clothes and turn on the shower. Forever seems to pass before the hot water warms my cold bones. Only then do I wash my hair—having to add water to the shampoo bottle because it's nearly empty—and scrub away the remaining stench of jail.

Clean and shiny and smelling like something wonderful, I wrap my body in a big fluffy towel and smear the steam on the mirror with my hand. I look rough—tired. My brown hair, a usual, curly tangled mess, is straight from the weight of the water and hangs halfway down my back. My olive complexion glows even darker against the white towel, making the gold flecks in my hazel eyes, shine even brighter.

I rummage through the drawers by the sink and find a brand new toothbrush and some toothpaste. Then I towel dry my hair and wipe the remaining water from my skin.

Dressed in nothing but a towel, I peek out of the bathroom and find that I'm alone. Jake must still be in his office. Cam must be doing whatever it is he does. And the fear that Jake might kill me if he found me in his apartment must have washed away in the shower. Because suddenly, the idea of watching T.V., wrapped in that warm blanket, curled up on his couch doesn't scare me in the least.

Despite the scalding water from my shower and warmth of the living room, I still feel chilled. I have a stuffy nose. My head hurts. Bones are achy. I pray like hell I'm coming down with a cold. I'm a sucker for a damsel-in-distress, and though my *That Guy* has proven to be a pain in the ass on both our encounters, I'm positive he'll take pity on me and nurse me back to health.

In between my fantasy thoughts of him exiting his office and gathering me in his arms, reality surfaces and I'm forced to think like an adult.

Today could've gone a lot differently. What if I hadn't made that call to Jake's office? What if I was stuck back in that cell with Big Bertha? What if Jake had called the police and had me arrested when he came home last night? Or when I showed up today? What if he does once he discovers I'm still here?

I need a phone charger. I need to call Emily. Upload my video. Reschedule my flight. Make Jake fall in love with me. Write a bestselling novel about me and my *That Guy*. Introduce Cam to Emily. Write another bestselling novel about the two of them. Find a shark to loan me money until I get my millions.

Someone knocks on the door. I mute Judge Judy and glance at Jake's office, waiting for him to charge from it to see who is here. When the knock sounds again and no one moves to answer it, I take it upon myself to do it—because answering the door in a house that doesn't belong to you is exactly what people with no sense do.

The man on the other side of the door is Jake Swagger—forty or so years from now. Other than the white hair and lines around his mouth and eyes, he looks just like him. Strong build. Hard jaw. Brooding expression. Oceanic eyes. He even glares at me in annoyance and distaste. Probably because I'm only dressed in a towel, but still...these damn mean-mugging stares are getting old.

"Hello, Mr. Swagger." Something about knowing who he is without really knowing makes me feel less inferior to him.

"Let me guess...you're Miss Sims."

Here we go with this shit again...

Without waiting for my reply, he pushes past me. He makes some noise in the back of his throat as he does—disapproval? Disgust? Both?

"Actually, I'm Miss Hart. But you can call me Penelope."

"Where is my grandson?"

I knew it! I want to smile. Fist pump the air because I was right. But I refrain from celebrating. I will not let my small victory interfere with my mission—to make a good impression on the future Jake Swagger.

"He's taking a call in his office." *Maybe.* "Can I get you something to drink?" I offer. But Ol' Pee-Paw Swagger makes himself at home. He pulls open the cabinet on the entertainment center and grabs a decanter and a glass.

I stand, willing myself not to fidget, as he pours a drink then turns to me. He studies me while he sips his whiskey. At eight in the morning. But hey, who am I to judge?

"Do you not have clothes?"

I flush and let out a nervous laugh. "It's a funny story, really—"

"I doubt I'd find humor in anything pertaining to your line of work, Miss Sims. So please, spare me the details as to how you ended up answering a door that doesn't belong to you, dressed in only a towel."

It's hard to hold your chin up and be proud when you're dressed like I am, looking up at a man who carries himself with an air of authority. Not Steve Jobs-authority. Not Henry Frick-authority. Fucking Hitler authority. Good thing I'm not easily frightened.

"My name is Penelope."

He makes that fucking noise again. I'm not as forgiving about it as I was a few minutes ago. He has about one more time to—

"I sure hope he pays you well. Although I can't imagine there's any sum of money that would be worth a person's dignity." He looks me up and down with a slow shake of his head. His lip curls into the same scowl Jake wore when he found out the bag on his bar was full of dog shit.

What in the hell?

I frown in confusion. "I'm not sure I understand."

"You should. I used small words."

Why this old bastard...

"Are you insinuating that I'm stupid, Mr. Swagger?"

He says nothing. Just stares at me with this hard, stoic expression. His attempt to make me feel inferior awakens my pride. My pride fuels my anger. My anger charges my words. And my words spew from my mouth before I can stop them. "I asked you a question, Mr. Swagger. I'd appreciate an answer."

His brow twitches a tiny bit. The movement is so miniscule, I might have missed it if I wasn't studying his face so hard. "Your southern accent is genuine. As is your pride." He takes a seat in one of the overstuffed leather chairs—crossing his legs like a lady might, yet he makes it look so masculine. "That couldn't have come cheap, but I'm sure you're worth every penny." He lifts his glass to me as if he just gave me a compliment or some shit.

"He's *not* paying me."

"Did he pay you to say that, too?"

Something is going on here. There are a number of reasons as to why I haven't quite figured it out—exhaustion. Dehydration. Flu-like symptoms. Shitty day. But I'm collecting pieces of the puzzle. And I'm pretty sure the mysterious, missing Miss Sims is a—

"If you're not here because Jake hired you, then why are you here?"

Because I broke into his house. Got kicked out. Set a bag of dog shit on fire. Went to jail. Called Jake's office. He thought I was Miss Sims using my given name. Sent someone to get me. Discovered the truth. And now I'm waiting on Cam to finish finding his hired help to take me home before Jake kills me.

He doesn't seem like the kind of man who wants to hear all of that. Besides, he's kind of a judgmental asshole, and I'm not sure how many more of his insults I can take. "How long do you have?" I ask, stalling until I can think up a believable lie.

"Long enough, Penelope."

I wither under his stern gaze. And melt a little because he remembered my name. Which is kind of sweet. Already I start to forgive him for being such a butthole.

The door to Jake's office opens and I'm saved from the truth. And graced with another view of his naked torso.

"Grandfather." Jake gives him a quick nod before drinking me in. His perusal slow. Real slow. Like cream rising on clabber, slow. Pouring peanut butter, slow. In a nutshell, Jake Swagger—the young, hot one—is looking at my naked arms, legs and the top part of my bare chest like his grandfather isn't even in the room and he has all the time in the world.

Did I mention that his slow gaze is hot, too? Like fire hot. Lava hot. Throw-me-on-an-open-flame-until-I-disintegrate-to-ashes hot. His look suggests he wants to eat me. It's all I can do not to rip this towel from my body and spread myself open on his pristine white couch like a Sunday morning Shoney's buffet.

"So this is the girl, hmm?" *Grandfather* asks, a hint of something I can't decipher in his tone. "She's a far cry from the women I'm used to seeing you with." I flush at his...compliment? Maybe? "I'm impressed. She's charming. Polite. Genuine..."

Jake straightens a little and that glint of slow fire fades from his eyes. "And you discovered all of this in less than five minutes?"

Grandfather stands and pulls at the cuffs of his jacket. "I don't believe it's been that long. Which is why I'm impressed. In the same given time I've spent with the women you usually surround yourself with, I come to much different conclusions. They're entitled. Selfish. Rude. They're...overpriced whores, Jake. And everyone knows it."

Another puzzle piece slides into place.

Jake pads across the room—barefoot—to the decanter and pours himself a drink. *Do these people not know it's only eight in the morning?* "I've never been one to care about what anyone thinks. You should know that by now."

"Nevertheless, the gesture is appreciated."

"Yeah? And what gesture is that?"

"That you would be so kind as to go to such extreme lengths to hire someone who could actually pass as a lady."

Jake snorts at that.

I want to flip him the finger. And remind Grandfather, again, that I'm not being paid. But he speaks before I can.

"You may not care about what anyone thinks, Jake, but your actions reflect on all of us."

"You mean you."

"Precisely." Grandfather glances over at me with a hint of a smile on his face. But his eyes are still hard. Still cold. I bet he has some evil in him. And his look along with the standoff between these two powerful men, has my writer brain going crazy.

Jake probably works for his Grandfather's company. Grandfather is retiring. Wants Jake to take over the company. Do things his way. Jake has other plans. But he can't act on those plans until he's President. Which means he has to do whatever his Grandfather says until he's released from his metaphorical hold. Even if that means being someone he isn't. Which is probably why Jake is an asshole. Why he's hardened himself against his true feelings. He's really a nice guy, but he has to be a dick to appease his Grandfather so he doesn't look weak.

This book is going to be so fucking good...

I tune back into the conversation that is somewhat lighter, but still tense. Grandfather pulls something from his pocket. I can't see exactly what it is, but it looks like a business card. I move closer.

"I know you have a soft spot for small-time entrepreneurs." Grandfather passes Jake the confirmed business card.

"Canton said he'd never sell."

"He has no choice. Put all his capital into another idea and lost it to an established patent from the late nineties. His company isn't of much interest to me. But with a little help from you, it could go places. Still, he'll be a hard sell. He has a lot of pride." At that, his eyes move to me. I drop my head and study my nails.

"I'll give him a call next week."

"You'll talk to him at the party tonight." Grandfather's tone leaves no room for negotiation. Jake's jaw tightens but he doesn't say anything. "Until then." He nods to Jake then to me, turns on his heel and walks to the door in long, purposeful strides.

The instant he leaves, I whirl around and face Jake. "Miss Sims is a whore, isn't she?"

"You ask that question like you expect me to answer it."

I throw my hands up. "Of course I expect you to answer it, considering he thought I was her. You know what he asked me when I told him you weren't paying me? He asked me if you paid me to say that, too."

Jake's not listening to me. He's looking at my chest. I look too. And my tits are just about to bulge out of the towel. I cross my arms and take a seat on the couch. Then pull at the end of the towel to try and cover more of my naked legs.

Where the hell is that blanket?

"So is she? A whore?"

"Penelope...*please*," Cam says, striding into the room. "*Whore* is so 1996. Jake prefers the term escort." He drops down on the ottoman, never looking up from his phone.

Jake shakes his head. "Do you ever shut up?"

"What? You do."

"How about we discuss what's really important. Like what the fuck she's still doing here. I told you I wanted her gone."

Cam shrugs. "You said to find Miss Sims, too. I believe that takes precedence. So take a seat. Calm the fuck down. Let me do my job, then I'll get rid of her."

Get rid of her...

Shit.

What is he going to do? Get me out of town or feed me to the fishes?

Cam's speech mellows Jake. At least a little bit. He runs his hands through those beautiful, black locks and takes a seat on the opposite end of the couch.

One cushion separates us.

We're that close.

So close, I bet I could smell him.

While his focus is on Cam, I pull in a deep breath through my nose. My left nostril makes this weird, snotty noise before it clogs up and cuts off my air. It's the most disgusting thing ever.

Maybe Jake didn't hear it...

He heard it.

I get his usual glare. Not really repulsive, just his signature anger. Or more like raw, undulated hatred.

He says nothing as he stands and *swaggers* to his office. I wait for the door to slam, but he returns carrying a suit jacket. He pulls something from the inside pocket, tosses the jacket across a chair and reclaims his seat.

Then, to my horror and amusement, he offers me a handkerchief.

A real one.

Like, a cloth one.

I take it, wondering if it's the first time he's had the opportunity to use it. I bet he carries one every day in hopes some woman with a runny nose will come along and make all the trouble of remembering to put it in his pocket worth it.

I hide my grin behind the handkerchief and dab at my nose. I want to just blow the shit out of it, but that'll have to wait until we reach that level of comfort all couples do once they fall in love. For us, I'm guessing it'll only take a couple of days.

Judge Judy calls a lady a moron. I focus my attention on that rather than the eyes burning in the side of my head. Chill bumps break out across my skin. I wish I could say it's from his arctic glare. Truth is, I'm freezing.

"Are you cold?" Jake's tone is flat. Uncaring and bored as if he asks only because he absolutely has to. Still, an unforced shyness takes root inside me at his attempt to be...polite.

"A little."

Without a word, he grabs the blanket from the floor and passes it to me. I try to touch his fingers—you know, so I can describe the "spark" I feel from our connection. But he ruins it by pulling away before I can.

"Thank you."

He shakes his head. "Don't."

I tuck the blanket around me and my legs beneath me until the only thing visible is my head. "Don't what?"

"Don't feign sweet innocence. Don't act all shy and submissive…"

Submissive.

He said submissive.

He's a dom.

I fucking knew it!

"…Grandfather fooled, but not me."

"Huh?" *Stupid day dreams.* "Sorry. Could you say that last line one more time?"

His lips thin and he pulls in a deep breath through his nose. *What I'd give for his nostril to clog up…* "I said, that little act you performed earlier might have my Grandfather fooled, but not me."

"What are you talking about? What *act?*"

"I've seen your true form. Remember that."

I draw my head back and look at him like he's lost his friggin' mind. I'm sure I have three chins in this position, but I don't care. "*Your true form?* Who the hell talks like that? What does that even mean?"

"You're prancing around *my* house in *my* goddamned towel, answering *my* fucking door, charming *my* Grandfather into believing you're some sort of saint." He pokes his chest every time he says *my*. I look at the red spot forming. He'll definitely bruise there.

I must've said that out loud. Because he laughs. Without humor. Don't think that's possible? It is. It's a bark-type laugh that people do when they find something unbelievable and have no words to say. Of course Jake always has *something* to say.

"You're un-fucking-believable."

"Um, no. What's unbelievable is that being an asshole really is hereditary. You should be proud. You and your grandfather proved a theory. I mean, even if I was an escort for hire, he didn't have to be such a prick about it. I'm glad Miss Sims wasn't here to listen to all those awful things he said about putting a price on one's dignity."

"You finished yet?"

"No. I'm not. Why do you need to hire someone anyway? You're like… rich. And hot. You could have any woman in Chicago."

"I got this, Jake." Cam leans forward, resting his elbows on his knees. "You see, Penelope, important people like Jake here don't casually date. He doesn't even have any female friends. Hell he barely has any male friends. He's all work and no play. Which is why it's both convenient and necessary for him to use an exclusive, very discreet, private escort service when they need a...female companion. Like for holiday functions. Balls, galas, charity parties..." He looks at Jake and smirks. "Grandfather's retirement ceremony."

But Jake is looking at me. As if he's anticipating my reaction. I try to remain indifferent. On the inside, I'm doing cartwheels. "So he hired Miss Sims to attend his grandfather's retirement party?"

"Yes. Although Miss Sims is a just a generic name we use. It rolls off the tongue a bit better than escort. Or...whore."

"I still don't see why he can't just ask like a friend or a colleague. Or why doesn't he just go alone?"

"*He* is sitting right here," Jake says, and damn it I don't want to, but I turn to look at him. And when I see his beautiful, chiseled face, I can't stop the questions from coming. I know I shouldn't ask. I know it'll piss him off. But this is important. I have to know.

"Do you use the escort service because they have to sign a NDA?" His brows draw together in confusion, but he doesn't ask me to elaborate. He doesn't have to. "Is it because you have a secret sex fetish you don't want people to know about? I can see how discretion is important for a man of your...status." He stiffens. I should reassure him. "I'm not judging." I cross my finger over my heart. "This is strictly for research. I promise."

"Research?"

"Yeah. You know...for my book."

He nods slowly as if he just remembered I'm a published author with four thousand followers and eighty-three reviews on Goodreads. Four-star average, thank you very much. "Your last one didn't do too well. Is that why you want to put me in this one? You hope people might actually buy it?"

I ignore his jab. "I don't want to put *you,* you in it. Just someone like you."

"Someone like me?"

"That's what I said."

"Do you even know who I am?"

"Of course I do," I lie.

"Enlighten me."

Shit.

"Well, I mean, I know your type."

"My type?"

I shrug. "Rich. Single. Works too much. Takes life too serious. Controlling. Ambitious. Secretly generous." I take a breath. "You're driven. Independent. Loyal. You have a soft spot for your mom. An issue with your father. And you've spent your life trying to get out of your Grandfather's shadow."

"I'm inferior to no one."

"But you don't have your Grandfather's respect."

"I have his respect."

I tilt my head and study him through narrowed eyes. "Do you?"

He smiles but it doesn't reach his eyes. Or that vein that's about to pop out of his forehead. "I know you too, Penelope Hart."

I thought I'd melt hearing him say my name. But all I feel is the ball of nerves in my throat that threatens to choke me. I'd blurted out my thoughts on his personal life with no regard to how they might make him feel. And now he was about to do the same to me.

Fair enough.

I force down my worries and flash him a smile. "What do you know about me? Other than what your grandfather said." I put my finger on my chin. "What was it he said again? I can't remember. I know he left out irresistible, but that one is already pretty obvious..."

"I remember exactly what he said." His voice is cold.

I throw his words back in his face and smirk. "Enlighten me."

"He said you were charming."

"I am charming..."

"Polite."

"I'm that too..."

"Genuine."

"Fake isn't even in my vocabulary."

"And my favorite." His eyes sweep over me. Not slow. Not hot. But quick. Callous. He's about to say something to hurt my feelings. I brace myself for it.

"He thinks you could actually pass as a lady."

"Jake..." Cam warns, but Jake ignores him.

"Now my Grandfather's definition of a lady is a woman with class, which you most definitely do not have. A woman of beauty...I'll be generous and give you a six on that. A woman who has achieved success."

"I'm successful!" I snap in my defense. "I've accomplished something millions of people only dream about."

"Setting a bag of dog shit on fire doesn't count, sweetheart."

I bite my cheek to keep from screaming at him. Or kissing him because he called me sweetheart. Even if it was in an indignant way. But that's just my crazy hormones talking. Truth is, the previous dig at my writing career and now his blatant disregard of it hurts my feelings.

Back in my hometown, I'm infamous for being the eccentric, mischievous daughter of the estranged, sorrowful lady who creates wood art and bakes the best lemon pie in six counties. When I was crowned queen at the Watermelon Festival my senior year in high school, people congratulated me and my mom for months. They figured that would be my greatest achievement. I mean, what more did a girl like me have to offer the world after being born out of wedlock, ditched by a sperm donor while still in the womb and raised like a heathen by a single woman who had turned down every advance from every available—and some unavailable—man in town?

I knew what the blue haired ladies said about my mother during the beauty shop discussion held every Saturday. I'd witnessed her name on the prayer list at church on Sunday morning. I'd heard them *bless her heart* for having such a nuisance as a child more times than I could count. Eyes might roll when I walked into a room, but daggers were thrown at my mother's back every time she walked out of one.

After high school, I enrolled in a local junior college. I'd exceeded the expectations of my small town, though I wasn't trying to, and because they didn't have anything bad to say about me, the gossip died down. The reprieve lasted until what will forever be known as *The Big Break-up* that happened my final semester of my second year in college.

With six hours shy of an associate's degree under my belt, a broken heart and that fucking Watermelon Queen trophy on the mantel in the living room serving as a constant reminder that the unspoken words of *I told you so* lingered behind every set of lips in Mt. Olive, Mississippi, I decided to write a book.

For my mom.

For me.

For the right to stick my middle finger up at every blue-haired old lady in town so they'd have something to really pray about.

So I did.

And three years later I still do—flip off the old ladies, that is. But I do it behind their backs because the Senior Citizen Center donated the money for a big billboard with my picture on it at the city limits that reads, *"Welcome to Mt. Olive. Home of Bestselling Author, Penelope Hart."*

Gotta love a small town.

What I'd do to be there now eating a slice of my mom's lemon pie. Watching Jeopardy and not having the question to a single answer. Instead I'm eight hundred miles away. Sitting on a couch that costs more than my Chevy. Eyes locked with a man who I thought was my *That Guy*.

He blurs in my vision and I blink the moisture from my eyes before tears can pool. The urge to cry is strong. I want to sob. Break down. Let go. But I can't. I refuse to be weakened by this man's words. If he threw me through a window or rammed my head through the T.V. screen, then yes—I'd cry. But shed a tear over hurt feelings?

Never.

And what happens when we don't process our feelings? We lash out using a different emotion. Mine is anger. Or at least that's what my anger management coach says.

"You're a real asshole, you know that?"

"You seem to keep forgetting that you broke into my fucking house."

I roll my eyes. "Are you not tired of saying that yet? Geeze, you've said it like, forty times today."

"You know what I'm tired of? You being here."

"Fine. I'll leave." The cover falls to my feet as I stand. "May I use your phone? Please?"

He gives me a snotty look. "So the country bumpkin does have manners."

"Fuck you." I stomp out of the room and into his office—ignoring his objections. I take a seat in his big chair and pick up the receiver. Cradling it against my shoulder, I punch in the number then lift my eyes.

Jake lingers in the doorway. His arms braced on the frame. His torso is long. Cut. Ripped in abs. My tongue darts out to wet my lips at the sight of his bacon grease splatter scars. Hell, his belly button is even hot. And the position has those already low rise pajama pants hovering dangerously close to the base of his shaft.

He's a butthole.

He's a butthole.

He's a butthole.

Between the mantra, his twisted scowl and the ringing on the other end of the phone, I manage to quell the heat that builds in my belly. "Do you mind? I'm on a call."

He mumbles something about me being fucking ridiculous, how I need to make it quick and to not touch anything, before he pushes off the door and turns. I have to mentally smack myself to get the image of his ass of brass out of my head long after he's out of sight.

Jake Swagger is a jerk.

Chicago is stupid.

And I want pie.

It's time to go home.

CHAPTER SEVEN

My Mom goes through the five stages of grief every time I talk to her.

Step 1: Denial.

"You are *not* calling me from a penthouse apartment in Chicago asking me for money to get you home. Seriously, Penelope? How did this happen?"

Step 2: Anger.

"How many times have I told you to stay out of other people's business, hmm? Now what are you going to do if Emily takes this guy back and they get married? You did more than burn a bag of dog shit, young lady. You burned the bridge of your best friend's potential future husband well and good."

Step 3: Bargaining.

"I'll send you the money to get home only if you promise me that you'll stop these shenanigans of yours."

Step 4: Depression.

"Do you have any idea what it would do to me if something happened to you? I'm stress eating Oreos as we speak. I'll be big as a house by the time you make it home."

Step 5: Acceptance.

"I'm glad you're okay. That's all that matters."

By the time I hang up, I'm smiling. Mom's worry has a way of doing that. It feels good to have someone care. Perhaps that's Jake's problem. He wasn't loved enough as a child. It wouldn't kill me to be a little more understanding. After all, I have brought him nothing but grief since I've known him.

Ugh. Why does talking to her always trigger empathy?

And why can't Jake be more like her and love me unconditionally despite my flaws?

For that, I make sure to leave lots of fingerprints all over the freshly polished wood of his desk. And because I'm petty and childish, I lift my towel and wiggle my naked ass on his chair.

I walk back to the living room feeling lighter. Better. I'll soon be saying my goodbyes, but I'm not sad. Though it was never his intentions, Jake gave me so much while I was here—material for my book. A limo ride. A view of Chicago and his half naked body. Pizza. Bacon. A get out of jail free card.

Well, he didn't really give me any of that. I stole it. But technicalities are overrated.

"I'm not fucking doing it, Cam. Forget it." I linger in the doorway of the office, hoping to catch more of the conversation. Jake spots me immediately.

Always crushing my dreams...

I smile to show him he's forgiven. I'm ready to tell him I'm leaving. Say my goodbyes. But he scowls at me and storms out of the room and up the stairs. Just like that, I'm pissed all over again. And the thought of leaving is fleeting. I'd rather stay until he kicks me out again for the satisfaction of knowing that once more, I got under his skin.

"It's not you he's mad at, babe." Cam's lips tip a little in an apologetic smile. It's cute and all, but I'm still mad.

"Do you always make excuses for him?" I make my way to the liquor cabinet. Drinking doesn't sound like a bad idea right now.

"When I need to."

I pour myself a glass and toss back the smoky flavored, burgundy liquid. *Shit that burns.* I cough a couple times. Then fix another and take a seat across from Cam. "You're a good friend. I don't know why, but you are."

Cam shrugs. "Jake's like an onion. He has layers."

"You just quoted Shrek."

He grins. "It's a good movie."

"So if he's not mad at me, who is he mad at?"

"He's pissed about the situation with Miss Sims. And his grandfather always puts him in a shit mood."

"Well, he didn't have to take it out on me." I take a small sip. It goes down smoother. Probably because this is the kind of liquor you're supposed to nurse. Not chug.

"You did break into his house, babe." Laughter dances in Cam's eyes. I might laugh along with him if I were in a better mood.

I cross my legs and Cam's gaze drops to my naked knees a moment before it returns to my face. His grin widens.

I take a gulp of whiskey. Or scotch. Or brandy. Whatever this expensive shit is. There is no way I'm buzzed off two glasses. But I do feel less tense. A little warmer. And suddenly more passive about the situation.

"Look..." I pull in a deep breath. My limbs feel heavier when I release it. "What I did was wrong. I admit it. But me being here today? That's not my fault. I could've told his secretary I was Miss Sims. But I didn't. I could've asked him to bail me out. But I didn't."

A hiccup escapes my lips. It sounds exactly like a donkey bray. I take a couple more sips to chase them away.

"I hung up the phone, Cam. Hung it up." Another hiccup. "Do you know I chose death over involvin' Jake in my problems? My cell mate was gonna kill me if I went back in there. And I would've had to," hiccup, "go back in there if you hadn't come because they wouldn't let me leave unless someone pick-ed me up."

I finish off the glass.

Hiccup.

"I think I'm a little buzzed."

"That's a hundred and eighty-four proof single malt whisky you're chugging, babe. Normally, people sip two fingers over a period of time. Your first glass was about four fingers." He points at the empty glass in my hand. "That one was at least five."

"Huh." Hiccup. I study the crystal tumbler. *Probably shouldn't have filled this sucker to the top.* "You know if the tables were reversed, and Jake was at my house instead of this way, where I'm at his house, things wouldn't be like they are."

Cam chuckles. "Not following."

Hiccup.

"Well first of all, *he* wouldn't have had to pour his own drink. Second, *I'd* have offered him some of my breakfast. B, *he* wouldn't have had to," I lower my voice and give my best impression of Jake, "'*Prance around my damned house wearing my fucking towel,'"* because I'd have found something for him to wear. Or not, probably 'cause I'd want him in jussa towel. But I wouldn't have bitched about it."

Hiccup.

My head feels heavy. My neck not very supportive. So I keep my head down and run my finger around the rim of my empty glass. "He hurt my feelings, Cam."

He eyes me thoughtfully. "I'm sorry he hurt your feelings, Penelope." The sincerity in his tone is genuine.

"Thanks. Pee Paw Swagger's a dick. Jake's a dick. Alfred's a dick for giving me that stupid top hat. Ross's a dick for...well, Ross is okay. And you're okay."

Hiccup.

"Out of all y'all, you're the best, Cam"

"Aww, she said y'all. Can we keep her Jake?"

A bottle of water appears in my line of sight. "Drink this." I lift my heavy head and lean back, back, back until I meet the cool blue eyes of Jake Swagger. "All of it...please."

I snatch the bottle from his fingers. Try to, anyway. Good thing he has a tight grip on it. I snag it on my second attempt. "So the cocky butthole," hiccup, "does have manners."

"Don't push it."

I mimic him in my head as I drink the water. All of it. Like he demanded. With an underlying promise of spanking me if I didn't obey. And no. That is *not* the alcohol talking. Not my writer brain, either. I'm sure of it.

Hiccup.

Cam's phone rings and he looks down at the screen then up at Jake. "Don't be an asshole. I mean it. Don't be a dumbass either. Ask her."

Jake simply flicks his fingers in dismissal. His eyes on me. He ignores Cam who glares at him across the room. When Cam's phone rings again, he releases a heavy sigh and leaves the room—frustration evident in his voice when he clips a quick, "What?"

Jake offers me a second bottle of water. This time I don't snatch it. I take it and the crackers with a nod of thanks. "Ask who what? Was he talking about me? You want to ask me something?"

"No."

Geeze.

Hiccup.

"Whatever. Well, I need to ask you something. A favor. And I'm *pretty* sure you're not gonna mind this one."

"I'll be the judge of that."

So damn cocky...

Hiccup.

He sits down on the couch and gives me an expectant look. I make him wait while I eat a cracker and ogle him in jeans and a gray T-shirt. I can't decide if he's hotter like this or half naked.

"Can you give me a ride to the bus station? Or order me one of those you-bers? I don't know how to do it."

Hiccup.

His smile is bewitching. All those hard lines on his face melt away. His eyes lighten. This man is sexy when pissed. But he's devastatingly handsome when he's not. "Uber."

"What?"

"It's called Uber."

"Oh." I shove a cracker in my mouth. "They should spell it with two O's then. Shit's confusing. We don't have them where I live. We don't even have taxis."

"What do you do when you need a ride?"

I give him the best look I can that suggests he's stupid. "We drive."

He rolls his eyes. "I mean when you go out, smartass. Like to a bar or a club. You do have bars and clubs, right?"

"We have them," I say around a mouth full of cracker. And a hiccup.

"So what do you do when you go out to a bar, have too many drinks and can't drive home? Or do you hillbillies just drive around drunk?"

I nod. "Yeah. We mostly just do that."

"Jesus Christ," he mutters.

"Don't say the Lord's name in vain."

"I didn't. I was calling on him to bring the rapture to Mt. Olive, Mississippi, ASAP."

I shoot him a toothy grin. "You're funny."

"You're drunk."

"I drank nine fingers of whisky."

Hiccup.

"And you're dropping crumbs all over my thirty-thousand-dollar couch."

"There's probably some pizza crust from the other night between the cushions too."

His eyes close and he shakes his head. But he doesn't get angry. I like him like this—un-pissed. He would wait until I was leaving to start acting nice.

"So will you take me to the bus station?"

He looks at me for a long time. I'm not sure exactly how long, but I've ate four crackers. If I could hit rewind, I'd have been drunk the entire time I was around him. It's easy this way. Less intense. I can handle his long, silent, stoic stares without fidgeting or feeling self-conscious. Although it could be that this is the first time he's looked at me without condemnation.

"Today was my fault," he says. I shoot a glance across the room expecting to see a big blimp pass outside the window that says, Psych!

"Are you apologizing to me?"

Hiccup.

"No. But what you said to Cam was true. Yesterday was all on you. But today is on me."

"You eavesdropped on our conversation?"

He glares. "You can't eavesdrop in your own house."

"You did."

His eyes fall closed. I think he's praying again. More for patience than the rapture. I mouth an, "amen" when he finishes.

And hiccup.

"You're impossible."

"I can see where you might think that."

He squeezes the bridge of his nose in exasperation, but I can see a hint of a smile. And suddenly, I just want him to kiss me.

Maybe it's the alcohol.

Maybe it's my hormones.

Maybe it's because he's the sexiest man I've ever seen in my life and I don't think I can go one more moment without feeling his lips on mine. Even if I have to climb into his lap, straddle his hard thighs and steal it, I need this kiss.

If he rejects me, who cares? If he hates me, it won't matter. I have nothing to lose and everything to gain. I'm leaving here soon. Possibly within the hour. He'll never have to see me again. If I don't kiss him, I'll always regret it. But if I do kiss him, even if it's terrible, at least I'll forever have the memory. And maybe a restraining order. But those things sound a lot worse than they really are.

Not that I've ever had one or anything...

"Can I have another bottle of water?" I'm breathless and he hasn't even kissed me.

"Yeah." He takes the empty bottle from my hand but instead of going to the kitchen, he walks to the little mini bar across the room.

So much for having the time to form a decent plan...

It's now or never.

I scramble off the couch. Catch my footing on step three just before I face plant the floor, and am two inches from his lips when he turns around.

"What the f—"

Say "fuck."

Do it.

Right now.

Notice how your teeth sink into your bottom lip on the "f?"

Well...that's the exact moment I pressed my mouth to his. So instead of kissing soft, puckered lips, then coaxing them apart with my tongue and swallowing his moan as I devour his mouth that tastes like whiskey and mint, even though nobody ever tastes like whiskey and mint, I end up licking his teeth.

Gums too.

All while he just stands frozen in place.

You know, any decent human would at least attempt to salvage the kiss. I mean, he doesn't have to just stand here and continue to let me humiliate myself. He could easily pull away. Cup my head. Angle his head. Something. But does he? Nope. And I can't do any of these things because I'm literally pressing my tongue against his teeth to keep from falling on my face.

At least the hiccups are gone...

I grab his shoulders and push myself back from him. He doesn't even flinch. Even when I stumble, he doesn't move to catch me. His teeth are still pressed into his bottom lip. Brows drawn together so tight I'm afraid the skin at his temples might split.

After I find my balance, I cross my arms and shake my head at him. "You have got to be the suckiest kisser on the planet."

"Me?"

"Yes. You. You suck at kissing."

"Are you fucking serious right now?"

"You just ruined it for me," I whine, throwing one hand up in the air. I stumble again. He doesn't right me again. So I put my hands on my hips to steady myself because it's obvious I can't depend on him.

His face relaxes a little and he runs his tongue over the indentions in his lip. I should be thinking about how those lips felt on mine. How that tongue felt. It should turn me on to see him licking his lips.

It doesn't.

"You tried to lick the enamel off my teeth, Penelope. I think it's safe to say that you're the bad kisser here. Not me."

I look away from him and mumble, "I imagined it different in my head." *Which reminds me...* "You could've at least attempted to save it."

"There was no coming back from that."

I glare at him. "Is Cam still here?"

He gives me a wary look. "Why?"

"Because I had it in my head that I was going to leave here kissed. And I always get what I want because I'm stubborn like that. And since my attempt with you didn't work out—"

"Yeah, not exactly."

"Well, I'm not going to rub it in your face—"

"Shut up."

"Hey! Don't be ugly to me—"

"Shut up, Penelope."

I stomp my foot. "I will not sh—"

Say "shut."

Do it.

Right now.

Notice how your lips pucker on the "sh?"

Well...that's the exact moment Jake Swagger kissed me.

His lips are smooth, but no soft. They're too powerful. Too demanding. Too *dominant* to be considered soft. His tongue? It's soft. He drags it across my bottom lip. Then my top. Bypassing my teeth because unlike me, he's not an enamel licker. And unlike him, I'm not an asshole. So I take the hint and open my mouth wider so he can devour me. And taste me. And I can taste him. And guess what...

He tastes like whiskey and mint.

I don't know where the mint came from, but trust me the cool hint of spearmint is there. I make a mental note to see how much a bottle of that twenty-four-hour mouthwash he uses runs on Ebay.

I whimper when his hand slides into my hair. He growls at the noise. Tightens his hold. Curls his other hand around my waist and pulls me closer to him. This time when I stumble, he catches me. Or should I say his chest catches me. Either way, I'm pressed against that unyielding, concrete slab he wears beneath his shirt.

Slow.

He kisses me so slow. How can something so languid, so tantalizing, so consuming be so damn passionate? Hell if I know. But this guy? He can do it.

I never want it to stop. *God please don't let it stop.* His hand slides to the side of my neck. Cups my cheek. Thumb rubs along my jaw. He pulls his tongue back but keeps his lips on mine. Pressing soft, sweet kisses across the swell of my bottom lip. I fight the urge to jab my tongue back into his mouth because I know the kiss is coming to an end.

I'm boneless when he pulls his mouth from mine. But he keeps me pinned to him. So close I can still feel his warm breath on my bruised lips. My eyes flutter open and I gaze up to meet his. Those whirlwinds of color darken by the second with some unspoken promise that I pray is something dirty and erotic.

"That, Penelope, was a kiss."

Fucking right it was.

"Ahem..."

Jake releases me so fast my head spins. He keeps a grip on my elbow but takes an immediate step away from me. Then his hand falls away and there's all this space between us. I don't want the space. I want his heat. His chest. His penis in my vagina.

Stupid Cam and his stupid throat clearing.

"Sorry to interrupt."

"You didn't interrupt. What do you want?" I'm shocked Jake can so easily act like his mouth wasn't just suctioned to mine. I'm pretty sure I just fell in love with him over that kiss. And I'm almost positive he's in love with me too.

How can he not be?

I'm a great kisser.

"The agency called."

Jake whips around to face Cam. It takes me a minute but eventually I mirror his stance—arms crossed. Eyes narrow and fixated on Cam. Silently killing him with a look because he just ruined the best moment of our lives. He doesn't even look apologetic about it either.

Smug bastard.

"Miss Sims took the train to Milwaukee and got a flight back home.

She has no interest in coming back. Just like I knew she wouldn't. Which is why I told you to ask her."

"Fuck!"

Here we go.

The Jake show is getting boring. I roll my eyes and take a seat on the couch, then pull the blanket tight around me and snuggle into the cushions. I think I'll just take a nap. Maybe relive our kiss. My lips tingle and I smile.

"You think this shit is funny?"

I peek up at Jake. "Huh? What? The Miss Sims thing? No. Why?"

"This is your fault."

I shrug. "Eh. Maybe. But even if it wasn't you'd blame it on me because I broke into your house."

He does that silent stare thing. I think he experiences some internal battle when he does this. Like maybe he's trying to talk himself out of killing me.

"Do you have any idea how much money you cost me when you got in the backseat of my car?"

I yawn. I'm totally not feeling this conversation. "You forget. I didn't even know how to pronounce Uber until just a little while ago. So no. I have no idea how much a car ride cost you."

"Not the car ride...." He pauses and presses his mouth in a thin line. Either he's trying to squeeze the lingering taste of me from his lips, or... yeah. That's what he's doing. Pretty sure of it. "Fifty thousand, Penelope."

He has my attention. "Jake say what?"

"I spent fifty thousand dollars just in agency fees to find the perfect woman to take to my Grandfather's retirement party. Ask me why."

"Why?"

"Because despite what you think, I would move heaven and earth for that old man. Not because I'm trying to earn his respect, but because he has mine. So when he asked me to find someone who wasn't the usual, obvious whore I wear on my arm to these events, I promised him I would. That promise didn't come cheap. And now she's gone. All because you stole a bag of fucking dog shit."

Actually, I bagged the shit myself. But whatever.

"That's very admirable of you to go to such lengths for your grandfather. But did you really pay fifty grand for one night with this chick?"

"I did."

"You couldn't find like a coupon or something?"

"For fuck's sake...."

"What? I'm just saying. I would've done it for half that."

"Is that so?"

"Yep. Pay me twenty-five grand and I'll be whoever you want me to be for the night."

Jake smiles. It's...a scary smile. I don't like it. "I'm not going to pay you twenty-five grand, Penelope."

I shake my head at him. "It was a joke. You couldn't pay me to hang out with that butthole grandfather of yours."

"Good. I'm glad you feel that way."

I eye him warily. "Why?"

His smile only widens. "Because you're going to do it for free."

CHAPTER EIGHT

"Is this like that time you told me Jason Aldean knew we were going to be on his tour bus, and then we got arrested for trespassing?" Why, three years later, does Emily still try to make me feel like shit about that? And why now? After I just gave her the best news of our lives?

The first thing I said after Jake told me I would be going to the party with him was, "Oh shit! I have to call Emily!" So I did. And now she's coming at me with this blast from the past instead of just being happy for me.

She's probably just jealous.

"So we got arrested for trespassing. It's not like we were charged. I got those dropped, remember? And you got a selfie on a celebrity's tour bus. And remember that pair of underwear I smuggled out for you?"

"They dropped the charges so they wouldn't have to see your face again, Penelope. You didn't do anything."

"But you got to take selfies."

"They confiscated our phones and deleted all of the selfies! It was part of the deal when they dropped the charges."

"Those underwear though...."

"You sold them to the deputy—"

"Yeah, yeah, yeah, for a half-eaten Subway sandwich and a bag of stale potato chips. Say what you want but that food saved our lives that night. We probably would've died from alcohol poisoning without it."

"I got alcohol poison that night." Her tone is bitter. "Probably because you refused to share the fucking sandwich."

"You're missing the point, Em. A billionaire just asked me to go to a party with him to impress his grandfather. I'm living our dream. Be happy for me. And most importantly, lie to my mother and tell her you're surprising me with a trip to New York and that we'll be back in a week."

"Fine."

"And don't forget to stay indoors and keep all the lights off so she doesn't drive by and get suspicious."

"How about I just take a bunch of pills and sleep for the next three days? Or eternity?"

"Don't be dramatic. We can't afford those kind of pills. And I hear a Tylenol overdose is very painful."

Her laughter is music. "You're such a dick."

She still doesn't know I succeeded in my plan to avenge her broken heart. I decide to save that for when I get home. Maximum praise and all that.

"I gotta go. I'll see you soon. Fuck Luke Duchanan."

"Fuck Luke Duchanan."

"Did you just say the name Luke Duchanan?"

I jump at Jake's voice. Drop the phone. Fumble with it several seconds before finally placing it in the cradle.

"Huh? No. I don't even know that name. What's up?" I'm rambling. Because I'm lying. And I wouldn't have to if he wasn't eavesdropping, again. And I'd probably be able to breathe if he wasn't standing in the door of his office, again. Arms braced on either sides and looking too fine, again. But I can't even speak without stuttering because I'm turned on by the vision of him, again. Having thoughts about what riding his face might feel like...again.

He doesn't believe me. But thankfully, he lets it go. "Come on. Alfred just brought Miss Sims' wardrobe up. Let's see if anything fits." He turns and saunters away. I take a second to appreciate the view. Or a minute. Long enough for him to snap at me over his shoulder. "Penelope! Now!"

"Coming!" *Almost literally*.

I follow him to the guest room where there is a luggage cart overflowing with several garment bags, round and square boxes with fancy ribbons and an assortment of smaller bags stuffed with colorful tissue paper.

"All of this for one night?"

"She was staying the weekend." When I shoot Jake a hopeful look, he shakes his head. "You're not."

Fun sucker....

He hands me another bottle of water. I guess he wants me to sober up. But the truth is, the excitement has done a pretty good job of sobering me. Actually, I could use another drink.

Jake rummages through the packages, tossing boxes and papers and bags to the floor as he flings garments on the bed. I grab a black, silk nightie and hold it against my chest. It fits me. Like, it's my exact size. And even over a towel, it looks really good on me.

"Put this on. You have an appointment in an hour." He throws a cream colored cashmere sweater and a pair of jeans at me. The nightie falls to the floor as I scramble to catch them.

"Appointment?"

"To prep you for tonight. You didn't think I was going to let you go like that, did you?"

I look down at my towel dress and frown. "I guess not."

"Didn't think so. Get dressed. Ross is waiting in the lobby when you're ready. He points to a blue bag hanging from the rack. "There are three different phone chargers in that bag. Charge your phone and stay out of my office."

My phone!

Facebook!

Toy Blast!

"By the way, who the hell travels all the way from Mississippi with just the clothes on their back, a Passport, a maxed out credit card and a crumpled up dollar bill?"

"I have a debit card, too."

"There's less than fifty bucks in your account."

"Well, it's the end of the month. I get paid on the first...wait." I cross my arms and glare at him. "How do you know all that stuff?"

"You're staying at my house, Penelope." He says it like that's reason enough.

"But *how* do you know all of that?"

"I went through the pockets of the clothes you so kindly left scattered on my bathroom floor." *Oh my God... Did he see...* He smiles. "Yeah. Saw those too. I wasn't aware they made underwear with *I'm your Huckleberry* printed on the ass of them."

I can't do anything but stand here and blink.

"Like I said, you're staying in my house. You have no secrets anymore. Now, get dressed. Ross is waiting."

With that, he turns to leave and I'm left with the realization that he knows everything about me, and though I know plenty about my That Guy, I know absolutely nothing about Jake Swagger.

"MOTHERFUCKER! Yep. That's it. I'm done." I scoot up on the table and scissor my legs around the head of the woman who has been so intimately eyeing my vagina for the past twenty minutes. She also removed the first layer of skin from my crack to my clit—after she waxed every other hair on my body. She's lucky she didn't catch a foot to the face.

"We're all done, anyway. Told you that last strip would be the worst." She winks at me, this *Alexandrea*, like she finds this shit funny.

It's not funny.

None of this is funny.

It sucks.

If beauty is this kind of pain, I'd rather be a hairy hippo.

From the time I walked into this upscale spa with its serene atmosphere and flute music, I've been anything but relaxed. The deep tissue massage nearly had me in tears. The facial burned like Hell's fire. My fake nails are too long and I got a nasty look when I said so. And then they send me to get waxed. I thought it was just going to be my eyebrows. I was wrong.

"Trust me, Miss Sims. You'll love it."

Oh. And everyone thinks I'm a whore.

"I won't love it enough to do it again. Trust *that*." I tighten my robe and follow her out of the room toward the next torture chamber. If they weren't so uptight about cell phones, I'd text Jake and tell him how much I hate him right now. And demand that he kisses every scarred inch of my hairless body until it feels better.

I'd love to think Jake booked this waxing session for me because he plans to fuck me crazy and prefers his woman hairless. But I was informed by him before I left the house that, other than hair and makeup, he didn't know what all they had in store for me today. Miss Sims had made the appointments herself. I was simply taking her place.

Miss Sims is a friggin' masochist.

We walk into a hair salon that is all white walls and huge mirrors. And, thank you, Lord, no flute music. There are no other clients in the room. Actually, I haven't seen a single soul other than the people who work here. Did Miss Sims rent out the entire spa?

"Look at this *face*!" I don't know who this guy with the flipped hair and brilliant smile strutting toward me is, but I like him.

His hands move to my face. Slow. Cautious. Like I'm some elusive piece of art and he fears his mere touch might damage me. "Finally, a challenge."

"Hey!" I slap his hands away. "Don't be a dick."

He throws his head back and laughs. "No, my sweet southern peach, I meant it as a compliment." His smile is warm and his eyes sparkle with praise as he drinks in all of my features. "Fixing ugly is what I do. But it will be a true test of my skill to make you any more beautiful than you already are."

Oh.

Well since he said it like that.

"Come. Have a seat." He waves me over to a chair that faces a mirror, then makes a big show of flapping the cape before covering me with it. "My name is David Michael. Jake Swagger is a *personal* friend of mine." I lift a brow at him. He dismisses the look with a wave of his hand. "Not in a sexual way, unfortunately. But his loss."

"Definitely his loss."

"He told me about you, Penelope Hart." Surprised, I look up at him, but he's studying my hair. "You're quite the clever girl. But I have to ask, did you mean for things to go this far?"

His eyes meet mine and I shake my head. "I just wanted to escape a crazed man and his dog."

Again, he throws his head back and laughs from his gut. I like how he expresses himself without reserve. It's infectious—his disregard for everything that isn't what he's feeling. And I find myself laughing with him.

When he settles into a quiet smile, he locks eyes with me in the mirror. "And now you're Cinderella going to the ball."

"I guess I am."

"Well then, let's not waste any more time. Jake wants you to fit in so you don't draw any attention. Which means he wants me to make you look like all of them."

"All of them?"

"The Miss Sims of Chicago. The plastics. The fakes."

"Ahh. I see."

"Of course I agreed because Jake is not just my friend, but a client. One who tips well enough to cover my rent for the entire month."

I nod. "I understand."

"But..." He shoots me a mischievous look. "Jake's not here. To hell with what he said. You deserve to stand out."

The idea of standing out, walking into a room like some Cinderella, stopping the show and having all eyes turn on me has my stomach knotting with nerves. "You know, I really don't mind blending in. But maybe we could take an inch off these nails?"

He snaps his fingers and a woman appears and takes my hand in hers to study my nails. Then she pulls a file from her smock and starts filing away. *This isn't so bad...*

I watch her work for a few moments, then David Michael's hands squeeze my shoulders. When he has my attention, he leans down to make his head level with mine as we both stare at me in the mirror.

"Be honest with yourself, gorgeous. You're not the kind of girl who blends in. You're most definitely not Miss Sims. You're not some Disney Princess, either, are you? So, Penelope Hart, tell me the truth. Who do you want to be tonight?" His voice drops to a whisper. "What kind of girl is it going to take to bring Jake Swagger to his knees?"

Jake.

On his knees.

I whimper a little at the thought.

There's only one girl who can bend a man like Jake Swagger.

"That girl."

CHAPTER NINE

M y Instagram be like:

#DONTHATEMECAUSEYOUAINTME
   #hotaf
   #nofilter
   #thatgirl
   #romcom
   #author
   #research
   #flamingdogshit

"SMILE, CAM!"

Immediately, Cam goes into selfie mode. Arm on the console, head angled toward the center of the vehicle next to mine, he cups his chin and grins. He looks...gah. He looks gorgeous. Sexy. Arrogant. Rich. All the things girls love. I snap the picture and upload it to Instagram along with the other three I've taken.

Once David Michael was finished transforming me into the most beautiful human on the planet, I'd called Ross to come get me. He was with *Mr. Swagger.* So it was Cam who showed. I'm so glad he did. My followers are going to eat his ass up.

"So...you like?" I gesture with my hand over my face and hair.

"You know I do."

True. He had whistled at me when he walked in. Acted interested when I showed off my long lashes, fancy hair and waxed underarms. Twirled me several times like I was wearing a ball gown and heels instead of the bathrobe and slippers the spa provided. He'd grinned from ear to ear and said, "Country ain't so country no more," in his best attempt at a southern drawl.

That was ten minutes ago.

This is ten minutes later.

And I'm needy.

"Am I prettier than the other Miss Sims? Huh? Am I? Am I?" I tease, wiggling my eyebrows at him.

He laughs. "I can honestly say that you are very different from all the others." He lets me stew a second on that before adding, "And much, much prettier."

I was only teasing, but Cam's response is genuine. And I flush from the compliment. David Michael did a great job on my hair and makeup, but I still look like me. Anyone who knows me would recognize me immediately. That makes the compliment from Cam even more rewarding. But it doesn't have the same effect on me as Jake's opinion. Speaking of him....

"When is Jake going to be back?"

"Not sure. He was in a shit mood when he left so my best guess is, something went wrong at the office."

"Isn't he always in a shit mood?"

Cam smirks. "Only on days that end in *y*." We come to a dead stop in traffic and Cam shifts to face me. "He's not happy about this...arrangement. Partly because he doesn't like you for what you did and partly because he doesn't have control over the situation. He got backed into a corner and taking you was his only option."

"He doesn't like me?"

"He doesn't like what you did."

"You said he doesn't like me."

"For what you did."

"Same thing, Cam."

"No it's not, Penelope. So stop frowning."

Jake doesn't like me.

Of course he doesn't like you, idiot.

This sucks.

This is your punishment.

I'd rather have a spanking.

The night is young.

"You know, me going to this party isn't the only option. He could always go alone."

"That will never happen. If Jake, one of the most eligible bachelors in Chicago, walks into the room without a woman on his arm, he might as well wear a sign above his head that says, 'rich, successful, single man looking for a one-night stand.' Plus, his grandfather insists he has a date."

"Why?"

He shrugs. "That's just the way he is. He says these events are for networking with clients, not getting your dick wet. And bringing a date with you helps eliminate distractions. Crazy talk if you ask me. Getting my dick wet is the only reason I go."

I picture Cam's dick in my head. Then feel guilty about it.

After all, he *is* my best friend's future boyfriend.

But I keep picturing it.

And it's...nice.

I need a distraction.

"So, tell me about tonight. What can I expect?"

"To be envied by every woman. Hit on by every man. Scrutinized by every employee of Swagger Corp. Disapproving looks from gramps. A moody Jake. Nosey reporters..." He shoots me a smile. "Sounds fun, doesn't it?"

"No. It sounds terrible. Will there be anything good at this party?"

"Duh. Me. And alcohol."

I laugh. "Yeah. I'm sure *grandfather* will love that. Me getting drunk, grabbing the mic and staggering on stage to tell corny jokes in between hiccups that make me sound like a donkey."

"You do have an interesting hiccup sound."

"I have some pretty badass dance moves too."

"I have no doubt that you do. And you'll need them." Our conversation is interrupted by his phone. He presses a button on the steering wheel. "Yes, Mr. Swagger?"

The shuffle of papers and the sound of drawers opening and closing fills the car. Then Jake speaks and my heart does that pitter patter thing in my chest. "Where are you?"

"Almost back at your place."

"She with you?"

"She is."

"And?"

"And...what?"

"How does she look?"

Cam winks at me. "I have no doubt she'll be the Belle of the ball."

Jake grunts. "Until she opens her mouth."

That peckerhead....

"Is this the part where you promise to fill it if I don't keep it closed?" I ask, much more blasé than I actually feel.

The only sound coming from the other end of the call is Jake's breathing. No words. No background noise. No grunts of disapproval. Just deep, heavy breaths that I wouldn't notice if I wasn't listening so hard for his reaction. Or if Cam's Bluetooth speakers were not state of the art.

Cam has his hand over his mouth trying to hide his smile. He too seems to be waiting for Jake to say something. What we get is a dial tone.

"Well...." Cam chuckles. "That shut him up."

"Indeed it did."

"You should use little sexual innuendoes like that more often when you want to render an asshole speechless."

"Perhaps I will."

"I bet that line would work on an even bigger asshole than Jake."

"There's a bigger asshole than Jake?"

I look at him confused.

He grins.

Then it hits me.

There is a bigger asshole.

"Grandfather."

And there's no fucking way I'll ever say something like that to him.

Surely.

Maybe.

Lying.

I totally would.

And I probably will.

———

THIS GIRL?

The one in the mirror?

The really good looking one staring back at me?

Yeah.

She's not Penelope Hart.

But whoever this girl is...well....

She's fine as hell.

The "dress" Jake had altered especially for me, is a sheath column, V-neck, gold sequined gown with a court train. It hugs curves I didn't even know I had. My C cups look like D cups. My ass looks like a Kardashian's. The two slits that start mid-thigh on either side of the dress show off my legs that look longer and more toned thanks to the matching six inch strappy heels.

And this color is *definitely* my color. My freshly-waxed, olive skin glows against the gold fabric. Add that to my long black lashes, natural glossed lips and simple, yet elegant, side ponytail hairstyle David Michael hooked me up with, and voila!

That girl.

I strike a pose.

Snap a selfie.

Send it to Emily.

Wait for a reply telling me how stunning I am.

I get a middle finger emoji.

So jealous.

I know how to walk in heels. And a dress with a train. The first rule is to *not* look at your feet. But that's exactly what I'm doing when I crash into Jake's chest in the hall. His hands grab my arms to steady me and, have mercy.

His touch is warm and strong and a fire ignites in my panties—if you can call the little strip of lace I'm wearing under my dress panties.

My gaze travels over him.

He's dressed in a tux.

A black one.

With a bow tie.

Not much different than the suit he normally wears. I mean, why do women get all bent out of shape when they see a man who always wears a suit, wearing a tux? Other than that weird thing that goes around their waist that looks like a back brace, isn't it the same damn thing?

Still, he's smoldering. All blue-gray-green eyes and dark hair. Tall and

broad and cocky and brooding and studying me with a heated expression
—my heels. Dress. Breasts. Neck. Face. Eyes.

"D-do I look okay?"

He clears his throat and takes a step back, suddenly stoic. "You'll do."

I'm not even mad. I grin because I know he likes what he sees. And
he's just too much of a cocky bastard to admit it.

"We need to go over a few things."

I do a little heel-kick river dance, snap and point my finger guns at
him. "What's up?"

"First. Don't ever do that again."

I do it again.

He's not impressed.

He stares at me like I'm stupid until I compose myself, wipe the smile
from my face and nod. "Got it."

"Don't answer any personal questions about us. When someone asks,
and they will, how you know me, just keep it simple by saying we're old
friends. If they pressure you for more, politely excuse yourself. Don't give
anyone your real last name. If someone asks, say Smith. Or Jones—"

"How about Swagger?"

"Penelope...."

"Okay, fine. What else?"

"Steer clear of my grandfather. Hopefully, he'll be too busy with
everyone else to have much time to corner you, but I can't promise he
won't make time. He's curious about you, for some fucking reason." Jake's
brow furrows in thought as he mindlessly tucks a tendril of hair back from
my face.

"Is that all?" I'm a little breathless and he must notice.

He pulls his hand back and locks his gaze on mine. "This party is
important. So I need you to rein in the crazy a little bit. Can you do that?
Please?"

I beam. "Look at you. Sayin' please and shit."

"Don't say that either."

"What?"

"*And shit.*"

"You really need to work on your southern accent."

"Well, I don't have the best teacher."

"Fine. No *and shit's*. Anything else?"

"Yeah. Can you dance?"

I do my river dance again.

He pinches the bridge of his nose.

"Hey...." I pull his hand away from his face. "I'm kidding. I assume you mean ballroom dance. And yes. I can do that. Among other dances. Like the tango. The electric slide. The watermelon crawl—"

"I get it. Do you have any questions for me?"

"Yep. What exactly is it that you do for a living?"

He seems surprised. "You don't know?"

"I know you're the CEO of Swagger Corp, but I have no clue what that is."

"Do people in Mississippi not pay attention to the stock market? Nasdaq? Dow? You ever heard of that?"

"I've heard of it," I snap, glaring at him. "Are you going to tell me what you do or not?"

"I'm a venture capitalist."

"Like on the movie Wedding Crashers?"

"I invest in more than shirts and pants, Penelope."

"So you put money into people's ideas?"

"Sometimes. But I prefer to buy them out so I have complete control. If that's not an option and it's something I can't walk away from, I'll settle for fifty-one percent ownership."

Fitting. Considering he such a damn control freak.

"Have you ever been on Shark Tank?"

"No."

Of course he can't be That Guy and a T.V. star. "Figures..."

"Why does that...*figure?*"

"No reason. You know," I turn my head to the side and study him, "I had you pegged as a corporate merger. Like in Pretty Woman."

He gives me a tight smile. "That would be my grandfather. Whose party we're already going to be late getting to. You ready?"

"I'm not gonna get any prettier."

"Figures..." He grins proudly at the opportunity to throw my words back at me.

I roll my eyes. "Aren't you easily amused."

With my matching gold clutch tucked away under my arm, I follow him into the foyer. He presses the button for the elevator—eyeing me as we wait. He looks...curious.

"What?"

"I can't believe you didn't Google me."

"Did you Google me?"

"Yes."

I beam at his short response. "You did? What did it say?"

"Not sure. I got tired of searching after page four."

My smile turns to a scowl. "That's pretty cocky coming from a guy who has to buy people's ideas because he's not clever enough to come up with his own."

Surprisingly, he laughs. I'm so taken back by it, I don't even notice the elevator has arrived. He has to grab my arm and pull me inside before the doors close.

And in the tight space, our close proximity gives me something I've been searching for since I first saw him.

His scent.

Have mercy.

I'm like a damn bloodhound.

Seriously.

My nose finds his shoulder and I inhale so deep I can taste the scent of him on the back of my throat. I keep it there instead of the corner of the elevator as we descend. My eyes fall closed and I hum my song—getting a nice whiff of him over and over.

I'm not good at describing scents. I could never put a name to that distinct smell in blood until I read Twilight. *Coppery. Metallic.* Once Stephenie Meyer explained it to me, I wondered how in the Hell I had never figured it out.

So really, the best I can give you is that he smells exactly like you think a rich, hot guy would smell. Like soap and cologne and man and clean and money. Oh, and some really nice fabric softener. I'm pretty sure that's Downy.

When we glide to a stop, I'm reluctant to pull away. As I do, I feel his eyes on me.

"What?" I ask, not bothering to look up at him.

"Why did you do that?"

"I have a fear of elevators."

"Hmm." Thankfully, it's all he says.

Alfred meets us at the lobby door. He hands a coat to Jake then holds open a white fur coat for me. I slip my arms inside and nearly come at the feel of it.

"Is this real fur?"

Jake lifts a brow. "Yes. Is that a problem?"

"No. I was just curious."

...As to how many innocent animals had do die just to keep me warm...

We walk out into the blizzard and I'm thankful for all the rabbits or squirrels or whatever animal was sacrificed just for me. Ross holds open the back door of the car and Jake gestures for me to get in. I clamber inside, nearly ripping my dress and falling on my face, before I finally settle on the seat. Jake follows behind me. All grace and fluid.

"So, are you nervous?" I lean closer and drop my voice. "You know... about me being fake Miss Sims?"

"No."

"Because you have full confidence in me?"

I'm so close, when he angles his head to look at me, his lips nearly touch my nose. "No."

"Well, you must be sure I can do the job."

"I'm sure I can fix whatever you fuck up."

I roll my eyes and lean back. "You know, since I'm doing you a favor, you could be a little nicer to me."

"I could put you on an overcrowded bus and ship you back to Mississippi, too."

"But you won't. Because you need me. Don't you?" I tease, giving his ribs a poke with my finger. He doesn't flinch.

"I don't need you. I could always go alone."

"No you can't."

"You sound pretty sure of that."

"I am. Cam told me."

"Cam has a big mouth," he mutters, leaning forward to pour himself a drink. He doesn't even offer me one.

Rude.

I snuggle up to his side and wrap one hand around his bicep and squeeze his thigh with the other. His arms stills. His glass several inches from his mouth. He doesn't move his body, only cuts his eyes at me.

"If I forget to tell you later, I had a really great time tonight."

His lips quirk like he wants to smile. But he doesn't give in to it. "The night is young, Penelope. I wouldn't thank me just yet. These people are sharks. They'll chew a girl like you up and spit you out." His features darken and his tone becomes serious. "If anyone makes you feel uncomfortable, just walk away and come find me. Understand?"

I pull away from him. "I can handle myself. But, I promise, if I see an opening for a damsel-in-distress moment, you can bet your ass I'm going to seize it." I wink at him. But the truth is, I know I'm in over my head.

These people aren't like me. They'll likely laugh at me. Tease me behind my back. Even to my face. But it'll be me who gets the last laugh. That's one of the perks of being a writer. You get to put mean people in a book.

And then you get to kill them.

CHAPTER TEN

I'm not sure what I was expecting.

A red carpet?

Cameras flashing?

People screaming my name?

Crowd surfing to get a lock of my hair....

Yes, to all of those things.

No, to the boring ass entry that consists of us entering through the back and having to walk through the kitchen to get to the actual party.

"So much for a grand entrance," I mumble, handing my coat to a man who nods way too much.

Does dude have a tic or something?

I mean, why does he keep doing that?

Then I notice the way he looks at Jake. Eyes all wide. Fingers fumbling. Words a jumbled mess.

Oh.

He's star struck.

Perhaps I should've Googled him....

"Why did we come in through the back?"

"Because this is the Jessie Swagger show. Not the Jake Swagger show." For the first time, he seems genuinely humble. And embarrassed by, what I assume, is his fame.

"It's about to be the Penelope show when I bust a move on the dance floor." Before I can do just that—bust a move—Jake grabs my elbow and presses his big body against mine.

"Do that river dance shit again and I'll lock you in the cooler." His threat doesn't hinder my good mood in the least.

I wiggle my eyebrows at him. "So you can get naked and warm me with your body heat?" He just stares down at me. "What if I have a fever? You gonna check my temperature? With your big...thermometer?"

That smile pulls at his lips again. And again, he doesn't give in. He pulls away and straightens, offers his arm to me and thanks the coat guy in the only language he knows—a nod.

I take a deep breath as Jake leads us out of the kitchen and down a wide hall. I can hear the music. The chatter. The laughs. The clink of glasses. My heart pounds harder against my chest.

I'm both excited and nervous.

More nervous than excited.

I think.

I don't know.

Shit.

This is crazy.

I'm here. At this super-rich party with all these super-rich people and I don't own a fucking thing with a Prada label.

I glance up at Jake.

This majestic motherfucker....

He's in *That Guy* mode. He exudes confidence. Radiates power. Emits authority. There's precision in his every step. Every breath is controlled. Too bad he's not very intuitive or he would know I'm over here about to lose my shit.

This is the part where all the heroines in the romance books "channel courage from this force of a man." But they don't explain *how* they do it. So I have no clue. I'm just trying everything—narrowing my eyes on him. Pressing my finger to my temple. Zapping his brain with my imaginary laser beams.

"What the fuck are you doing?" He stops walking and looks down at me like I'm stupid. Which is exactly how I feel when I relax my face and eyes and lower my finger from my head.

"In case you haven't noticed, I'm a nervous fucking wreck...and shit," I add, just to spite him. "We're about to walk into the wolf's den and you haven't said a single thing that might boost my confidence."

"You were chanting some shit about calling the four corners. Which I wish I could say is out of the norm for you, but it's not. So you can't possibly be pissed at me for not giving you a pep talk."

"I was calling the four corners?"

"Yes. Stop watching *The Craft*."

I toss that over in my head and nod. *Maybe I know a little something, something about channeling power from heroes after all....*

"Why do I get the feeling you're experiencing some kind of epiphany?" Jake's confused expression makes him look quite boyish.

"Because it worked."

"What worked?"

I study him and nod thoughtfully. "Yep. It definitely worked. I learned how to channel your energy. You're losing control. I'm gaining it."

Jake looks around to make sure we're alone, then turns on me. He looks a little angry. Which I understand. But he doesn't have to point his finger at me. "Get your shit together, Penelope. I mean it."

I slap his hand away and glare up at him. "Would it kill you to say something nice to me? How in the hell am I supposed to face the kind of people in that room if all you do is make me feel like the village idiot?"

"Well, when you're walking down the hall mumbling, *light as a feather, stiff as a board*, how else am I supposed to treat you?"

Yeah. I get that.

But I'll drop dead before I admit it.

I stand my ground and meet his glare head on. Pretty damn proud of myself for holding his gaze without wavering.

"For fuck's sake..." He runs his hand through his hair. Puts them on his hips. Looks down at me. Licks his bottom lip.

He's about to say something nice to me.

Probably tell me I'm a vision.

That he's in love.

That if this was the Jake Swagger show, he'd be proposing tonight. But he can't because he respects his grandfather and all that bullshit.

"It's about time you showed up."

Fucking Cam.

"Damn, Penelope." His eyes move very, very appreciatively over my body. This is the first he's seen me in my dress. And the way he looks at me is almost embarrassing. And I don't really get embarrassed. Ever.

He's forgiven.

And too fine in his black tux. Even though, like Jake, I've seen him wear a suit, he looks different in full formal. Hotter. Sexier. Maybe because he doesn't have that CEO vibe.

"If you're finished eye fucking my date...." Jake's agitation is evident. He wants me all for himself. I knew it.

He's forgiven too.

Cam smirks. "For now. Save me a dance?"

Give you my virginity....

If I had it.

But I don't.

I smile. "Of course."

Jake doesn't bother to offer me his arm this time, he just grabs my hand and tugs me along beside him. I look back over my shoulder to find Cam ogling my ass. I almost throw a hip out swaying it for him.

"Remember what I said, Penelope."

I let out a sigh and turn back to Jake. "Yeah, yeah, yeah. Keep my shit together."

"No." He's thoughtful as he looks at me. His hand hovering on the handle of the door that will lead us into the party. "You find me if you need me."

"Geeze, Jake. Are these people humans or comic book villains? I mean, is fucking Lex Luthor on the other side of this door? The Joker? Shredder? Loki? And if Loki is here, is Thor here too? Not comic book Thor but the *real* Thor? As in, Chris Hemsworth?"

His lips thin. "You watch way too much fucking T.V., you know that?"

"And you're way too paranoid. I'm from a small town in the south. We have snakes and bears and Bigfoot. I can handle some snotty rich people. Trust me."

"If you say so. Now, smile."

I smile.

He smiles.

I melt.

He opens the door.

We walk in and every eye in the room turns to us. We really should've just came through the front. I can't imagine we would get any more attention if we had. People stop talking and turn toward us. Men straighten. Women all but foam at the mouth. Everyone seems to be waiting for the perfect opportunity to come say hello.

It's fucking weird.

And the room is a little...blah. There is nothing fancy about this place other than the massive chandeliers. It's just an ordinary hotel ballroom. There's not even a banner to congratulate ol' Pee Paw.

Poor hateful bastard.

My eyes fall on a flash of flaming orange and I stumble a little. I want to stop and gawk, but Jake is steady in his steps—forcing me along beside him.

"Jake." I squeeze his hand. "Jake. Jake. Ja—"

"You're losing your shit, sweetheart," he mutters around his smile.

"Yeah. I know. Cause that's Ed Sheeran. Like, right there."

"For fuck's sake, Penelope. Don't point."

"You think he'll let me get a selfie?"

"Pull yourself together."

"I don't think I can."

Fucking Ed Sheeran.

Right. There.

Jake pulls me closer and dips his head to my ear. "Keep it together and I swear I'll make sure you meet him, get your tits signed, take a selfie—"

"I want him to sing to me."

"Whatever you want. Just...chill the fuck out."

I nod. Pull in a breath. Force myself to look away from Ed, even though I'm sure he just waved at me.

"Jake! How are you?"

"Marvin, great seeing you here. Thanks for coming. This is Penelope." I smile and nod at the old fart with the receding hairline who is blocking my line of sight to the stage. Jake continues to speak to him for a few minutes. Asking boring questions about family. Laughing at stupid jokes. I'm thankful when we move on, only to be stopped three steps later by someone else.

"Good evening, Mr. Swagger."

"Tonight it's just Jake, Charles." He introduces me then nods to the woman next to Charles. "Stephanie. How are you liking The Windy City?"

Flustered, Stephanie rambles a minute before concluding that she is enjoying the city. I'm introduced and don't miss the heated stare from Charles. Or the look of hatred from Stephanie. If Jake notices, he's unaffected.

He's the amiable prince.

The charming investor.

The fakest fucker in here.

For the next half hour, it's the same thing.

Walk three steps.

Stop.

Introductions.

Curious looks.

Small talk.

Repeat.

I'm bored. I'm hungry too. Seems if I'm going to enjoy myself at this party, I'm going to have to strike out and do it on my own.

I break Jake's hold while he's mid-sentence. He pauses and turns to me. I smile at him and then to the couple he's talking to. "I'm just going to visit the ladies room."

Jake doesn't look pleased, but he nods. "Of course."

The moment my back turns, I roll my eyes. When they settle in my head, I see a familiar set of blues watching me from across the room.

Grandfather.

I look away and move quickly toward the bathroom Thankfully, it's empty. I consider hiding out in here, but Ed Sheeran is out there. And I have some pretty awesome dance moves I'm ready to show off. I also saw a buffet on my way in. I've never been one to turn down a free meal and I would *kill* for a chicken wing.

I bet they have the good chicken wings, too.

Loud chatter fills the bathroom and I cringe a little at the hoard of beautiful females who walk in. They're all so...*tall*. Like, super model tall.

I wonder if they had their knees done....

"Penelope!" The blonde standing center of the group beams at me. I guess she's the leader. I suddenly feel like I'm on an episode of *The Secret Life*.

"Hello." I give a little wave to the woman who I have never seen before in my life. I'm guessing she only knows me because the name of Jake Swagger's mysterious date has spread.

"I love that dress. Valentino?"

What? Is that Spanish for something? She did say it with an accent....

She blinks at me a few times when I don't say anything. "The design, sweetie. Is it Valentino?"

"Oh!" I snort a laugh—a very, snorty one. "*Valentino*. Yeah. I have no clue. Could be Jalapeno for all I know."

The synchronized head movement they all perform as they study me like I'm some alien is a little strange. Did they rehearse that shit before they got in here? Are they robots? One of them mumbles something I can't understand and they all nod—again in synchrony.

"Are y'all gonna like, turn into a Camaro or something?"

"Excuse me?" Bimbo Barbie Blonde One asks.

"Nothing. Enjoy the party." I give them a tight smile and move to leave. They seem to panic, realizing they missed their opportunity to drill me.

As I pass, one of them asks, "So you and Jake are old friends?"

"Yep," I call over my shoulder, not bothering to turn around as I push open the door.

In the hall, I'm met with three other women. All tall. All beautiful. All almost identical to each other.

There's some weird shit happening around here....

"Well hello there, mystery girl." This plastic actually sounds like she could be a nice person. "You are the topic of every conversation in this building."

"No shit?" My surprise is genuine. I mean, fucking Ed Sheeran is here. I feel like I need to tell them that. So I do. "Did y'all know Ed Sheeran is here?"

Tinkly little laughs ring out. "Yes, Penelope. Ed's a good friend of my husband's."

"Are you married to Taylor Swift or something?" I point to where I last saw him. "Because that's not some washed up singer from the nineties. That's Ed Sheeran."

Her eyes are amused but warm. "I'm Caroline. My husband, Carver, is Mr. Swagger's CFO."

"Which Swagger?"

"The mean one."

"Which one is that?"

She grins. "Jessie. But from what I hear, Jake can be a pain in the ass too."

I'm still not sure about this Caroline. She seems nice, but she looks too much like all the others for me to fully trust her. So as bad as I want to tell her that what she heard was true, I refrain. Jake might be an asshole, but I'm not going to admit that to her.

"It was nice talking with you, Caroline. I hate to run, but..."

"Ed Sheeran." She nods. "I know. But you do realize he's not here to perform. He's here as a guest."

"What?"

She lifts a dainty finger in the air. "That's not his voice you hear, is it?"

I listen harder.

She's right.

It's not Ed's voice.

Hell, it's not anyone's voice. It's some classical shit.

"So you and Jake? How did that happen?"

"You wouldn't believe me if I told you."

She winks like she knows some big secret. "Try me."

"Some other time. See you around?" I walk away before she can respond and disappear into the crowded room. A waiter walks toward me with an empty tray of champagne glasses. I lift my chin to get his attention.

"Yes, Miss?"

"This is gonna sound strange, but do y'all have any beer?"

He fights a smile. "I'm sure I can find something. Any special preference?"

"Anything domestic. Bud. Coors. Miller. I'm not picky."

"Two minutes?"

"Hell, take a smoke break and make it ten. I'm in no hurry."

He chuckles at that. "I'll be right back."

From where I'm standing in the back corner of the room, I can see everything. There are little clusters of people scattered throughout the area. Some sit. Some stand. Some even dance to the elevator music.

They could've at least hired a band.

Bought a flower arrangement.

Rented a fog machine.

The waiter is back sooner than expected and hands me a Budweiser. "Here you are, Miss." He offers me a wine glass, but I've already turned up the bottle. The beer is delicious. So cold it has ice shivers. Just the way I like it.

"Good?"

"Perfect. Can you keep 'em coming?"

"Absolutely."

"Thanks, and I better get that glass," I say, knowing Jake will have something to say if he sees me chugging a bottle of beer in the back of the room.

"Allow me." The waiter pours it without spilling a drop and hands it to me. From a distance, my Bud could pass for Moscato.

I want to ask if they have chicken wings, but my phone vibrates in my clutch that's tucked beneath my arm. The message is from Emily.

How's the party?

Sucks balls.

I hit send, thank the waiter again and start making my way through the throng of people in search of Ed. I find Jake first. And I can't say I'm disappointed. He's so relaxed. Carefree. Happy. Laughing—like I've never seen him before.

He stands with four men. They remind me of the cast from Magic Mike. Except they wear suits. And smirks. And have matching 2011 Justin Bieber hairdos. But even as hot as they are, they don't compare to my *That Guy*.

Jake spots me and his smile falters. He just looks...hungry.

His eyes flit to my beer, my chest then to my face. He crooks his finger at me—his lips curling at the corners to reveal a sexy half smile. I hadn't even realized I'd stopped walking. With tentative steps, I go to him.

"Penelope," he says in a deep drawl that causes my knees to tremble. His fingers graze my elbow and he leans in to kiss my hair.

Except he doesn't.

"Where the hell have you been?" he growls before pulling away—his smile back in place. If his fingertips on my elbow didn't feel so good, I might pull away and punch him. "Gentlemen, I'd like you to meet my date, Penelope."

Jake may take my breath away, but I'm the kind of girl who can appreciate a good looking man when I see one. In this case, four men. I bat my lashes and give them my full mega-watt smile. "Hello."

I shake hands with three of them. Jake tells me their names, but they're forgotten the moment he says them. Only one name sticks. Briggs. The name of the man who takes my hand, brings it to his lips, kisses it and then says in the hottest English accent *ever,* "Pleasure to meet you, Penelope. You are fucking stunning."

Someone in the group snickers. I think Jake sighs. But all I can focus on are his words. And that there's something...off...about this guy.

"Jake," he says, his beautiful hazel eyes never leaving mine. "May I steal your lovely date? For a dance?"

"Careful, Briggs." Jake's voice is tight. A little annoyed.

I can't find it in me to care. At least this guy is showing me a little attention. Jake has barely spoken to me since we've been here, much less asked me to dance.

I thrust my glass in his hand and let Briggs lead me out on the dance floor. Apparently, there is a band. They're not playing yet, but they're setting up. Doesn't matter. I'd dance with Briggs to the Oscar Mayer bologna theme song. This classical elevator music will do just fine.

With one hand still clasped in his, he pulls me close and wraps the other around my waist. He holds me like a lover as we spin in a slow circle. A little too tight. Somewhat uncomfortable. I can feel every hard plane beneath his suit. Feel his heat. But we just don't really...fit.

"You are a vision, Penelope."

I smile. But I really want to frown. *It was supposed to be Jake who told me that....*

"You're not so bad yourself, handsome." Over his shoulder, I find Jake talking to a woman. He's laughing. His head dipped so he can hear her.

Briggs' gaze follows mine and he smiles. "Jealous?"

"Nope." *Liar.*

He says nothing. Just...stares down at me with those sparkling eyes. His lips curved into a permanent amused smirk.

"So, how do you know Jake?" I ask, wishing he'd hurry up and spin me back around so I could see what else Jake was up too. And maybe get a better view of the woman he's speaking with.

Maybe she's old.

Pregnant.

His sister....

"We went to college together. I was new to the states. Jake took me under his wing. When we graduated, he convinced me to stay. The rest is history."

"Oh. Well that's nice."

"Mmm..."

I'm distracted. Jake is walking away with that woman. Who is prettier than me. Am I jealous? If so, why? Jake isn't mine. I'm not his. I'm not anyone's. I'm free to fuck Briggs in the bathroom if I want. And I just might. Call me a slut. I don't care.

We twirl two more times. Jake's still gone. My mood has turned sour. This twirling is getting old. Briggs is too quiet. I miss my beer. I still want chicken wings.

"Do you offer freelance services?" Briggs' question pulls me back. But I'm not sure I heard him right.

"Excuse me?"

"A couple of hours is all I really need. I don't see the point in contacting the agency and having a contract drawn up for such a small amount of time."

Confused, I stare at him. First, because his accent slipped. Which explains why I felt something was off about him from the beginning. Second, because I have no clue what he's talking about. Then I remember I'm supposed to be Miss Sims. Who is a whore. And though I should be offended, I'm only curious.

"How much are you willing to pay?"

"Name your price."

Well that was stupid of him to say....

"One hundred thousand dollars."

He laughs. "No piece of ass is worth a hundred grand."

"In my opinion, it is."

"Funny. I didn't think whores were allowed to have an opinion."

This cocky sack of shit....

"Well, we are. We also give out advice when it's needed. And I'm going to offer you some free of charge." I stop spinning and drop my hands at my sides. His still lingers on my waist. "Keep the accent. It's the only shot you have at getting laid."

With his pride hurt, his arrogance comes full frontal. "I doubt that, considering I could have any woman in here."

"And I doubt that, considering you just offered to pay me to have sex with you. Thanks for the dance." When I move to step away, his hand that was warm and soft in mine only moments ago, wraps around my arm. He squeezes tight and I can feel his fingertips bruising the sensitive skin on the back of my arm.

I channel my inner Denzel Washington. My eyes zone in on his grip and everything else becomes a blur. I'm about to reenact a scene from *The Equalizer* when someone snaps his name.

"Briggs!"

His grip immediately loosens on my arm when someone snaps his name. It's then I notice that the three men from earlier have crowded around us. But Jake isn't here. And for some reason, that stings.

I jerk free of him and this time Briggs releases me. The men are talking to him in low voices. Telling him it's time to go. I'm still in Denzel mode, so I'm all cool, calm and collected when I turn to walk away.

I've taken two steps when I hear him call out to me. Because I refuse to cower to this asshole, I spin on my heel to face him. His eyes are dark.

His glare angry. He points a finger at me. When he speaks, his voice is a low growl, but clear enough for it to carry over the noisy room.

"If it weren't for men like me, tramps like you wouldn't even have a place in this life."

"Yeah? Well you know what?" I pause for dramatic effect and then give him a sweet smile. "If the rabbit hadn't stopped to shit, the dog wouldn't have got him."

CHAPTER ELEVEN

They don't have chicken wings.
They don't have cocktail weenies.
No cheeseball.
No chips and dip.
Not a single fucking thing wrapped in bacon.
What kind of party is this?

A waiter sets a tray of some fancy finger food down on the table. I snatch it and make a beeline to the kitchen where Jake and I came in. The nodding guy isn't here. But I remember the door he went through and I follow it and come to a small employee lounge.

I take a seat on a bench and set the tray of hors' d'oeuvres in my lap. My nose scrunches at the sight of the cucumber slices, slathered in white shit, topped off with some sort of raw meat shavings and a little sprig of grass.

Gross.

"Good evening, Miss Hart."

My head snaps up and I find Grandfather looking back at me. *Great.* Just another person I didn't want to see. Well, I'm not in the mood for his shit either.

"Pee Paw Swagger. What brings you here?"

"This is my party, Penelope. Why wouldn't I be here?"

"Okay...allow me to rephrase. Why are you slumming it back here with the hired help?"

"I thought Jake wasn't paying you."

"He's not. I meant the hired help as in the kitchen staff. Not that it matters. You don't believe me anyway."

He studies me a minute. I don't look away. Even though I really want to because his look is super intimidating.

"You're not anything like the other women here."

I give him a big, cheesy, fake smile. "Well, thank God for that."

"You don't approve of them?"

"Have you met them? Besides, I thought you were expecting someone different. Which is why you were convinced that Jake must've paid a pretty penny for me."

His eyes crinkle a little like he wants to smile, but can't bring himself to do it. He looks down at the untouched platter in my hands. "You don't like the food?"

This time, it's me who studies him. "I'm not sure if you just want to hear what I have to say, or if you're really asking all these questions because you don't know the answer."

"I like hearing what you have to say."

"You sure? Because you may not like this."

"Oh, I'm sure. Please. Don't hold back."

No problem, old timer.

I take a breath and lean back against the wall. "I spent last night in jail. I've had no sleep. What was supposed to be a relaxing day at the spa turned into an afternoon in hell. I've been poked and primped and plucked and waxed in places I didn't know I had hair. My feet hurt. This dress is uncomfortable. Everyone here looks at me like I'm a whore. Jake is an asshole. As are his friends. I'm hungry as a hostage. And this shit looks like something a vegan barfed."

"Interesting. But I only asked about the food."

"And I only wanted a fucking chicken wing. Instead, I got this crap and a conversation with you. So I guess we both got more than we bargained for."

He gives me a healthy dose of that Swagger silence then says, "Come with me," before he turns and walks out.

I was not expecting this....

I don't know what to do.

Follow?

Run?

Scream?

I stand and poke my head out of the door. He's walking toward the kitchen. At least there are witnesses there. There are also knives.

You are not a punk, Penelope Hart!

I look down at the platter, unsure if I should bring it with me to my doom.

"Leave the tray, Penelope."

Pee Paw Swagger is a witch!

I set the tray down. Smooth my hands over my dress. Take a deep breath. Lift my chin. One foot in front of the other...that's all I have to do. By the time I join him in the kitchen, the sinking feeling in my stomach is at its worst.

"Of course, Mr. Swagger," the chef says with a bow. Then he barks a command in a language I don't understand and the entire kitchen staff disappears.

Pee Paw stands with his back to the massive industrial sized stove. His eyes are on me as he takes off his jacket, folds it over a chair then starts removing his cufflinks. He nods his head toward a stool next to the prep counter. "Sit."

I sit because I'm scared to fucking death.

He rolls his sleeves up and grabs an apron from a hook on the wall.

What the hell?

"Would you like something to drink? Perhaps a beer?"

Of course he would know I had a beer.

He opens the refrigerator and grabs two bottles of Budweiser from the case sitting on the top shelf. "Phillip, the waiter you asked to bring you a beer, had this in the trunk of his car." He twists off the caps before handing me one then keeping one for himself. "He was told to personally make sure you were accommodated with whatever you wanted. Lucky for you, he shared your taste in beer."

"Really? Who told him to do that?"

"My grandson."

My heart warms. And I want to kick myself because I could've had chicken wings after all.

"Jake always goes above and beyond to make sure his...*guests*...are taken care of. From what I can tell, he's treated you no different. So imagine my confusion when you tell me he is an asshole."

Blood floods my face. Hearing this, I feel I'm the true asshole. But my stubborn pride has me grasping at anything to aid in my defense. "He has yet to say something nice to me. You know, he didn't even tell me I looked pretty. He said, 'You'll do.'"

"Do you really need to be told you're pretty?"

"Yes," I deadpan.

"I see."

"He also told me he'd introduce me to Ed. Even get him to play me a song. He hasn't done that either."

"Ed?"

"Ed Sheeran. The singer. He's here. At your party. Where have you been?"

He ignores me as he melts butter in a skillet. "I heard you had an issue with Briggs tonight."

I cringe at the reminder. "Something like that."

"Would you like to talk about it?"

"Sure wouldn't."

"Are you okay?"

"Sure am."

He shoots me a chastising look then grabs a knife to cut the loaf of fresh bread next to me. "I have the feeling that if I ask you to tell me the truth about the reason you're here, you will."

"All you have to do is ask."

He tosses the bread in the skillet. Slathers it with cheese. Adds some spices. All while I watch him work. Sipping my beer. Enjoying comfortable silence with a man I never thought I'd enjoy comfortable silence with.

"Eat first. Then we can talk." He sets a plate in front of me.

He cooked me a grilled cheese sandwich.

I would cry if I wasn't so damn hungry.

Within minutes, I have devoured the entire thing. "That was delicious."

"I know."

I grin at the cocky man. Surprisingly, he grins back. And like Jake, he is stunningly handsome when he smiles.

"So you want the truth...why? What does it matter?" I ask, propping my elbow on the counter and getting comfortable.

"It doesn't matter. Jake is a grown man. He can do whatever he wants. I'm just curious. And I can't get answers from him, so I'm asking you."

I take a swig of my beer. With it, I find a little courage. "Can I be frank with you, Mr. Swagger?"

"I'd very much appreciate it if you were."

"You're full of shit."

His brow lifts. Before he can say anything, I continue.

"You didn't seek me out to make me a sandwich. Just like you didn't leave your guests just to satiate your curiosity. The truth matters to you. And if you want me to be the one to give it to you, then I'm going to need to know the real reason why."

He curls his lips in a lopsided grin. "Perceptive little thing, aren't you?"

"No. I'm just really nosey."

He says nothing for several moments. Then, as if he's decided to not give a damn, he loosens his tie and leans back in his chair. "Jake never acts on a whim. His strategy is to be three steps ahead at all times. He's meticulous like that. Always has been. I know my grandson well enough to know that you were never part of his plan. He acts as if he had no choice but to bring you here. And I need to know why the man I'm about to give my company to is acting so out of character."

"Wow. Yeah. That's a good question. Wonder why he wouldn't just tell you the truth instead of risk you doubting his ability to run your company?"

"Probably because he doesn't know I'm leaving it to him."

I nearly fall off my stool. "What? He doesn't know?"

"No. And I'd appreciate it if you kept it between us."

Why must he burden me with such a huge secret? It'll nearly kill me to hold this in. Like, literally take all my willpower not to chant, *"I know something you don't know."*

"So if he doesn't know you're giving him the company, what does he think will happen when you retire?"

"He assumes I'll remain sole owner after and leave the board to run the company for me. But the only way for me to fully retire is to walk away completely. So I plan to give him sole ownership and he can decide whether he wants to appoint a board, run it himself or merge his company with mine."

"Wait. Y'all don't work together?"

"We are two separate enterprises. He invests in people's ideas. I buyout entire corporations. His passion is helping people. Mine is money. I've worked hard my whole life so that one day I could enjoy the fruits of my labor. But I don't want to watch everything I've worked for fail without my leadership. I don't see Jake giving up his company to run mine, but I have no doubt that he will make sure the company continues to thrive under his ownership and the direction of the appointed board. He won't fail. He doesn't know how.

"But what if he says no? That he doesn't want the company?"

He chuckles at that. "Power is a very addictive thing, Penelope. Jakes possesses it now, but with my company, he'll define it. And he'll have my company and everything that goes along with it. Nothing you say will change my mind about that. But it will satiate my curiosity. And though you doubt that's my reason for being here, I can assure you it's not. I just want to know the story behind my grandson's unusual behavior."

I sigh. Why couldn't I have been born into a wealthy family? Jake is so damn lucky. He's going to be a gazillionaire. Thanks to me. And I'll get nothing.

Story of my life.

"Okay, Pee Paw. I'll tell you." I point my finger at him. "But if I do, then you owe me one."

He nods once. "Fair enough, Miss Hart.

"Well...I guess I should start from the beginning. So you should get comfortable. And probably have another beer."

———

"In my head, I'm thinking robots. And when I think robots, I think Transformers, right? So with a straight face, I asked..." I pause to stifle another giggle and then tilt my head to the side and narrow my eyes. "Are y'all gonna like, turn into a Camaro or something?"

The entire kitchen erupts in laughter. Loudest of them all is the deep, baritone of Jesse Swagger. Grandfather. Or as he's now agreed to let me call him, Pee Paw.

We, along with the kitchen staff, have spent the past half hour making fun of all the Miss Sims at the party. The employees had some interesting stories to share. I, of course, had mine. And Pee Paw simply listened. He shook his head in disgust at some of the things the women had done, and laughed heartily when they got back a little bit of what they gave—which seemed to always be the case.

But before the staff had returned and the fun times began, I told Pee Paw everything. From start to finish. Again, he just listened. Once the truth was out, we'd talked about my life back in Mississippi. My mother. My writing. The ups and downs of living in a small town.

Then he'd opened up about his life. About his late wife who passed when Jake was only two years old. About his son, Jake's father, who'd married Jake's mother, his high school sweetheart, his first year in college. That he was an English Professor who didn't have a corporate bone in his body. And, along with Jake's mother, had joined the Peace Corp later in life and was now teaching English to children in a village in Africa.

I'd had so many questions. I wanted to know about Jake's childhood. When the last time was that he saw his parents. Were they close? Did he have commitment issues? On a scale of one to ten, what were my chances of getting him to marry me?

But then the staff returned. In the few seconds we had left alone before they made it to us, Pee Paw took my hand in his. Fixed me with a thoughtful gaze. And did something I'm sure a man like him has only done a few times in his life.

Apologize.

He told me he was sorry for accusing me of, basically, being a whore. And for treating me as such by insinuating I had no dignity, lacked intelligence and was beneath him—a man who made an honest living.

I accepted his apology.

A bond was formed.

And now I'm pretty sure he loves me. I wouldn't be surprised if he started sending me birthday cards with hundred dollar bills and telling people I'm his long lost granddaughter.

A throat clears.

Silence descends.

I don't have to look to know it's Jake standing behind me. He has the typical *That Guy* presence—the kind that can be felt before it's seen. I glance over my shoulder anyway. Because it's been a while since I last saw him. And though I've spent the past hour staring at the older version of him, there's nothing quite like the real thing.

His gaze moves to me, perched on my stool. Cold bottle of Bud in my hand. Legs crossed. Split in my dress exposing an indecent amount of thigh. Then he looks over at Grandfather. Jacket off. Sleeves rolled up. Tie loosened. Beer in hand. Lit cigarette dangling from his lips. Leaned back in a swivel chair he'd snagged from the employee lounge.

Jake takes in the rest of the room—wait staff, chef and prep cooks in white coats all sipping whiskey or beer. Sitting on counters, milk crates and a couple leaned casually against the wall. Eventually, his eyes find me again.

"Penelope."

I nod. "Jake."

I applaud his stoic expression. For the most part, he appears unaffected by the scene before him. But I can see the questions in his eyes. The uncertainty. The burning need to storm over to me, grab me from my stool, haul me in the cooler and demand I tell him what the fuck is going on.

Then check my temperature with his big thermometer...

Grandfather stands and unfolds the sleeves of his shirt. "It's been a pleasure, but I believe it's time for me to get back to my guests." He fastens his cufflinks and takes the jacket offered to him. "Thank you, Geoff. It's been a pleasure. As always."

"Pleasure is mine, Mr. Swagger. Congratulations on your retirement."

They shake hands. Grandfather makes eye contact with each employee, silently acknowledging them with a nod. Which I find sweet. Then he turns to me as he straightens his tie. "How do I look?"

"Like a stud."

He glances at Jake and smirks. "Hear that? I'm a stud." He shoots me a wink, gives one final nod to the room and with a breath, transforms from cool Pee Paw, to Jesse Swagger. "I'll be making my speech in ten. I expect you there," he says to Jake as he crosses the room. He pauses when he's next to him and leans in to say something I can't hear.

I nearly fall off my stool in an effort to listen. Jake's eyes lift to me as Pee Paw claps him on the shoulder then strolls out of the kitchen.

The chef starts barking orders. The staff groans, but everyone gets to their feet and soon the kitchen is chaos once again.

Jake's big body shadows mine as he comes to stand right in front of me. "It seems you've bewitched my Grandfather."

I shrug. "Bewitching is what I do."

"Since when are the two of you best friends?"

"Since I finally convinced him I wasn't Miss Sims and he learned the error of his ways and apologized to me."

"Bullshit."

"Cross my heart." I cross my heart.

He helps me to stand and his hands fall to my hips. He studies me with a soft expression. I look up at him. At those lips. Wondering if he will kiss me. Suddenly needing it so bad I almost ask for it. His eyes follow his hand as he lifts it to my face and tucks back a loose strand of hair before he feathers his thumb across my temple.

"What am I going to do with you, Penelope Hart?"

Fuck me.

Love me.

Marry me.

Feed me chicken wings....

I swallow hard. "I have a few ideas."

"I have a few of my own, baby."

I'm not sure if it's his words, how he whispered them, the softness in his eyes, the fact that he just called me baby—the most original, yet swooniest endearment ever—or the gentleness of his touch that has me feeling tingly all over. Like I have Pop Rocks in my veins. The back of my ears tickle. A heavy warmth weighs in my chest. Yet there's this hollow ache I can't describe. It's one thing to be turned on by him sexually. This... this is something different.

I like it.

But I don't like that I like it.

Loud applause and cheers can be heard from the ballroom. Jake blinks and the mist in his gray/green/blue eyes fades.

"We need to get back to the party."

He takes the beer from my fingers and tucks my hand in the crook of his arm. I spend the entire walk trying to distract myself from the feeling. I do this by thinking about turtles.

Snapping turtles.

Sea turtles.

Box turtles.

Ninja Turtles.

Turtles in a half shell.

"Turtle power!"

Fuck. Me.

"What is it about this hallway that makes you say stupid shit?" Jake asks, never slowing stride as he stares down at me with that you're-out-of-your-fucking-mind look.

"You try not chanting the song when you think about Ninja Turtles."

"I don't have to. Because I don't think about Ninja Turtles. Or any of that other random shit in your pretty little head."

I gaze up at him and smile. "You think I'm pretty?"

"I didn't say that."

"You said my head was pretty."

"Well it better be for the amount of money David Michael charges." He opens the door to the ballroom before I can respond.

Pee Paw's voice commands the entire room. Deep and strong. His words smooth. Confident. Powerful. The speech is more than a thank you or a farewell. It's a testimony to greatness. A promise that anything is possible with a little patience and a lot of hard work.

Shit's good.

When he thanks the entire room for forty years of memories, we're standing just to the right of the makeshift stage next to Cam. And I'm clapping the loudest. I really want to pull a Julia Roberts and roll my fist in the air while I let out a "Whoop, whoop, whoop!" But Jake would probably kill me. And Pee Paw probably wouldn't approve of the outburst either.

"As you all know, my dear friend Ed Sheeran is here tonight..."

Pee Paw looks at me. My mouth falls open. I silently relay him a message as he waits for the crowd to stop clapping.

You shut the fuck up, Pee Paw Swagger! You didn't tell me he was your friend! Ed who... You sneaky, studdly old fart!

"And as a favor to me, he has agreed to perform a song so that I may return a favor I owe to my Grandson Jake's lovely date, Penelope."

Where the fuck is my phone....

Emily is not *going to believe this shit!*

"Ladies and gentlemen, Mr. Ed Sheeran."

I'm still gaping. Staring at the fiery orange hair of one of my celebrity crushes as he takes the stage. Willing him to look at me. So that I may use my silent message relaying power to tell him, "Yes. I will have your babies."

But before I can wave like a fool to get his attention, Cam pries my opened clutch from my hand. Then I'm whisked around and embraced in the arms of Jake Swagger.

And I

Cannot

Breathe.

That Pop Rocks, ear tickling, warm chest, gaping hole feeling is back. Because Jake's smile is...everything. Maybe it's for show. To prove something to his grandfather. Keep the women from sinking their teeth into him. So he looks handsome in the pictures being taken by all these damn flashing cameras. And it scares the shit out of me because I don't care if it's fake. It feels real.

He doesn't hold me like a lover.

He holds me like a woman.

And it's not awkward.

Or crowding.

It's possessive.

And comforting.

We fit.

We are the *perfect* fit.

The song is *Perfect*.

Seriously.

Ed's singing *Perfect*.

"Relax, Penelope. Or do you just want us to stand here and not dance while every eye in the room is on us?"

I look around and sure enough, they're all watching. The dance floor is empty. It's just us. I take a breath and relax into Jake's firm hold. His smile widens and he winks. Then we're moving. Not in that slow spinning circle way like how normal people dance. No, he has to Jake Swagger the shit out of it and waltz us across the floor in long, graceful strides. And I have no clue what the fuck I'm doing. But somehow, I'm doing it. Backwards at that.

I mirror his steps. Move when I feel his push. His hand at the small of my back reassures me. If I miss a step, I have no doubt he will just tighten his hold, pick me up and carry me around the floor. My credentials for *That Guy* didn't even include being a good dancer. This is all Jake.

"Ready?"

"Huh?"

"To turn. You ready?"

"What?! No! Wait—"

Too late. He pushes me away from him. Releases my waist. Tightens his grip on my hand. Spins me. And before I can fuck it up, pulls me back to him. Never breaking stride.

"Don't do that again," I snap, still trying to wrap my head around the fact that I just did a swirly spin move and didn't fall on my face.

He laughs. The sound reverberates through his chest and thunders against mine. "You told me you knew how to dance."

"I do. I'm gonna show Ed my river dance as soon as this song ends."

He laughs.

Again.

His chest does that rumbling thing again too.

I really like it.

He twirls me.

I do not *like that.*

"Would you quit?"

"Why? What are you afraid of?"

"Um...falling on my ass and embarrassing myself in front of Ed."

His eyes flit toward the stage. "First you tell my Grandfather he's a stud. Now you're worried about impressing Ed? Are there any other men I need to know about?"

My smile falters a little.

His does too.

"I should have never left you alone with Briggs."

"How did you know about that? You weren't even around." I refrain from saying he was with a slut. Even though I really want to just so he can assure me he wasn't.

"The pregnant wife of one of my senior officers asked me to settle a friendly dispute between her husband and his assistant about whether they could determine the sex of the baby from an ultrasound picture. When I returned, you they were escorting Briggs out. I followed to see what happened. I'm sorry, Penelope. You didn't deserve that."

I'm trying to quell my excitement at the beautiful woman being married. And pregnant. Nonchalance is hard for me in the moment, but I manage it like a pro. "Meh. It is what it is."

"No." He shakes his head. "Don't disregard what he did. It was wrong."

"Maybe. But that's not your fault."

"It is my fault. You're with me tonight. It's my job to protect you. And I didn't. But I assure you he's been dealt with."

I perk up at that. "Oh! How alpha male of you. What did you do? Rough him up in the parking lot? Break a limb? Tell me, tell me, tell me."

His brows draw together. "No."

Spin.

Double spin.

"Would you stop that? I mean it."

He ignores me. "This isn't some juke joint or river bank in Mississippi. This is the corporate world, sweetheart. We don't fight with our fists. We fight with our lawyers. It's a lot more painful than a black eye. Trust me. I hit him where it really hurt."

"If you had hit him in the nuts, that would've really hurt. I'm just saying."

He grins. "Well the next time I have to defend your honor, I'll try your approach."

Spin.

Spin.

Spin.

"You're gonna make me puke on your shoes."

"Nah." His lips form a crooked smile. "I'll just spin you toward Cam and let you puke on his shoes."

"I wouldn't do that. I like Cam."

I'm not sure if his frown is real or not. "I thought I was your *That Guy.*"

"Yeah, but Cam told me I was pretty. He whistled at me. Twice. I've even been called a vision tonight. And stunning."

His eyes darken.

Spin.

"I want you to forget everything Briggs said to you tonight. Even that."

"Maybe I could if I had something better to remember."

He shakes his head. "So needy."

I shrug. I am needy. I don't care that he knows it.

He licks his lips. Gives me a solemn look. Just like he did the last time he almost said something nice to me. "Do you remember when we were sitting on my couch and you said I could have my pick of women? That you didn't know why I needed to hire someone?"

"Yes."

"Well, you were right. I could've chosen any woman in Chicago to accompany me here. Instead, I chose you. Do you know why?"

"Because I was your only option. I've already told you this. Remember? In the car on the way here? When I said Cam told me and you said he had a big mouth."

"I remember. And Cam's full of shit. That's not why I brought you."

"So why did you bring me?"

"I saw the dress." His eyes sweep me from head to toe. "This dress."

Spin.

Spin.

I don't scold him. I'm too anxious to hear what he says next.

"While you were on the phone with your mother, Alfred brought it up. And I just couldn't get the image of you in it out of my head. That's why I asked you, Penelope. Because I had to see you in this dress. Then I did. And in that moment I knew there was no fucking way I was coming to this party without the most beautiful woman in Chicago on my arm."

Go away, weird feeling. Go away. Go away. Go away. Take them flapping ass butterflies with you. And get me some water for this dry mouth. And a tissue for my watery vagina.

"I-I don't know what to say."

Spin.

Twirl.

Spin.

Spin.

Stop....

Dip.

"Nothing, Penelope. You don't have to say a damn thing."

I'm hovering above the floor. He's leaning over me. His arm muscles stretched tight against the fabric of his tux. Those lips slightly parted and a hairsbreadth from mine. Gray/blue/green penetrating. His nose skims my nose. Our breaths mingle. Mine labored. His controlled.

He straightens—pulling me with him. I'm lightheaded. More from his admission than the spins and awkward bent back position I was just in. I don't let go of his arms. He doesn't release me. He stares one second longer then turns toward the gathering crowd and smiles.

I lick my dry lips. Try to control my breath. Slow my heart. Smile. Not look like a love-struck idiot. It's harder than it sounds.

Then a flash of color appears. And the strange feeling dissipates, replaced with overwhelming excitement at the sound of the Irish accented voice.

"So I hear someone has some pretty bad ass dance moves."

CHAPTER TWELVE

"**N**o, Cam. This isn't cowboys and Indians. You don't make the *pew-pew* sound when you pull out the finger guns. You can make that clicking sound with your tongue and wink, but that's it."

We're in the back of the limo. Me and Victoria—Cam's date—on one seat, Cam and Jake on the seat across from us.

Cam shoots me with his finger guns. He makes the *pew-pew* sound. Blows the smoke off his revolvers. Holsters them. Then tips his imaginary hat. "That's how it's done, little lady."

I laugh so hard my side hurts and I lean against Victoria. She cringes and edges away from me. I laugh harder. Cam laughs too. I guess he's confident he's getting laid tonight no matter what he does, since he paid for it. Jake on the other hand? He doesn't laugh. Actually, he hasn't said or done a damn thing since we got in the car other than fuck me with his eyes.

At the party, he was a completely different person. We both had too much to drink. But Jake handled it better than I did. Where I'm carefree and charismatic and awesome all the time, it took him an ungodly amount of fancy liquor to get that way.

After Ed's performance, I'd shown him my river dance moves. He showed me some of his own. Jake seemed proud to introduce me as his date. We laughed. Danced. Joked. He kept his arm around my waist when

I was near. I leaned against him just to feel his grip tighten. Then I'd watch as he ignored whomever he was talking to, to look down at me and see if I was alright. When he discovered I was, he'd smile. Sometimes he'd wink. And I'd get that feeling.

But now that he's gone silent and brooding and all sexy-eyes, I have another feeling. It's not warm. It's hot. Fire hot. Horny hot. Crotch-about-to-set-the-seat-on-fire, hot.

I shake it off and turn back to Cam. "You ready for the next one?"

"Yep. If it's good, you get the guns." He shows me his finger guns. "If it sucks, you get the fingers." He flips me both his middle fingers.

"Put those away, cowboy. This is a pistol shooting rhyme if I've ever told one."

"I'll be the judge of that."

"Are we almost there? I'm getting a headache."

I turn to Victoria and level her with a look. "Victoria. Are we giving you a headache?"

"Yes," she deadpans.

"Well, lucky for you, I have something that will help."

"Oh, thank God." She straightens in her seat and holds her hand out to me.

I shake my head and tsk her. Downside of me drinking? My mouth loses its filter. "Laughter is the best medicine, Victoria." I hold my hand up. "And before you start getting splinters from that stick in your ass, just hear me out. If you don't laugh at this one, I won't say another word the rest of the ride."

She looks doubtful. "Really?"

"Scout's honor." I give her the Vulcan hand signal. *She doesn't know the fucking difference.*

"Fine."

"Are your finger guns ready?"

She heaves a breath, holds up her finger guns and gives me a sarcastic head jerk. "Happy?" I almost lose it when she actually holsters them. Cam turns his head to hide his smile and even Jake's lips curl.

"Yes. Thank you. So...There once was a man from Gent. Whose dick was so long that it bent. To save him some trouble, he folded it double and instead of coming he went."

Cam shoots up the car. Jake lifts a glass. I look over my shoulder at Ross who gives me a thumbs up. Victoria is trying like hell not to laugh. And failing. With a resigned breath, she shoots her finger guns.

Me and Cam cheer. He points at Victoria. "Your finger guns are so fucking sexy."

Then Victoria gives him a dreamy look and says, "I can't wait to swallow your cock."

Wait.

What?

Just...where the hell did that come from?

Awkward silence.

Even Cam doesn't know what to say. He does shift. And groan. Which makes it even more weird because now everyone in the car knows he has a hard-on.

"Mr. Swagger." Ross announces our arrival and quickly closes the partition as the car slows to a stop. Poor guy. It's going to take forever to drive across town to Cam's place in this weather.

"Don't fuck in my car, Cam. I mean it," Jake says, just as the door opens. I think I hear Ross mumble a thank you, but I can't be sure.

Jake helps me out and holds my hand as we enter the lobby. But he releases me once we're inside. "We got it, Alfred." He lifts his glass to him and Alfred nods.

"Have a good night sir."

Jake's voice is gravel. "I plan on it."

Holy shit.

What does that mean?

He keeps a respectable distance from me on the walk to the elevator. Once inside the box of death, I stand in one corner while he stays in the other. I hum my elevator song. It's all off key because I'm so distracted by the sexual chemistry thrumming between us and all the sexy questions in my head.

Is he going to fuck me?

Will we do it all night?

Like six times?

Just like in the books? Even though we're both buzzed and nobody wants to wake up at four in the morning with a hangover and sticky thighs to satiate their insatiable desires?

I follow him to the door of his apartment. He opens it and steps back, motioning me inside. My hands fidget with the fur on my coat. Afraid I might pluck the damn thing bald, I take it off and lay it over the chair. Then I walk to the windows. Because I need a distraction. That doesn't help. I just feel like I'm in a bubble.

Bubble.

Bubble gum.

Juicy fruit.

Winterfresh.

Doublemint.

"That's the statement of the greatment in doublemint gum."

I river dance a one-eighty until my back is to the window. I had a great finishing move but Jake isn't wearing his jacket. His bow tie is off. The first three buttons of his shirt open. And thank you, tuxedo gods, he's not wearing that weird back brace thing.

"So it wasn't just the hallway, I see. You say weird shit all the time, don't you?"

"Yeah. I kinda do. That. A lot. Especially when I'm nervous."

He walks toward me. Slow. Predatory.

Breathe.

Swallow.

Pull it together.

"Are you nervous, Penelope?"

My back hits the wall of glass behind me. He cages me in. One arm braced on the window beside my head as he stares down at me. I can smell the whiskey on his breath. My eyes fall to the glass and he lifts it to my lips. I take a sip.

"That's disgusting," I say, trying to keep from choking on the liquid fire scorching my throat.

His lips curl. "I asked if you were nervous."

"N-no. I'm not nervous. Uh-uh. Nope."

"Your pulse tells a different story." He traces my throat with his finger.

"Must be the whiskey."

Heart! Stop beating so hard!

"Did you like when I kissed you, Penelope?"   •

Why does he say my name like that? Like it's dirty talk. Like we're in the bedroom and he whispers in my ear, "Take your panties off."

I shiver.

"I'm going to assume that is a yes."

"Yes. It's a yes. I liked it. It was good. Great...good. Yeah."

"Hmm." He drags his finger down the center of my chest. The bottom of the glass in his hand sliding over the side of my exposed breast making me squirm. He finishes off the last of the whiskey and sets the glass on the table beside us.

He leans in. His eyes move from my eyes to my lips. Back and forth. Back and forth. "Can I kiss you?"

I nod so hard the back of my head hits the glass. I don't even feel it. "Say it."

Um. Okay.

"Kiss me, Jake."

And he does. His kiss is soft. Sweet. Sensual. Erotic. He deepens it and the whiskey and everything Jake and everything me mixes in the most delicious flavor I've ever tasted.

He kisses me stupid. Kisses me careless. Kisses me into another universe. Until Chicago is no longer at my back, but worlds away.

"My, my, my, Penelope." He breaks away from my mouth to whisper the words against my lips. "What a sweet mouth you have."

"Thank you." That sounded so stupid. Why did I say that?

"For what? The compliment or the kiss?" he teases.

"Both? Mostly for the kiss though. I mean, the compliment was nice, but that kiss was really nice."

"I'm glad you enjoyed it." His voice dips. "But that wasn't the kiss I asked for."

Hands.

They're sliding down my waist. Over my hips. Under my dress. Up my naked thigh. He lowers his body in front of me—dropping to one knee in the slowest, most seductive way imaginable. Eyes on mine the entire time as he grabs the lacy strap of my panties and inches them down my legs. He lifts my foot to free one side, then the other before tossing them over his shoulder.

With just his fingertips, he makes his way back up my leg. Caressing my ankle. My calves. Knees. Behind my knees. Higher. Taking my dress with him until it's fisted in those big hands at my waist.

He can see everything.

I think he likes what he sees.

He sure is staring at it hard.

I'm blushing everywhere. Wiggling with insecurity because his perfect face is positioned right in front of my bare sex.

Thank you, wax chick. Thank you. Thank you. Thank you.

Those green/gray/blue eyes lift, hazy with lust and nearly hidden beneath his long dark lashes. When the corner of his mouth lifts in a sexy smirk, I want to eat his face.

"Tell me the truth, Penelope. Have you ever been kissed..." his eyes dart back to my sex a moment then back to me, "here?"

Oh my God.

What do I do?

Lie?

Tell the truth?

Bladder check....

Okay, I'm good.

So what do I do?

Say something snarky?

Say nothing at all?

Tell him to quit wasting time and just do it already?

Truth. I'm going to tell him the truth. And I won't be ashamed. "No."

"No, what?"

I swallow hard. I know what to say here. I read books and shit. "No, sir."

He gives me a devilish grin. "I meant I want you to say the words, Penelope."

Fucking hell...Perhaps that isn't a playroom behind that locked door after all.

"I—" I close my eyes and take a breath. The fact that my vagina is still centered in front of his face doesn't relax me or make me think any clearer. "Could you please repeat the question, sir?"

I did not just do it again.

"So respectful. That's never really been my thing, but I think I like hearing that word on your lips."

I crack open one eye to see him peering up at me. He's clearly entertained. I'm thoroughly humiliated. And he hasn't even licked me yet.

His thumbs draw a circle on my inner thigh. My body jerks and I whimper in the most woeful way. I'm embarrassed. Shy. Nervous. All these things I'm not used to feeling. And he must notice because he takes pity on me.

"Look at me, Penelope." The grin is gone. There is no humor in his eyes. Only feral desire and raw possessiveness. "Has any man ever kissed you here? Yes, or no?"

I shake my head. "No."

His eyes drop and he growls. "Well that's a goddamn shame."

My head falls back. Fingers claw at the window in search of something to latch onto. Vocal cords open up and a cry erupts from deep in my chest.

His *mouth* is on my *vagina*.

His *tongue* is on my *vagina*.

Licking the seam of my sex.

Sliding between my lips.

Exploring.

Tasting.

Devouring.

He shifts beneath me. Lifts one of my legs to rest on his shoulder. It opens me up. Gives him full access to—everything. I moan so loud it drowns out the pounding in my ears. Whatever he's doing to my clit, is making me a shameless, horny, crazed maniac who selfishly just wants more of this...tongue-circle-mouth-suck-lip-kiss-repeat thing he's doing.

My hands find his head. Fingers thread through his hair. I hold him steady. Right where he is. Pleading loudly, "Yes. That. Just like that."

He groans.

I vibrate.

My knees almost buckle.

His grip tightens.

Have mercy.

This man is on his knees. Making me feel what I've never felt. Kissing me in a place I've never been kissed. No restraint. No teasing. Just sucking and licking and bringing me higher and higher and higher.

I never imagined it could be this good.

Never knew what I was missing.

But even if I did have experience in this type of kiss, I doubt any man other than Jake Swagger would know how to touch me like he does. How to give me exactly what I need. How to take what he wants because he knows I want it too.

You can paint it pretty and call it beautiful, but there is only one true way to have an orgasm.

With reckless

fucking

abandon.

So I do.

I don't hold back. I can't. It's not physically possible. But even if it were, I wouldn't. Because Jake Swagger not only expects me to give it all to him, but the man fucking deserves it. He's earned the right to know what he's doing to me. What he's done. How he's taken me from everything I know, away from where I am and everywhere I've ever been and transported me to a place where the only thing that matters is his mouth.

On my vagina.

I'll save you the details of my cries and tremors and pulsating waves of exquisite pleasure and just say this: I come.

He kisses his way up my body. Hands slide to my back and he lowers the zipper of my dress. He pushes the fabric off my shoulders and it puddles at my feet. His mouth dips to my breasts. He kisses one nipple while he pulls at the other with his fingers.

I tremble. Goosebumps cover my flesh. Not from the cold, but from the aftershocks of what I just experienced. I'm still trying to recover from the best orgasm of my life. And his touch on my oversensitive body isn't helping me come down from this high—it makes me want more.

I'm lifted. My legs around his waist. Hands still in his hair. His cupping my ass. Mouth trailing wet kisses along my neck. My back hits the couch. His big, warm body covers mine.

"I've wanted to fuck you on this couch since the moment I came home and found you on it."

I nod. "Yeah," I pant, breathless. "Me too."

He strips off his shirt. My fingertips skim his chest. Stomach. Nipples. Shoulders.

"Your touch is as good as your taste."

I lift my eyes. He's watching me. On his knees between my thighs. Palming his cock through his pants as I explore him with my hands.

"I wouldn't know."

He arches a brow. "You don't know how you taste?"

I shake my head. "I've always hoped it was like sunshine. Or rain. Or Skittles. But I'm not a very clean eater. And I danced a lot tonight. So I fear it may taste like cheap beer. Or armpits. Or heaven forbid, the sea."

He laughs. "I swear, if your innocence wasn't so damn sexy or your body this gorgeous or the way you come so fucking cock hardening, you could kill a mood with the shit you say."

Hmm...well now that's the nicest thing he's ever said to me. And it makes me a little shy, to be honest. I bite my lip to hide my demure smile and look away.

His thumb slides over my sex. He gives my clit a little rub, then dips the tip of his thumb into my opening. I whimper when he pulls away. And whimper again when he makes a show of licking and biting the pad of his thumb.

He leans over and touches his nose to mine. I inhale. Deep. He grins. Then kisses me just long enough to fill my mouth with my taste.

"Well?"

I frown. "I'm not sure. I can't really put a name to it. But it's definitely not armpits. Or of the sea variety."

"No, it's not."

"I wouldn't call it cheap beer or rain, either. And sadly, it doesn't taste like Skittles."

"Sunshine, then?"

"Don't be ridiculous, Jake." I roll my eyes. "Nobody knows what sunshine tastes like."

I really like it when his laughter rumbles against my chest. And when he dips his head to plant a kiss to the side of my throat, I like that too.

"Would you like to know how you taste to me, Penelope?" His mouth moves down my neck and he kisses a trail across my shoulder.

"O-okay."

"Like the sweetest kind of sin." He kisses his way back to my neck. "Like sexy innocence." He nibbles my earlobe. Licks the shell of my ear. Then growls, "Like my goddamn kryptonite."

I've been accused of a lot of things. Being someone's kryptonite isn't one of them. I'm not even sure it's a good thing. Nevertheless, it ignites something inside me.

I pull his mouth to mine. Kiss him hard. Inhale my sin. Taste my innocence. Use that recently discovered radioactive power I possess to force him to give me what I want. Which is him, naked. And inside me.

My fingers fumble with the button on his pants. He flicks my hand away and does it himself. Then he pushes his pants just over his hips. Pulls out his cock. Strokes it a couple times. Then while he retrieves his wallet from his back pocket, I marvel at the big thing that is somehow supposed to fit inside me.

Yes, I know this is overused in every romance novel. The, *will it fit,* line followed up by the, *don't worry baby, it'll fit,* response. But seriously. How the fuck is it going to fit?

This thing looks like a damn sixteen-ounce Coke can. Simple vaginal stretching just won't do. I'll have to fucking dilate to accommodate this monstrosity. And that's not happening. Sex? Between us? Yeah, that's not going to happen either.

On a side note, I now understand what heroines mean when they say a penis is beautiful. I never thought a cock could be beautiful. This one actually is. Well, for a cock. I mean, it doesn't compare to like a sunset or a clear blue sky or the long awaited birth of a famous giraffe's baby, but to the other penises I've seen—in real life and on T.V.—it's beautiful.

"Hey...." Jake's soft voice pulls me from my thoughts. Concern is etched on his face. "You okay?"

"Huh? Oh. Yeah. But um, yeah. No. That," I point to his cock, "that's not going in this." My hand sweeps up and down my entire torso. I'd motion all the way to my throat, but I'm being realistic here. No penis is that big.

A slow grin spreads across his face. "That's more flattering than *sir*."

I lean up on my elbows. "Really? I figured you'd be mad."

"Because you said my dick was big? Baby...please."

He keeps calling me baby and I'll let him put that thing in my butt.

"I almost came just hearing it."

"Want me to say it again then? Is that how you want to get off? Because I was serious when I told you that this isn't happening." I do the finger-point-torso sweep again.

His head tilts a little and he studies me with a mixture of hope and disbelief. "Are you a virgin?"

"Did you really just ask me that?" I shake my head at him.

"So, no?"

"No, not no. I was shaking my head in disbelief. It wasn't my answer."

"So, yes?"

"That is a very personal question, Jake."

"We crossed the personal boundary when you were pressed up against my windows, screaming my name, coming on my face. I think it's safe for me to ask if you're a virgin."

Fair enough.

"I'm not a virgin. I've had sex. Not a lot of it, but enough to know that your cock is way too big for me. I have a narrow channel, Jake."

He groans as if he's in pain and strokes himself. "That mouth of yours is killing me, baby."

Okay. He can have it. If he rips me in two? Totally worth it.

Kidding.

He can't have it. When a man says, *I'm going to ruin you for every other man on the planet,* it's supposed to be in reference to him being great in bed. In this case, Jake would ruin me for an entirely different reason. Hot dog down a hallway kind of reason.

"I'm scared." My admission comes as a shock to me. Why did I say it? Why did I whisper it in a voice tinged with fear? Why does looking at his handsome face with all its softened features make me feel like I said exactly what needed to be said?

Jake stuffs his rigid cock that is now sheathed in a condom, into his boxers and pulls his pants up over his hips—not bothering to zip them. Probably because he can't. He stands and holds his hand out to me. "Come on."

I take his hand and let him pull me from the couch. He grabs a blanket and wraps it around my shoulders before leading me into the kitchen. There, he lifts me to sit on the counter, pours us both a glass of wine, hands me one, clinks my glass and takes a big sip.

I guzzle mine until there's nothing left.

He pours me another one.

"Better?"

I nod. "Yes. Thank you."

"It's not that big, Penelope."

My eyes roll. I thought we were having a sweet moment. He just wants to get me drunk and fuck me. "Have you done research on this? How many penises have you actually seen, Jake?"

"Probably more than you. And wipe that look off your face. No. I'm not nor have I ever been, gay. But I am a man. Who has pissed in a public urinal. And watched porn. And may or may not have measured my dick along with all of my frat brothers in college."

"And how did you measure up?"

He takes a sip of wine.

"That's what I thought."

The way he looks at me—curious like I'm a mystery, yet captivated by what he's already unveiled—has me feeling that feeling again. The way he licks the corner of his lip and drops his eyes to my legs has me rethinking this whole, *it won't fit,* thing. And when he tucks my hair behind my ear, looks me dead in the eye and whispers, "You truly are a vision, Penelope Hart," I swear I can feel my vagina widening just for him.

What the fuck am I doing?

Is it really *that* big?

I don't even drink sixteen-ounce cans of Coke.

I can't recall the last time I saw one.

What do I know?

And aside from the fact that I'm sitting naked, on a kitchen counter, in a penthouse, that belongs to Chicago's most eligible bachelor, who just so happens to be the hottest man on the planet, I have an opportunity to get some hands on, real life experience with my *That Guy*. This is research. Nobody made the *New York Times'* bestseller list with a book they didn't do some research on.

Sigh....

The things I do to be a good writer.

I finish my wine. Grab his glass and finish it too. Shrug the blanket off my shoulders. Wrap my hands around his neck. Pull him to me. Lock my legs around his waist. And fist his hair in my hand.

"Kiss me, Jake."

Within moments we're back on the couch. Our movements frantic. Mine because I need him. His because he's probably afraid I might change my mind. But that can't be right. Because he grabs my wrists. Pins them over my head. Gives me a long, thoughtful look and then asks, "Are you sure, baby?"

Baby.

Gah.

If I wasn't sure before. I'm sure now.

"Please."

His mouth is on my nipple. Hands cupping my ass. Hips grinding against me. He moves lower. Lower. Lower. That tongue of his finds my clit and performs that tongue dance he's so good at. He slips a finger inside me. I'm a little embarrassed by how easily it slides in. He adds another finger and there's not much resistance there either.

It doesn't take long for me to reach that point where I don't care if a small SUV can drive in there. I'm coming so hard, screaming so loud, flying so high, feeling *so. Damn. Good.* I fear I may lose consciousness.

He asks me something and I nod. I have no clue what I just agreed to, but it doesn't matter. If I die, I'll go out knowing that sparks really do explode behind your eyelids when you have the right kind of orgasm.

You know, I'm ashamed to even look Jake in the eye right now. Because that big Coke can cock of his that I swore wouldn't fit, slides right up inside me without anything more than a slow, persistent thrust. Jake does the whole, "*So fucking tight,*" speech on a *pained cry*, and I know it's just to make me feel better.

"You have to relax, gorgeous. Trust me. I won't hurt you."

I just stare at him. *Really, asshole? Did you have to say it out loud?* It's obvious he isn't going to hurt me. Because it's also obvious that I'm not as narrow as I thought I was.

To humor him, I let out a loud breath and relax every muscle. It's like someone let the air out of me. I just deflate completely and sink about three inches into the couch cushions. I hadn't realized how tense I actually was.

I hadn't realized Jake wasn't even halfway inside me either.

I can't help it. I smile. Big cheesy grin. You know...because narrow channel and all that.

"Pretty proud of yourself I see." He pushes deeper and my smile turns into an O. He slides out, thrusts back in a little more and I groan. The next time steals my breath and he pauses to kiss me stupid and remind me to breathe before pulling out and burying himself in me completely.

Oh.

My.

Fuck.

It's so much. So, so much. I've heard this sensation described as feeling full. I'm past full. I'm in cock overload. I can feel this motherfucker in my spine. One wrong move could result in paralysis. This shit isn't natural.

"Penelope...."

I hope like hell that strangled cry is because he's just come and this is over and he can get out of me while I still have feeling in my legs.

"If you don't stop squeezing my cock you're going to kill it."

"What?"

He chuckles. Mutters something. Lowers his mouth to mine. I melt. The moment I do, I understand what he's talking about. He doesn't shrink in size. My vagina doesn't get any bigger, either. But without the Kegel death grip, the feeling changes. Still more than full, but not at all unpleasant. The great thing about big dicks? They can reach places that elicit sensations most women don't even know exist.

Take my word for it, though. They exist.

"You think too much." His hips swivel and I gasp. "If I can't make you forget everything but me, then I'm not doing something right."

"You're right." I grin up at him. "Perhaps you should step up your game, Mr. Swagger."

His smile is wicked. "My pleasure, Miss Hart."

I really need to learn to keep my mouth shut.

I'd have been fine with plain ol' vanilla sex—me on my back. Him thrusting and grunting inside me while I moan and claw at his arms. But when Jake Swagger steps up his game, it's like going from Pee-Wee football to the NFL. Just...one minute you're a three-foot-tall quarterback, missing your two front teeth, pausing mid-throw so your mom can take a picture, and the next you're six two with a Nike endorsement, a Maserati, a supermodel to cook your dinner and another to lick your balls.

Jake Swagger doesn't fuck around.

Before I can even process what's happening, I'm flipped on my stomach. Hips lifted. Knees spread. Ass up. Back arched. Hair fisted. Head pulled back so I can see our reflection in the windows.

I love how he touches me. How me slides his hand up my back and across my ribs to palm my breast, instead of just directly reaching and fondling it. It makes the lewd position I'm in feel sensual. Makes me feel sexy. And makes him a good lover.

"When I fuck you like this...on your knees...that pretty little ass of yours in the air...you're going to feel all of me." His hand slides down my stomach to cup my pussy. "This sweet cunt is going to feel me for days." The tip of his middle finger dips inside me. Then he drags the wet digit through my lips to circle my clit. "We'll start nice and slow. You tell me when you want more. I'll let you set the pace, baby." His voice drops to a whisper. "But I decide when you come."

He kisses me softly on my temple, like I'm someone to be cherished. Like I mean more to him than an ass in the air and a quick fuck. The intimacy contradicts everything in this moment. It's exactly what I've always wanted from sex. Yet I never knew it until now.

My entire body thrums with this pulsing energy that will not fade. When he releases my hair to drag his hands across my spine and to my hips, I break position on a sigh. He's quick to correct me.

"Ass up, gorgeous. Hollow your back. I want to see every inch of you. Watch your pussy swallow my cock."

Fuck. Damn. Oh. My.

I do as he says. He wastes no time pushing inside me. I look over my shoulder and tremble when I see those gray-green-blue eyes hooded with lust. Darkened with desire. Lips parted as he breathes deep—his chest rising and falling as slow as his thrusts. The sight of him is as much of a turn on as what he's doing to me.

He's deep—so deep. I'm deliciously full. Stretched wide. The size of him elicits sensations that border on pain which only heightens my pleasure. My response is a continual song of loud moans that are like a cathartic release. I can't control them anymore than I can control the build that stirs in my depths. Or the sweat that beads on my skin—fighting the fever that burns inside me. Or the need for something more. Just a little. Just enough to push me over the precipice.

"More, Jake."

He drives a little harder. It's not enough.

"More."

His hips move a little faster. It's not enough.

"More...please."

His words get a little dirtier.

"...Love how greedy your fucking pussy is..."

Still, I can't find my release. He pounds inside me, pistoning his hips mercilessly. Bruising the back of my thighs with his own. Spreading me open with his hands. Baring every part of me and reminding me how much the sight turns him on. But without the touch of his tongue or his fingers on my clit, I just...can't.

"Jake, I—" My voice cracks. Frustration builds. Need becomes overwhelming. I push against him. Meet his thrusts. I'm a wet, wanton mess with no shame. No humility. Filled with desperation.

"Tell me, baby." He shifts behind me and the movement causes me to stiffen. He doesn't stop, only slows his pace a fraction while I adjust. Within seconds, I'm pushing back against him again. Hoping this is the angle I need. But my release is still just out of reach.

I whimper. If I don't come soon, I'll combust or at the very least, my vagina will be ravaged beyond repair.

"Please, Jake. I need...I need..."

"I know what you need, sweet girl." *Oh...the way he talks.*

The deep tenor. The reassurance. The unspoken promise of delivery. Right now I'd do anything for this man. I've never felt the desire to please anyone as much as I do him in this moment.

His hand wraps around my stomach and he lifts me. My back to his chest. His mouth on my neck. Hands on my breasts. Then...*oh.*

Oh.

OH.

"There's the sweet spot," he murmurs, rocking into me with long, smooth strokes. His hand slides down my stomach. Finds my clit. He rubs me in the slowest, most torturous way. The build climbs, but at a pace I'm not patient enough for.

"Relax. The less you rush it, the better it'll feel." He kisses my temple again. "I promise."

I do as he says and relax. The feeling intensifies the higher I get until I'm to the point I'm scared of what awaits me at the top. I stifle a sob. "Jake...."

"I know, baby."

"I can't—"

"Shh...."

My nails dig into his thighs. My entire body becomes rigid. Breath leaves me. Behind my eyes are flashes of colors against darkness. A dull almost silent ringing sounds in my ears.

I shatter around him.

Pleasure consumes me in waves.

Over and over and over until I'm lying limp against him. I don't have the strength to do anything. My limbs are flaccid and the only thing keeping me from falling is the hold he has on me.

He pulls out of me and gently lays me on my side on the couch. A blanket engulfs me in warmth. My shoes are removed from my feet.

His steps are silent as he walks away. Probably to get a warm cloth to clean me like all the good *That Guys* do. The lights go out. *Or perhaps that's what he was doing.*

I anticipate the feel of his lips on my temple again kissing me good-night. I shiver with the idea of him sliding beneath the blanket and pulling me into his arms. I fight my sleep just to wait for his return.

He never does.

CHAPTER THIRTEEN

"Penelope."

The deep voice calling my name isn't Emily's. The big hand shaking my shoulder doesn't belong to her either.

It's all coming back to me.

Flaming dog shit.

Jail.

Jake.

Party.

Sex.

Mmm...sex.

"Penelope. Get up."

I groan and pull the cover over my head. "Go away."

Loud, dramatic exhale. "Cam, do something."

Silence.

More silence.

I'm curious now.

I roll over and peak out from beneath the blanket to see Cam sitting on the ottoman less than two feet from me. He grins. "Good morning, princess. You look like hell."

He looks like perfection in a suit. "It's Sunday. Why are you dressed like that?"

"Because I'm at work."

I look around the living room. "You work here?"

"I do."

"In Jake's house?"

"When I need to." He holds up a steaming cup. "Coffee?"

"I prefer Mountain Dew in the afternoon." I look out the window. It's as gray as it was yesterday. "It is after noon, right?"

"It's eight in the morning."

I can't keep the edge out of my voice. "Then why are you waking me up?"

"Because I was told to."

"You work for Jake, don't you?"

He tweaks my nose. "Nothing gets past you. Now, get up. Seriously."

A wave of sadness washes over me. "Are you taking me home?"

"What is she still doing on the couch?" Jake's thundering voice turns my head. He's freshly showered, dressed in jeans and a sweater. He stomps over to us and takes a seat in the chair. Man, he looks good this morning. My thighs tingle at the reminder of how good he looked last night.

I glance at the window. At the exact spot where he sank to his knees. Out of the corner of my eye, I see his gaze follow mine. I'm looking at him when he turns back.

He smirks. "The things we do when we're drunk."

Ouch.

That probably wouldn't sting so bad if it didn't trigger the reminder of what else happened last night. What I've been trying all morning to forget. At the party, something sparked between us. He'd told me I was the most beautiful woman in Chicago. We shared that dance. He'd held my hand for the greater part of the evening.

Then we came home. And he fucked me like I've never been fucked. Kissed me where I've never been kissed. Said things to me that made me feel like I meant something to him. I'm not stupid or naive enough to think that he'd hopelessly fallen in love with me and last night was the start of our happily ever after. But I'd expected more from him than this— left on the couch, alone.

He treated me like a Miss Sims.

I feel like one too.

He slips his shoes on and stands. His towering position over me makes me feel small. The dismissiveness in his eyes makes me feel insignificant. And the pain in my chest worsens.

"I have a very important client coming over today. I need you to stay out of sight while he's here. You can use the guest bedroom. Take a nap. A shower. I don't care. But under no circumstances do you come to my office. Understood?"

I have nothing to say, so I simply nod.

"My assistant is working on travel arrangements for you. We should know something by the time my meeting is over."

Why is he acting like this?

I've never been one to feel sorry for myself. This time is no different. So Jake Swagger wants to send me home. Today. And he hurt my feelings. It's not the first time. And just like the first time, I bottle up those feelings. I can think about them later. Or never. Right now, I'm going to spend what little time I have left here focusing on my revenge—the one thing I know better than *That Guy*.

"Fine."

I stand with the cover around me. It slips and nearly exposes my breast, but I catch it just in time. And I don't miss the flash of possessive heat or the warning in Jake's eyes as he plants himself in front of Cam's line of sight.

I turn to hide my smile and attempt to sashay out of the room. That doesn't work. My poor vagina took a beating last night. And I'm feeling it today. So I end up taking tentative steps that I hope aren't too obvious.

But leave it to Cam to shit on my dreams.

"Someone slung the D last night...."

Asshole.

I'M NOT SHOWERING in the guest bedroom. After the morning I've had, I deserve a nice hot bubble bath in the aquarium-sized tub in the master suite. I probably shouldn't have added all those bubbles and turned on the jets, though. Turns out that shit can get out of hand in a hurry.

By the way, when heroines claim they're, "deliciously sore," after a rough fuck with a hot hero, they're lying.

There is nothing delicious about the way I feel today. It hurts. Everything hurts. My wallowed out narrow channel is battered. Thighs bruised. Clit raw. My limbs are achy and stiff. Nipples tender to touch. And my head feels like it might explode. Partly from alcohol, partly from the hair pulling.

Jake Swagger should have his ass beat for not checking on me, massaging me or offering me some numbing crème for my lady parts. The first thing he should've done this morning was ask me how I was feeling. Then tell me he was going to take care of me today. That's what swoony *That Guy* would do.

But did Jake do that?

No.

Why?

Because he's an asshole.

I have no clothes, so I slip into Jake's closet and sift through his. I choose a gray dress shirt that hangs nearly to my knees. After rolling up the sleeves, I examine myself in the mirror and make a mental note to steal this before I leave. If I belted it at the waist, and paired it with some heels, it would be a super cute outfit.

"He'd be pissed if he knew you were in here."

I meet Cam's laughing eyes in the mirror and shrug.

"You like pushing his buttons, don't you?"

"Prove to me he doesn't deserve it and I'll stop." I spin to face him. He's leaned against the doorway, arms crossed over his chest. "What are you doing in here? I thought you were working."

He lifts a shoulder. "He's pissed at me. So I walked away before he could hurt my feelings." His smile tells me he's not the least bit worried about his feelings.

"Why is he mad at you?"

"Because of what I said about you and him," he shoots me a wicked grin, "...fucking."

Oh.

"I'm assuming he doesn't kiss and tell?"

"Well, see that's the thing that has me so confused, Penelope. He always kisses and tells. And that comment I made is one I've made plenty of times. This is the first time it's pissed him off."

I blanche. "You mean you've watched other women do the bow-legged walk of shame?"

He laughs. "No. That was a first. But the just-fucked hair and the hungover woman on the couch always means the same thing. Someone got the D."

Cam just confirmed my worst fear. He did treat me like a Miss Sims last night. And that bottle holding my hurt feelings is just about full. But I make room. And focus on something that will make me angry instead of sad. Like the fact that Jake has ruined yet another fantasy about *That Guy*.

If he's the hero and I'm the heroine in this story, then he should've fucked me in a place he's never fucked another woman.

It's official.

Jake Swagger is not *That Guy.*

He is That Asshole.

"Always thinking." Cam grins at me and pushes off the door. "I'm out of here. You need anything?"

"Nah. I'm good. But it'll probably be the last time I see you, so should we hug? Also, I need your number to give to my best friend, Emily, because I need you to fall in love with her."

He shakes his head at me. "You're nuts. And you'll be here when I get back. I'm sure of it." I want to bombard him with questions. Ask him why he's so damn sure that I'll still be here. But he does that mysterious, sexy wink and leaves me on a cliffhanger.

Whatever. I'm glad he's gone. I have shit to do anyway. Like find some food. Make a plan. And fuck up whatever Jake has going on in his office.

"...EVERYTHING else is negotiable, but I promise you we'll stand firm..." Jake's voice trails off as his eyes meet mine.

I'm standing in the doorway of his office. Holding a silver platter with a bunch of random shit I found in Jake's kitchen in one hand. The other hand on my hip. Wearing nothing but his shirt and a smile.

That vein in Jake's forehead makes its presence known as he shifts in his seat. Instead of sitting in his desk chair, he sits next to his client—a middle aged man dressed in a Stetson, cowboy boots, Wranglers and a blazer.

Perfect.

"Figured you boys were hungry," I say, in my thickest southern drawl.

The man stands. Jake, in his stunned/angry state, is a little slower to follow suit.

"Well, now," the man says and smiles warmly at me. "Who is this?" I detect a hint of an accent in his voice. Definitely not from around here. Not as deeply southern as mine either.

"Mr. Canton, Penelope Hart. Penelope, this is Mr. Canton. He's here on business." Jake speaks with an edge of annoyance that he attempts to conceal with a smile that doesn't meet his eyes.

"Pleasure to meet you. Cracker?" I hold out the tray.

"No thank you, dear. I had a big breakfast." He rubs his slightly bulging stomach.

"Drink?"

"We're good—"

"A whiskey if you have it?" Jim cuts in, shooting Jake a sideways glance.

"Of course. I'll help you with that, Penelope," Jake says, walking toward me and mouthing something about killing me once he's out of Jim's sight.

"Thanks, Jake." I thrust the platter into his hands and ignore his clenched jaw and hard eyes as I step around him and claim his seat. "I can tell by your accent you're not from around here." I keep my gaze on the man so I don't have to face Jake's glare. But I can still feel the daggers he shoots at me.

Jim chuckles as he settles back in his seat. "I could say the same about you, Miss Hart."

"Call me Penelope, please."

He tips his hat to me. "Alright, Penelope. And you can call me Jim. What state below the Mason Dixon line are you from?"

"Mississippi. And you?"

"Kansas. I've been here a week on business. I was supposed to fly out a couple days ago but the weather took a nasty turn."

I gasp and lean forward to lightly slap his knee. "Same thing happened to me!"

"Are you here in Chicago on business as well?" He winks at me. "Or some other reason?"

"Definitely some other reason."

"Really?" His smile is warm and suggestive. Like maybe I'm here for Jake. "And what might that other reason be?"

"To set a bag of dog shit on fire."

His brow furrows. "I beg your pardon?"

"You know, put some dog shit in a bag. Set it on a porch. Light it on fire. Ring the doorbell and wait for someone to run out and stomp on it. It's quite entertaining to watch. But rather difficult to pull off." I lean forward, shield the side of my mouth with my hand and drop my tone. "You wouldn't believe how protective these people around here are of their dog's shit."

Jim stares silently at me for several long moments before he bursts into a fit of laughter. Jake walks in and looks between the two of us confused. I just smile.

"This..." Jim points at me while he pauses to catch his breath. "This girl is something else, Jake. I like her."

Jake's fake ass laugh has me rolling my eyes. "She is definitely something else." He moves out of Jim's sight and mouths, "What the fuck did you do?"

I shrug and take the other whiskey glass in Jake's hand that's clearly for him and not me. But these damn morning drinkers are turning me into an alcoholic. Until I take a sip and nearly barf.

"You must come to dinner with Jake tonight."

"Unfortunately, Jim, she can't. She's busy."

"No I'm not."

Jake levels me with a look and a cool smile. "Sure you are."

"Mmm...." I pretend to think on it a second. "Nope. I'm free."

"Great!" Jim stands and holds his hand out to Jake who immediately transforms into a charming, gracious host. "I'll see you both there. My girls are going to love her." His expression turns solemn despite his smile. "Might make convincing them a little bit easier. No offense, but the corporate world can be intimidating. It'll be nice for them to see you surround yourself with people who are a bit more what we're used to."

Jake seems genuinely happy now. "I understand. We'll be there." He walks him out while I sit and wait for the explosion to happen.

When Jake returns, he walks around to his desk and takes a seat in his big, important chair. He's stoic and I can't read him. I'd almost prefer him angry.

"That man was convinced that his daughters wouldn't agree to sell their stock in the company. I've spent the past thirty minutes trying to renegotiate our deal because this is an investment I refuse to walk away from. Nothing I said persuaded him to give me the chance to pitch my offer to his family." He pauses and takes a deep breath. I can tell he's about to say something he really doesn't want to. And it makes me *so* happy.

"But whatever random shit you said or crazy shit you did in the two minutes I was gone was enough to convince him otherwise. And I don't know if I want to throw you through those windows, fuck you senseless against them or drop to my knees and do what I did last night until you can't stand up on your own."

I don't know where I put that bottle of feelings I'd planned to pull out to remind me of who Jake really is, in the event he tried to turn his charm on me. Because, suddenly, I'm mush and hormones and heat. But I keep it together—barely—and remain unaffected on the outside. "A simple thank you will suffice."

"Not a chance in hell. What did you do?"

"I didn't do anything."

"You did something. What the fuck was it."

I roll my eyes. "Really, Jake. I didn't do anything. People just naturally gravitate toward me. I'm a pretty remarkable person. But you're too busy being a self-centered asshole to notice."

He scoffs. "Self-centered? After all I've done for you."

Now, it's my turn to scoff. "What you've done for me? What about what I've done for you?" He starts to say something but I point my finger at him and narrow my eyes. "So help me God, if you bring up me breaking into your house, I will jump over this desk and ravage you."

Ravage....

Fuck.

That's not the right word.

"I meant, tackle you."

"Are you a woman of your word?"

"Of course!" I snap, not realizing I've taken the bait until he has me hook, line and sinker.

"You broke into my house."

I sit back and cross my arms. His eyes move to my exposed cleavage. "You can forget it, *sir.*"

"So you're not a woman of your word."

"I'm a woman who can barely walk today."

He frowns at that and the cutest little V forms between his brows. "Are you hurting?"

"Oh, now you care." There's no bite to my words. Truthfully, I didn't even want to say them. I'd much rather nod, pout, make my lip quiver, crawl in his lap and let him comfort me. But I have a little bit of dignity. Not much, but some.

He stands and makes his way to me. My heart pounds harder the closer he gets. And he keeps breathing all the air and not leaving any for me. He takes my chin in his hand when I refuse to look at him. That V is still there between his eyes.

"What can I do? Would you like something for the pain?"

I slap his hand away. "I was fucked hard. Not hit by a bus."

I'm mad because that's not what I want him to say. He shouldn't *ask* me anything. This is the part where he is supposed to scoop me up. Take me to his bed. Inspect me. Growl and say something about how much he wants me but that he'll have to wait. Then cover me up. Demand I stay put. Fetch me a glass of water, two Ibuprofen and insist that I take them and rest.

I'm so over him fucking everything up....

"What the hell is your problem, Penelope?"

"*I'm* not the one who has a problem."

He rears back like I slapped him. "Oh, so I'm the problem?"

"Yes."

"For fuck's sake, what are you so pissed about?"

I jump to my feet and poke my finger in his chest. "The fact that you don't know for starters."

"Why don't you enlighten me then?"

"Fine! I will."

Oh, there you are bottle of emotions.

I stomp around the room and make a big show of flailing my arms. "You're nice to me as long as you're drunk or trying to get your dick wet. Saying sweet shit to me. Calling me baby. Treating me like, oh...I don't know...a human! Then, the moment you're sober and your cock is dry, you treat me like I'm a pebble in your shoe. And I'm over here, doing all of this to save your ass, when all I really want to do is drop you on it."

He shakes his head while I catch my breath. "You can't even come up with an original line to threaten me with."

Though I already know, I ask, "What are you talking about?"

"That last line? The one about dropping me on my ass? That's a line from *Dirty Dancing*."

Hands on my hips, I glare at him while I scramble for a comeback. "Well...the fact that you know that line isn't gonna make me like you. So...whatever."

"Whatever?"

"What...*ever*."

"Kiss me."

"What?"

"Kiss me."

"N-No."

"Would you rather me ask? Fine. I'll ask. Kiss me?"

What the hell is happening?

"No. I'm not going to kiss you."

"I won't ask again, Penelope."

This motherfucker thinks he's so...suave....

"Then don't."

"Done."

Three steps.

That's the distance it takes for him to have me at arm's length.

Two breaths.

That's how long it takes for him to reach out, grab me around my waist and pull me flush against his chest.

One kiss.

That's all it takes to melt me.

I don't even know why I was angry. I mean, it's not like he owed me anything. I can take the good with the bad. Sure we had a spat, but if we're destined to be together, that's expected.

He pulls away from my mouth and lifts me around his waist. "You know why I can't be nice to you?" Words fail me, so I shake my head as he sets me on his desk. "Because when I am, you get this look about you." He pulls his shirt over his head. Rips open mine and groans. "This hazy, lust-driven look that drives my cock crazy."

His lips find mine on a frantic, impatient kiss. I return it with just as much fervor. I'm a panting, wanting mess when he grabs the back of my knees and pulls me to the edge of the desk. "How sore are you?" The intensity in his stare warns me not to lie.

Desperation overrules all sense of reason. "Not sore enough to say no."

He flattens his palm against my stomach and urges me down onto my back. The heels of my feet somehow find their way to the edge of the desk. My knees part and he's there, staring down at me. Completely bare.

He caresses the inside of my thigh with the back of his knuckles before dragging his thumb down my slit. "You're swollen."

"Yeah, about that. I got stung by a bee. Doesn't have shit to do with last night. I'm good."

And obviously desperate to say some random shit like that.

He chooses to ignore my stupidity and pushes one, long digit inside me. "Fuck, you're as wet as you were last night. Tighter than you were last night. You're swollen here, too."

Told y'all it was as big as a Coke can....

He removes his finger from my *stupid swollen vagina* to caress my thigh once again. He also frowns and has that little V of concern I thought was hot, but now I just find it annoying.

"It's nothing. Really. I'm naturally this tight. It's just my narrow channel, Jake."

"Penelope...please stop saying narrow channel."

"It's the appropriate medical term."

"Appropriate or not, I find it sexy as hell and I shouldn't. Not to mention I'm trying to *not* go against my better judgement and take you hard right here on my desk, bee sting reaction or not."

He said bee sting.

I giggle.

He glares.

"That cute little laugh of yours doesn't help either."

"Have you tried thinking about turtles?"

He says nothing.

"Bubble gum?"

More silence.

"Want to channel my energy?" I press my fingers to my temple.

He grabs my hand and pulls me to a sitting position. My feet fall with the movement and soon my legs are dangling over the side of the desk and he's in between them. He does that hair tuck, temple touch thing. "I took you too hard last night."

My body instantly ignites in flames. I whimper and shift on the desk. Lean into his touch. Reach out and try to pull him on top of me. He's an immovable steel force.

"Let me take care of you today."

Oh, now he wants to be That Guy and take care of me.

Now.

When I'm a hot, horny mess.

Well, this isn't swoony *That Guy's* moment. This is Jake Swagger's moment. The fuck you with my big dick and you'll take it and like it because I said so, Jake Swagger.

"If you really want to take care of me...."

"Mind out of the gutter, Penelope." He sweeps me off the desk and plants me on my feet. Pushes the tattered shirt off my shoulders. Grabs his discarded one from the floor. Pulls it over my head then kisses my forehead like a fucking Daddy Dom. Which isn't my kink.

"Are you trying to pout that hard or does it just come natural?"

Pout....

A very *Daddy Dom* thing to say.

"If you pull out a sippy cup, I'm gone."

He eyes me a moment, shakes his head, then turns and walks out— mumbling under his breath, "The shit she says..."

CHAPTER FOURTEEN

S o maybe swoony *That Guy* isn't that bad. His timing is just off. Like this morning when I wanted him to care about me and he didn't. Then later this morning when I wanted him to not care about me and he did. In the end, I got what I wanted. Just not when I wanted it.

Well...some of what I wanted anyway.

I'd already had my lady parts inspected on his desk. Then he'd ordered us breakfast—even asking what I wanted. I'd settled for bacon, eggs, pancakes, fresh fruit and some of that oatmeal from McDonalds with the raisins in it.

Did you know that Uber will bring you food? In a blizzard? They call it Uber Eats. That might not be a big deal to some people, but when you're from a town where even the local Pizza Hut doesn't deliver, hearing news like this will blow your mind.

Anyway, after that, I finally got those two Ibuprofen and tall glass of water, along with the demand to rest. Which is exactly what I did. Only I slept on the couch instead of his bed, because I was too full from all the shit Uber Eats delivered to make it up the stairs.

After a three-hour nap, I took a hot shower to wake me up. When I got finished with that, I was instructed to, hurry the hell up before I made us late. I started to complain that I had nothing to wear, but then I found an outfit already laid out on the guest bed for me. And every cosmetic I could ask for was lying on the bathroom counter.

I left my thick curls untamed so they were wild and crazy, but somehow stylishly cute. Spritzed them, my neck and my wrists with Chanel. Went heavy on the mascara to make my eyes really pop. Light on the lipstick so I had that glossy, natural pink, Kim Kardashian thing going. Marveled at my skin that glowed against the stark white, off-the-shoulder blouse that flared slightly at the waist. Thanked Emily for the Pilates class she signed me up for, which had tightened my ass and toned my legs, that looked really great in the black, leather, stiletto pants. And took seventeen pictures of the Louboutin heels that were white on top and red on the bottom.

"Penelope!"

I snap a quick, bathroom mirror, duck face selfie and send it to Emily. Wait for her response.

Get the same one I get every time I send her a pic.

The middle finger emoji.

"We've got to..." Jake's voice trails off as he drinks me in, fucks me down, turns me on and twists me inside out all with a look. "...Go."

"Do I look pretty?" I flash him a smile and curtsy.

"You look like dessert."

Heat is just...it's everywhere. Burning me the fuck up. I part my lips to get more air and pant while he takes his time looking at me. "Do you like dessert?"

He meets my eyes. "It's quickly becoming my favorite thing to eat."

Kryptonite...Still got it.

I'm feeling a little weak, too. The man is wearing a suit, which isn't unusual for him. But this one? All black. Jet black. Even his tie is black. He looks like a CEO bad boy. And that big Rolex on his wrist isn't helping to quell my desire.

I'm not a materialistic person or anything, but when you've only dated the kind of dudes who wear a Timex, you can't help but get a little excited over seeing a man with a diamond encrusted piece of jewelry that, no matter the quality, still just tells fucking time. Like, literally. That's it's *only* purpose. Hottest waste of money ever.

The ogling between us lasts a minute longer before he clears his throat and grabs the black leather jacket he'd laid out for me. His hungry prowl is that of a panther. And I'm a gazelle. About to be eaten for dessert. Because I look like dessert. Or, so says Jake Swagger.

Even in these heels that are every bit of four inches, he towers over me. When he steps behind me to assist with my jacket, I have to take a deep breath to steady myself. He takes a deep breath too. Only his nose is buried in my curls.

"You smell divine."

I turn to face him and the smoldering look he's giving me has my nerve endings sending signals to my brain that result in me doing that thing I always do when I'm nervous. "Still not of the sea variety, eh?" River dance, finger snap, finger guns.

"You are so fucking strange. Anyone ever told you that?"

I waggle my eyebrows. "Only the people who like me."

"It's because they want you to change."

I tilt my head and narrow my gaze. "But do they really?"

He grunts. "Let's go."

I'm shocked and a little flattered when Jake takes my hand. That fades when I realize it's so he can set our pace—really fast. I'm not surprised when he huffs about having to slow down because I can't keep up in these shoes. I'm not surprised when he gives me the stupid-stare in the elevator as I hum. Or when he keeps his head in his phone and doesn't speak to me the entire ride to the restaurant. This is typical Jake Swagger behavior.

But it's when we arrive at our destination that I discover a chivalrous side to Jake that makes this hopeless romantic swoon harder than I ever have. Like dancing, this isn't even on *That Guy's* list of must-have's. It's all Jake. Which somehow makes it even hotter.

The small Italian restaurant is tucked neatly between two massive brick buildings. The glass front with its view of the white linen covered tables, muted lighting, overhead awning and hanging baskets of greenery dusted in snow, looks like a picture of Paris. It's a burst of warmth on what could be the coldest day in Chicago's history.

But the front of the restaurant is just that—a front. There's no door for entry. And the parking lot in the back sits a good hundred feet from the entrance due to the garden patio. I take Jake's offered hand and step out of the car and into the bitter cold. The asphalt, though it's been salted, is an icy death trap for my Louboutin's.

With Jake's hand still in mine, I feel positive he'll catch me before I bust my ass. But I haven't even taken a step when my feet are swept out from under me. I let out a squeal, and feel my heart sink to my knees.

Jake's rumbling laughter cuts through the cold and hits me dead in my chest. Warmth spreads throughout my body when the panic passes and I process what's really happening.

He's carrying me.

One arm around my waist.

The other under my knees.

Looking down at me with a smile.

Closing his eye on a wink.

Teasing me with his words. "Those heels are for my viewing pleasure, baby. Not for walking on ice."

Lord, please let this restaurant have ice chairs. Because I'm pretty sure these pants are for his viewing pleasure, too.

"I'll probably go to hell for saying this, but I've never found praying hot until now."

"H-how did you know I was praying?"

He laughs. Bites his lip to stifle it only to end up chuckling. When he sets me down just outside the entrance, he grabs my chin, tilts my head back and gives me a handsome, devilish smirk.

"You said, amen."

Of course I did.

CHAPTER FIFTEEN

"**G**o *Penelope!"*
      "Go Penelope!"
      "Go Penelope!"

The crowd of people gathered around me chant my name as I stand on the bar of Chicago's most elite night club and do The Running Man. I wave toward Amber and Mary, Jim Canton's two daughters, to join me on the bar. Then everyone on the dance floor below joins in. Now the entire club is doing The Running Man.

Turns out, all Jim's daughters needed to persuade them to sell their stock was to see the numbers in black and white. When Jake slid the envelope containing his offer across the linen tablecloth to Amber, the oldest daughter, her eyes went wide and she screamed. Then she showed it to Mary who also screamed. It took several minutes for their father to calm them down.

Everyone was staring. It was weird. And I was sad because I didn't get to see how much the offer was. I mean, how much can an irrigation system cost?

Jim wanted to go back to the hotel room with Jake to review the paperwork before everyone signed and made it official. His daughters wanted to celebrate. So we all went back to the hotel and the guys went to the room. Me, Amber and Mary went to the hotel bar.

Things got a little crazy after that.

Jake, in a moment of stunned excitement, had very stupidly given me his credit card and told me tonight was on him. He'd also called Cam to come to the hotel bar to "look after us" and make sure we didn't get into any trouble. When the girls told Cam they wanted to party Chicago style, he told them he knew just the place.

That was hours ago.

Now, I'm drunk.

The sisters are drunk.

Cam is trying to get lucky.

And Jake just walked through the door.

Black suit. Black hair. Square jaw. Swaggered walk. Eyes searching. Scanning. Appraising. Following the chant. Lifting up, up, up, and finally settling on my face. I beam at him, though I half expect him to be angry at me for...something. Getting the Canton Sisters drunk and convincing them to dance on a bar seems like something he wouldn't approve of.

To my surprise, his lips turn up on one side in a sexy grin. I'm trying to stay in tune to DNCE's *Cake by the Ocean*. But that damn face of his has a way of rendering me stupid.

The same man who treated us like royalty the moment I flashed him Jake's black Amex card, walks up and greets him. Moments later, Jake is escorted to our VIP suite on the second floor. He disappears a moment from my view and my smile falls. Then it's back when I see him lean over the rail, drink in hand and immediately find me with his eyes.

I've got it so fucking bad....

I look up and give him a little wave. He wiggles his fingers at me and smiles. I've never seen him so content. I wonder if he's always like this when he closes a deal. Or if it's just this one in particular. I make a mental note to ask him later when we're alone. Maybe in those sleepy moments when we're cuddling in post-coital bliss.

"I'll be back!" I shout to the sisters who are too busy making a Cam sandwich to care.

I hold out my hands to two dudes below me and they're more than happy to lower me to the floor. I can't tell you what they look like. I don't know. Don't care. Doesn't matter. They won't compare to Jake.

The music dulls as I head up the stairs to the VIP suite. He's watching me when I finally make it to the landing.

"Nice moves."

"I know right?" I do The Running Man just for him. Then I switch to my river dance. By the time I snap my fingers and pull out my pistols, I'm touching his chest with the tips of my finger guns.

"That river dance of yours, though...."

I grin up at him. "Does something to you, doesn't it?"

"Mmm." His smile is wide. Teeth pretty and white and glowing in the black light.

"I wish you could've been here earlier. You missed me doing the Watermelon Crawl."

He tucks my hair behind my ear. "Someone had to work so the rest of you would have something to celebrate."

"You closed the deal? It's official?"

"We went over the details. But I need our lawyers to close. We'll set up a meeting sometime in the next couple of days, depending on the weather, to finalize it." His fingers ghost the neckline of my shirt. "Stay with me until it's done." He looks up at me from beneath his lashes and grins. "Just in case the sisters sober up and change their mind?"

OMG.

He's asking me to stay.

Shit!

I'm not sure I can.

"For how long?"

He smirks. "Trying to play hard to get?"

I shrug. I'll let him believe whatever he wants. But I still need an answer. And it takes him a few moments to realize I'm waiting on one. "You're serious?"

"Yes. How long are you asking me to stay?"

"What's it matter? Do you have to check your schedule or something?"

"Or something. How long?"

His eyes narrow. "A couple days at most."

"So, two days? That's it?"

"Yes, Penelope. Two days. Will you stay with me for two more days?"

I grin. "Okay. I can do two days."

"You are so odd."

"Tell me something I don't know. Like why you agreed to dinner with him and his daughters tonight if you weren't doing it to close the deal? I didn't think rich people did anything on their own. I figured you had a team that would handle things like that."

"I prefer a more...hands on approach"

"Was that a sexual innuendo?"

He laughs. "Not if I have to explain it."

His hand clasps mine and he leads me to a seat on one of the velvet couches and passes me a bottle of water from the wet bar. This VIP suite is the shit. They even have chicken wings.

"I do a lot of business with people like Jim Canton. People who put their heart and souls into their projects," he explains, taking a seat on the couch opposite me and leaning forward with his elbows on his knees. "A lot of them risked everything to bring their ideas to life. Invested everything they had. I admire that. I respect it. So I make it personal. I don't want them to feel like they're selling out to a suit. I want them to feel good about the decision to sell. And know that I'm going to treat their product like it was my own."

Wow.

Who knew he could get sexier?

"That room in my house? The one with the code on the door that you think is some kind of sex dungeon? It's where I keep all my files. The original copies of the blueprints on patents. All my clients' personal information. Prototypes. It's all there. Where I never have to doubt if it's secure. I don't even trust that kind of information in the hands of the people who work for me."

"That's...I wasn't expecting that."

"What part? How I make every investment personal or the locked room being a file room rather than a sex room?"

"Well, I'm disappointed the file room isn't a sex room." He laughs. *It's such a great laugh.* "But the other? You making it so personal? That's pretty awe-inspiring."

He sobers. "It's good business. And it's why I'm successful. Like you said, I'm not creative enough to come up with my own ideas." His left eye closes on a wink. My vagina quivers. "But I know business. I like investing in things that are often overlooked. It makes it even more satisfying when it becomes a global phenomenon."

"Global phenomenon? Really?"

He shrugs. It's just a lift of his shoulder, but the humble move says so much more about him. "I know something good when I see it."

His eyes sweep over my body. Like I'm something good.

I straighten, try to perk my tits up a little. Arch my neck. Pout my lips. I'm not very subtle.

He catches on quick and smirks at me. Then his eyes darken. And his lips part. And I feel like dessert.

"You want to get out of here?"

"Yes. Please. Yes. I do." *Idiot....*

I feel like I'm in a haze as we walk through the club. The mist is just a blur of lights and music, Cam promising to get the sisters home, Ross opening the door of the car and the hard wall of muscle sliding onto the seat next to me.

My drunken fog has nothing to do with alcohol. I'm stoned on Jake Swagger. High on sexual tension. Boneless and horny and jacked up on endorphins.

Lips are on my lips. Tongue dancing with my tongue. Thick, deft fingers flipping open the button on my pants. One masculine hand sliding beneath my panties. A feral growl in my ear. A harsh whisper confirming my desire, "Your pussy is fucking soaked."

I moan. He silences me with his mouth. But the closer he takes me to the edge, the louder I get. The harder it is to breathe. And soon, I'm breaking away from his mouth and panting as the build becomes too much. Too intense. I cry out and his free hand clamps over my mouth.

Motherfucker.

It's the hottest thing *ever*.

"I love how hard you come."

Okay...maybe *that's* the hottest thing ever. Maybe it's just all of it—his finger doing wicked things to my clit. His words that are rough and low and barely above a whisper. And that hand, clamped over my mouth. Muffling my cries of pleasure as my back arches off the seat. Hips buck. Legs wide. One thrown over him, the other spread lifelessly across the car.

Yeah.

It's all pretty damn sexy.

But wait.

He hasn't done the typical *That Guy* move which would be the sexiest move by far. And as I come down from my orgasmic high, I find myself staring at him expectantly. Waiting. anticipating the part that comes next. The part he's not doing.

He zips my pants. Kisses my shoulder. Squeezes his cock through his pants and groans. His eyes lift to mine and he blinks a few times before tilting his head to study me. "Are you having a seizure?"

"What? No. Why would you ask that?"

"Because you're staring at me like you're crazy. And you haven't blinked."

"Maybe I'm waiting for something...." I try to sound sultry. Bat my lashes. It just confuses him more. He analyzes every feature in my face. Looking for a hint. He thinks he has it figured out and smirks. But before he even opens his mouth, I know he hasn't figured out a damn thing.

"Don't worry, baby. You'll get that something and a whole lot more. But I'm not fucking you in the back of this car. It's going to take a lot longer than ten minutes to do what I plan to do."

Blah.

Blah.

Blah.

"That's not what I'm waiting for," I deadpan.

His eyebrows shoot to his hairline and he laughs. "Don't hold back, gorgeous. Tell me how you really feel."

"It's not about how I feel. It's about what I want." I button my pants, cross my legs and stare out the window so I don't have to look at him. "You sure do suck at being *That Guy* sometimes."

He slides one big digit across my jaw—the same big digit that he should be sucking on while his eyes roll back in his head and he groans deep in his chest because the taste of my essence triggers some overwhelming, primal desire to claim me.

He pinches my chin and turns my head to face him. Of course he's entertained by my pouty attitude and has that stupid smirk on his face.

"What?"

"What...what?"

"What do you want, Penelope?"

"It doesn't matter now, Jake. You've already ruined it."

He leans in. Kisses my top lip. My bottom lip. Still holding my chin between his fingers that are now so close to his mouth....

"Tell me. What *That Guy* move have I fucked up this time?"

"I know you think this is funny, but if you're ever going to learn, you need to know."

I pull away and put a little distance between us. His amusement only grows. He's barely able to contain his smile as he tries to look serious, holds his hands up and leans back into his seat. "Please. Enlighten me."

I waste no time. "In every romance novel, the hero, aka *That Guy*, always follows up a good backseat fingering with a move that sets the heroine's panties on fire. It ignites those feelings all over again, so that even as she comes down from her first orgasm, she's already anticipating the next one."

He's no longer fighting his smile. "So what did I do wrong?"

"You pulled your hand out of *my* pants and wiped your fingers on *your* pants like they were damp due to condensation from your water glass, rather than the sweet, sinful, innocently sexy kryptonite honey flowing from my vagina."

He shakes his head at me. "The shit you say."

"The shit you don't do," I fire back.

"Uh-huh. And what exactly was I supposed to do, Penelope? You know, with all that *sweet honey* of yours?"

"Um, duh. Lick your fingers. Growl. Say something possessive and profane."

"Lick my fingers?"

"Yeah. To get my taste. Because you can't help yourself."

His voice does that growl thing. "Why settle for just a taste?"

He shifts. Grabs me under my knee. Spins me to face him. Pulls me forward. Lifts my hips and forces me to my back. I land with an *oomph*. Then he unzips my pants. Jerks them to my knees. Leans in and licks the length of my slit. Over my satin panties. And somehow, that's better than being completely bare.

"W-what are you doing?" I glance at the blacked out glass separating us from Ross. Out the window at the passing buildings, wondering how close we are to his apartment. And finally, between my legs at him. He's hovering over me. A day's hair on his chin tickling me through the thin material of my underwear.

"I'm giving you something you want."

I shake my head. Swallow hard. Find my breath. And hope like hell I can be heard over the thundering in my chest. "Y-you said there wasn't enough time. Remember? Like, two seconds ago. Not enough time. That's what you said."

"There's enough time for this."

"But I just wanted you to lick your fingers."

"Sorry, baby." He drags his nose across my panties and inhales. I almost die. "Like you said..." He takes this big fucking dramatic pause and winks and I'm scared that whatever he's about to say might finish me off for good. "...I just can't help myself."

And...I'm dead.

CHAPTER SIXTEEN

I'm a coming machine.

Give me the pressure of a deadline, the possibility of getting caught and Jake Swagger's tongue and I can make it rain in this bitch.

Seriously.

Liquid kryptonite just...everywhere.

I thought I wouldn't be able to move considering the intense tongue fucking I just endured, but like I said....

I'm a machine.

And the promise of Jake's cock inside me puts an extra pep in my step as we exit the car, make our way through the lobby, up the elevator—me in the corner, humming like a crazy person while he watches—through the front door of his apartment and to his office.

I don't know why we're in his office. He just said, "office." And I listened. Because the idea of him fucking me on his desk, picking up where he left off this morning, has me abandoning this little voice in the back of my mind that says a repeat of last night isn't what I truly want, and has me stripping off my clothes to save time. But the walk is short so I'm still dressed from the waist down when I make it to his desk and turn to face him. And he's....

Have mercy, he's naked.

Not a stitch of clothing.

He's even managed to remove his shoes and socks.

Seeing this...vision.

This...Adonis.

This...yeah, I've got nothing else.

Because this man is the finest motherfucker I've ever seen in my life and there is nothing worthy of comparison to a naked Jake Swagger. I've never seen him completely naked. Witnessing him bare chested was hard enough. Add some masculine feet, the calves of an athlete, a couple muscular thighs and that thing I refuse to look at that hangs between those muscular thighs, to the picture and I suddenly feel like maybe I should've left my clothes on.

I thought I looked good tonight.

Compared to him? I look homely as hell.

It doesn't help my nerves any that for him to have gotten this naked in the thirteen steps it took us to arrive at his desk, he had to have pulled off some real magical shit.

"Abracadabra." I give my imaginary wand a twirl.

He advances on me slowly. "Why are you nervous?"

I've watched him pull his cock from his pants. Seen it fisted in his hand. But I've never seen it like this. Just...swinging between his legs like a pendulum.

I close my eyes to block out the sight.

But it's too late.

I saw it.

Swaying.

Helicoptering.

Oscillating like the blades on a Kim Jones box fan.

And I can still see it.

Behind my eyes.

Forever.

Likely the only thing I'll ever see again.

"Penelope?"

I keep my eyes closed. "Hmm?"

"You said 'abracadabra.' Because you're nervous. Why are you nervous?"

"B-because you're naked. Got that way really quick, too. Magician moves."

"Ahh...." I crack open one eye just in time to see him nod in understanding, three feet from me. "Magician." Two feet. "Explains the wand." He's in front of me. "Touch me."

Okay.

I'm so relieved for my fidgeting hands to have some direction, I slap them against his chest a little *too* hard. He stifles a groan. My palms tingle. His blood rushes to darken the handprints on his pecs. All my blood rushes to my cheeks.

"As charming as it is to see this shy and nervous version of you, I prefer the you that screams and thrashes and doesn't give a damn about anything other than how fucking good it feels."

My finger traces the outline of handprints. I open my mouth. Close it. Take a breath. Force myself to look him in the eye, and reveal a small truth to him. "It's only ever felt that good with you."

I feel his chest rumble beneath my touch, but hear no sound. He traps my wrists in his big hands and presses his forehead to mine. "That mouth of yours, Penelope Hart, will be my demise."

The kiss that comes next is a warning as much as it is a promise. A warning that he's about to ravage me. And a promise that I'll love every second of it.

Though his movements are rushed and greedy, they're precise and rewarding. He strips my pants down my legs in one, fluid motion. But when he kneels to remove my heels so he can free my pants from around my ankles, he takes a second longer to caress the arch of my foot with his thumb.

He cups my ass with his palms, lifts me to sit on the edge of his desk, steps between my legs and pulls me roughly against him. But his touch is soft when he drags a single finger down the center of my chest before flattening his hand on my stomach and urging me to my back.

His grip on my hips is rough. Fingers kneading then releasing. Eyes wild and hungry. Bottom lip trapped between his teeth. But when he slides the length of his shaft up and down my slit, he does it with a sense of tenderness. As if the need to feel me against him is greater than the desire to just bury himself inside me. It's confusing. And that voice in the back of my mind—the one telling me this isn't what I truly want—is back.

He fists his cock and teases me with the head. His eyes travel over my naked torso, worshipping every inch of my skin before meeting my hooded gaze. "I need a condom. But fuck, you feel so good like this."

The intensity in which he looks at me, as if he's trying to read my thoughts on the matter, takes me out of the moment and makes me question if beneath all his hotness, he's actually an idiot.

He's super rich.

I'm super poor.

Why would he take a chance on getting me pregnant? The only reasonable explanation is that he's fallen in love and wants to trap me for the rest of my life.

I'm good with that.

But it's another thought that has me forgetting that I'm naked, spread eagle on his desk with the head of his unprotected penis pressed against the opening of my vagina.

Why would he risk catching a disease from someone he barely knows?

Did you know, people can have a STD even if there are no visual signs of one? And that an unseen STD can still be transmitted without a current breakout? Not that I have any STDs, but he doesn't know that. Which makes him really stupid.

Does it make me stupid to sleep with him without protection? Considering he could have an STD and I could be on the receiving end of it?

Hell no.

Why?

Because he's rich. And if he gives me something that won't wash off in the shower, then I'm going to sue the shit out of him. He's smart, aside from this rare moment of stupidity, so he'll settle out of court. And guess what.

I'll be *rich*.

As.

Fuck.

A few million dollars makes having herpes totally worth it. Plus, there's all this advanced medicine these days. It's a win-win for me. For him? Not so much.

I mean, he didn't even ask me if I had a clean bill of health or confirm that he had one like all the heroes do. Which, by the way, blows my fucking mind. Like who does that? Just gets randomly checked for diseases, though they swear they've never fucked bareback in their life.

Romance novels, am I right?

"I'm almost positive that whatever crazy shit you're thinking this time, actually has the power to turn me off." His gaze might be stoic, but I can see the plea deep in his eyes that begs me to not say what I'm thinking.

"You're probably right. And just in case, we should use protection. I'm not on the pill." I add that last part because I don't want him to think he needs to use protection for any other reason than an unplanned pregnancy. Which is also why I don't tell him I'm on the shot.

He holds up a condom between his fingers. "Yeah. I decided that the moment you said, 'Rich as fuck.'"

My eyes widen. "It's not what you think. I swear."

I shut up when he places a finger over his lips and shakes his head. He flicks the condom and it lands next to my head. When I look over at it, I see it's just the empty wrapper. My eyes drift to his cock that is now sheathed in latex.

A—How did he manage to fit that thirty-three-gallon lawn and leaf bag covering his penis in that little bitty foil wrapper?

B—Just where in the hell did he get that condom?

C—When did he put it on without me knowing?

I look up at him and he smiles. "Abracadabra."

"Smooth, Swagger. Real smooth."

"I know."

"Well, if you're finished now, maybe we can move on to the next act in your magic show."

Without warning, he thrust inside me. Shit he's deep. I'm taken back to last night. Us on the couch. That fear of paralysis. Cock overload. Coke Can. Narrow channel. Yeah, I'm done.

"Breathe, sweet girl." Jake's body over mine keeps me from jumping off the desk. His words remind me that I probably do need to breathe. And his sweet kisses on the side of my neck liquefy me.

I adjust to him quickly. The initial punch to the cervix that nearly rendered me unconscious has softened to a dull ache. Not a painful ache. A desperate ache. When I hear that voice in my head again, a little louder this time, I drown it out with begging. "Oh, please. Fuck me, please."

His cock jerks inside me, but his body doesn't move. "Be careful what you wish for, baby."

Shit. He's right.

"Just...Don't...Well...."

"Say it, Penelope. I can't read you like this. When you're thinking too much. Tell me what you want, and I'll give it to you. When I do, you'll forget everything. Then I won't need your pretty little mouth to tell me what you want. Your body will." He places a kiss right behind my ear. And just like in the books, that's the spot.

"Slow, Jake. Fuck me slow. And touch me. Everywhere. I like when you touch me."

He does just what I ask. Slow thrusts. Deep and measured. Hands all over me. Caressing this. Cupping that. Lips here. Tongue there. But something isn't right. And though I know exactly what it is, and have known the entire time—thanks to that voice in my head—I can't bring myself to say it.

I don't want him to see me as weak. I don't want him to know how bad he hurt me. And I'm not sure if that's because I'm ashamed of how he made me feel, or because I don't want him to regret making me feel that way.

"Talk to me, baby."

God I want to.

"Just say it, gorgeous."

Even the endearments aren't helping.

He stills inside me. Kisses me softly. Looks at me even softer. Then the words I needed to hear fall from his lips like the sweetest kind of pained melody that has the power to twist you up inside and make you long for something you didn't realize you were so desperate for.

"Trust me, Penelope. I've got you."

Without giving it further thought, I surrender. And for the second time tonight, I give a little piece of myself to this man.

"I want this. But I don't want to feel like I felt last night. That's not who I am, Jake. I'm not...them."

Them.

The Miss Sims.

The others.

The women before me.

The hired whores left alone on a couch.

Fucked and forgotten.

I may not mean more to him than they did.

I may not be more to him than they were.

But I can't let him treat me like I'm just a piece of ass.

Not again.

He hasn't said anything. Not a word. Just pinned me with that stoic, thoughtful gaze of his.

Fucking hell.

I knew better.

I flatten my hands against his chest and avert my eyes. "Look...I...." I let out a breath of nervous laughter. I hate being this exposed. This vulnerable.

Stupid fucking trust.

Stupid fucking voice.

Stupid fucking Penelope.

"I'm sorry. I shouldn't have—"

He cuts me off with a kiss. A searing kiss that bruises my lips and completely negates the way he cradles my face in his hands like porcelain. It makes my head spin. His breath is controlled but a little harsh when he pulls away and whispers against my lips, "You are *not* them. Do you hear me?"

I nod.

He captures my mouth again. This kiss sweeter than the last. Softer. Slower. He wraps my hands around his neck. My legs around his waist. Keeps himself buried inside me as he stands with me in his arms. "You will never fucking be them."

Every few steps he kisses me. My lips. My neck. Cheek. Nose. Corner of my mouth. Temple....

Gah.

Those temple kisses....

I kiss him too. His jaw. Ear. Chin. Neck. Mouth...that is now claiming mine. I'm dizzy with lust and swimming in warmth that has to do with something that has nothing to do with sex. But I don't shake it away. I revel in it. I live in the moment. I let go so my pretty mouth doesn't have to speak and my body can do the talking.

And I learn very quickly that I should let my body do the talking all the time.

I'm on a bed. A large hand pins my wrists over my head. The other touches me in that way I love to be touched. It slides down my chest, across my breast, over my ribs and curls around my hip.

I look down at the sight before me. The body above me. The wide, chiseled chest dusted in hair. Ripple of eight pack abs that disappear into the V. And beneath that V, the thick, beautiful—for a cock—shaft that slowly pulls almost all the way out of me. Then Jake lifts his hips, pulls me to him and drives back in.

Over and over. Until I can't hold my head up anymore. Until I squeeze my eyes closed and move my body to meet his. Until I shatter beneath him when he tells me, "So fucking perfect." And when he says, "I'm not through with you yet, gorgeous," I mewl and cry and beg for mercy and more and something and everything until I have it all.

Mercy, when his thrusts become a little harsher so that the dull, distant, slow burning throb inside me becomes a crescendo.

More, when he shifts our bodies and finds that spot deep inside me so that the feeling is prolonged.

Something, turns out to be a pinch of pain when he pulls my nipple between his teeth and then soothes it with his tongue followed by a breath of cold air.

The everything both scares and delights me. It's the forbidden. The one place his mouth touches when he flips me to my knees, and then his finger finds when his cock is once again buried inside me. I pull away—shame overpowering desire.

"Easy, baby."

Easy for him to say. He doesn't have a finger in his butt.

"Stop thinking. Feel."

I do feel...a finger in my fucking butt.

Then I feel a deep thrust that steals all the air from my lungs. Sensation in my toes. And thoughts from my head.

I come so hard I collapse face down. Ass still up. He's still fucking my brains out and I can't find gravity. I don't want to find gravity. Fuck gravity. Unless gravity is Jake Swagger. Who can put whatever he wants in my butt as long as it feels as good as this does.

He comes on a warrior cry that has me arching my brow—wondering if maybe he's a descendant of Arminius. Or part werewolf. Not just from the cry either. But from his never-ending stamina. He has to be exhausted. He's done all the work. So werewolf or warrior descendant is the only explanation for where he finds the strength to kiss his way down my spine, then back up again, flip me over, position me in the bed so my head is on a pillow and walk to the bathroom to dispose of the condom.

All I did was grunt and I can't get these heart palpitations under control.

I'm almost asleep when he crawls into bed, pulls the covers arounds me, leans over and kisses the corner of my mouth. "How are you feeling, baby?"

The question strips me of my humor. I wear it like armor and without it I'm a coward. Which is why I pretend to be asleep so I don't have to answer because I'm afraid I might tell him the truth. And I'm not sure what he'll do with that truth. How he'll feel about it. Or how his reaction will affect me.

He doesn't ask again.

He doesn't leave me alone either.

He lays down beside me. Curls an arm around me. Pulls me to him and buries his face in my hair. Kisses my head. I feel his whole body relax against mine. It's in that moment I find my courage.

I want him to ask me again. I'm not strong enough to say it on my own, but if he asks, I'll tell the truth.

I pray that he asks.

My prayer is answered with his silence and the slow, deep breathing that tells me he's asleep.

So I stuff my truth into my bottle of emotions and save it for the next time he asks me how I feel. Which is nothing like Miss Sims.

And just like I'm falling in love.

CHAPTER SEVENTEEN

Emily is so selfish.

A good friend would have rationed the food in the apartment, so she could stay out of sight like I asked. But not Emily. She just had to go to the grocery store in broad daylight where she could've been seen by anyone. My mother wasn't in the store, but she was in her workshop when Emily got back to the apartment—the one located directly above my mother's workshop.

"I just can't believe you would go to such extreme lengths to lie to me. And to involve Emily...Penelope how could you?"

I throw my arm across my face and groan. "Mom. It's fine. Emily is fine. I'm fine. She needed some time alone and I needed some time away from her so I could do some book research on my *That Guy*."

"Penelope Lane Hart!" she whisper-shout-hisses. It's so loud, I have to pull the phone from my ear. "Are you still in that man's house?"

I peek from beneath my arm to find Jake lying awake next to me wearing an amused smile. *I guess he heard.*

She starts in on me again. And instead of me getting up and barricading myself in another room so he can't hear her, I turn on my side to face him and put the phone on speaker between us. Her voice fills the room mid-sentence.

"...could be a sex offender. You just never know about people these days. Especially people from *up there*." Jake lifts a brow and I grin. "They're not like us. I don't care how many fancy parties he takes you to or how rich he is or how nice Emily promised me he was, I don't trust him."

"Mom—"

"What kind of man looks like that and isn't married?"

"Mom—"

"Emily showed me a picture on the Google."

"Mom—"

"But she won't tell me how to do a background check."

"Mom—"

"I've already made a pie to bribe the sheriff."

"Mom!"

"Are you having sex with him, Penelope?"

Geeze Louise.

"Mom, you're at a nine. I'm gonna need you to bring it down to a three before you get your blood pressure up. Take some deep breaths."

While she does that, I share a smile with Jake. Usually, we're either arguing, flirting or fucking. But this feels normal. Comfortable. A little awkward considering my Mom is chanting a breathing exercise.

When I think she's had enough, I ask, "Better?"

"Much. Yes. Okay. I'm good. I'm still not good with you being there with that strange man but I'm putting it in the Lord's hands. Thank heavens the Bible tells us He always listens to our prayers for those who are living in sin. If that wasn't the case, He'd never hear me when I prayed for you."

Jake smirks at that.

"Thanks, Mom." My tone is dry.

"You make sure he knows that you have a mother who is going to be checking in on you regularly. So he better not try any funny stuff. I read in the newspaper, you know that column Connie writes about how to be an aware woman in a dangerous world? Anyway, just last week she said most pedophiles don't target women who have an active relationship with family and friends. They mostly target those who live lonely lives. Like..." her voice drops to a whisper, "whores."

I can't help it. I laugh. Jake rolls his eyes and gives me the finger.

That finger.

"He's a nice guy, Mom. You have nothing to worry about."

"I'm a mother. My job is to worry, Penelope." The sadness in her voice tears at my heart.

Jake reaches out and caresses my temple with his thumb. I force a smile that he doesn't return. He's thoughtful a moment longer. And then he does something really stupid.

"Ms. Hart?"

I dive for the phone but he grabs it and holds it out of reach. "What the fuck are you doing?" I mouth, but he ignores me.

"Ms. Hart this is Jake Swagger. Penelope has been staying with me?" He's all amiable and smooth. Voice warm and smile big even though she can't see it. But it falters when my mother's tone loses its sweet southern charm and becomes matter-of-fact.

"What can I do for you, son?"

I lean back and smirk. This may turn out to be pretty entertaining.

"I just wanted to let you know that Penelope is safe here with me. And she will be as long as she's in Chicago."

A beat of silence passes before she answers.

"Jake, was it?"

"Yes ma'am."

"Well, Jake, I appreciate that. And while I have you on the phone, there's something that I want you to know."

Oh Lord.

I know that voice.

"If my daughter comes home hurt, harmed, sick or crying…I'm holding you personally responsible. You do *not* want me to come to Chicago, Jake. Do you understand?"

"Yes ma'am. I'll take care of her."

"Don't make promises you can't keep, young man."

Jake grins. "I wouldn't dream of it, Ms. Hart."

"You say that now. But Penelope can be a handful."

"I am quite aware, I assure you."

"She's been that way her whole life."

"I'm right here, Mom. And my phone is about to die." Before she can say something about that, too, I snatch the phone from Jake, tell her I love her and hang up—not giving her a chance to respond, or Jake a chance to say goodbye. Which he chastises me for with a narrow, disapproving gaze.

"I'm hungry. Can we call Uber Eats?"

His face softens and he smirks. "You don't *call* Uber Eats, sweetheart. You use an app. And I've already ordered us something." He grabs his phone and swipes his finger across the screen then turns it so I can see. "It'll will be here in five minutes."

"Then I should get dressed so I'm not naked when Alfred brings it up." I roll away from him and untangle myself from the covers.

"Alfred has the morning off, but even if he didn't, he wouldn't come all the way up here and see you naked."

"You don't know that."

"Yes. I do. Just like I know Vance, the other doorman who is working today in Alfred's place, won't come in here just to see you naked, either."

"Whatever. I'm going down to meet the Uber." I wince as I stand. Everything south of my bellybutton is sore. And just like yesterday, there's nothing delicious about it. This just can't be normal. "I don't know Vance. He might be a pervert."

Despite Jake's laugh, I can feel the burn of his stare as I make my way very slowly and very nakedly across the room. "And no sex today," I say, doing my best to avoid looking at him sprawled out in bed wearing nothing but a sheet that's tented by that damn light pole he calls a penis. "Or tomorrow. Or maybe for the rest of my life."

He chuckles. "That's a little extreme, don't you think?"

"Nope. It'll probably take that long for my vagina to shrink back to its original size."

His groan is low and pained and I'd bet anything he's stroking himself. *Men.*

"Don't say vagina, Penelope."

"It's the appropriate medical term, Jake."

The guest bathroom seems a million miles away. I'd use his, but I need my toothbrush. ASAP. And as bad as I want to be just like every other typical heroine in a romance novel, I don't want it bad enough to use Jake's toothbrush.

There are some things I just won't do.

The blinds in Jake's room are closed, but the ones in the guest room give me a full view of the ominous gray sky. It looks like a scene from *The Day After Tomorrow.* Everything is still. Cold. Creepy. It pains me to look at it. But not as much as it pains me to see my own reflection in the bathroom mirror.

I have that just-fucked glow without the glow. My kissed-too-hard lips are a little dry. Messy and crazy, thick, untamed curls are everywhere. Day old mascara clings to my lashes and is smudged beneath my eyes.

Not that I've looked at it, but I'm pretty sure my vagina is in the same just-fucked state as the rest of me. I fear it may be ruined. I'd hike my leg up on the counter to visually survey the damage if I weren't so scared of what I might find.

Mouth clean, bladder empty, I dig through the Miss Sims wardrobe hanging in the closet in search of something normal. I spot something gray toward the back and get excited. I think it's sweat pants.

Please let it be sweat pants....

It's...pants. Comfortable looking ones. With a matching top that has a C looped through a backwards C logo on the front. I feel like I should know what that is. I'm pretty sure it's Coach. I look at the tag.

Chanel.

I thought they just sold perfume.

"Oh my God this feels amazing." I can't stop from running my hands over the fabric. It's so soft. I don't even know what kind of material it is. But I love it.

I find some *Chanel* slipper shoe things and slide those on—over socks, because I'm fashionable—and head to the elevator.

Nose to the wall, humming my song, I distract myself by thinking about what food Jake ordered. I hope it's not anything healthy like an egg white omelet or turkey bacon. He looks like the kind of guy who eats that shit. Although he is also the kind of guy who cooks real bacon shirtless. So, what do I know?

The lobby is warm and welcoming. The man sitting in his car honking the horn? Not so much. I thought he was supposed to come inside the lobby. Does he? No. He's a dick. And I'm forced to walk outside in the snow and meet him at his car.

And it's minus forty-two degrees.

The young punk that can't be a day over fifteen rolls down the window and I want to snatch the food, give him the finger and tell him to go to hell. Then I remember I have to pay him. And I have no money.

"I f-forgot your m-money." I wrap my hands around me to hold in the warmth while he stares at me like I'm stupid.

"You Mrs. Swagger?"

Mrs. Swagger.

Well, now...that has a ring to it.

"Y-yes."

"You paid with the app, lady." He holds his phone up like I'm supposed to understand the shit on the screen.

"Oh, w-well in that c-case...." I snatch the food off the seat. Give him the finger and stutter the best insult I can manage with frozen lips and jittering teeth. "G-go f-f-f-fuck yourself, you l-little shit."

"Penelope?" I straighten to find Jim Canton staring at me. Then his eyes move to the Uber driver. "Is everything alright?"

"Y-yes s-s-sir." *Shit. Fuck. Damn.*

"You better get inside, girl. It's freezing out here. Where is your jacket?" He holds open the door and ushers me inside, casting uneasy glances over his shoulder until the car drives away.

I move to the massive fireplace in the lobby. My bones are frozen. I'm sure of it. And I've only been outside a couple minutes. I've never felt cold like this. It's not right.

"This weather is something to get used to, isn't it?" He pulls off his thick jacket, dusts the snow from it and places it around my shoulders. Such a gentleman. *Man, I miss the south.*

"I have n-no intentions of g-getting used to it."

"So summers here and winters in Mississippi?"

"W-what?"

He pulls a chair closer to the fire and gestures for me to sit before getting a chair for himself. "You and Jake. Are the two of you going to spend winters in Mississippi? To avoid the cold?"

I manage a laugh. "Oh. I'm not sure what we're going to do. Or what we even are."

"Ah. I see."

Anxious for a change in subject, I nod toward the leather briefcase in his hand. "I didn't know you and Jake had a meeting this morning."

"Technically, we don't." His small smile is a bit sheepish. "I hate to just show up like this, but I was hoping he and I could discuss a few things this morning. And this darn cell phone of mine only works half the time." He pulls from the pocket of his shirt what has to be the original Nokia cell phone.

"Well, since Noah brought that thing over on the Ark, I have no doubt it doesn't work when it should." We share a laugh and now that my limbs have thawed and my shivering has stopped, I figure it's a good idea for me to phone Jake and let him know we're coming up.

"Give me just a second. I'm going to call Jake and let him know you're here so he'll be decent." *Fuck!* "I mean dressed." *Shit.* "I mean...yeah." I scramble out of my seat and across the room but not before hearing Jim's chuckle or seeing the glint of amusement in his eyes.

I grab Alfred's desk phone and hit the button labeled with a big *P.* It rings eight times. I know because I counted the damn things and cursed Jake on every ring he didn't answer.

"Penelope." My knees shake at his deep tone laced with the promise of so many orgasms.

"Jake..." I breathe, gripping the phone so tight I'm surprised it doesn't crack under my hold.

"Whose fucking jacket are you wearing?"

"What? How did you know—"

"I can see you. The surveillance cameras are linked to my phone. Now. Whose fucking jacket are you wearing?"

I look directly into the little black dome above my head and smile. "Are you jealous?"

"Yes. I won't ask you again, gorgeous."

Have mercy.

He's jealous.

Of me.

Kryptonite.

"Jim Canton is here. Just thought I'd let you know before we came up and caught you...busy."

"You didn't answer my question, Penelope."

I smile to myself and sway back and forth while I write *Mrs. Swagger* with my finger on the desk like a sixth grader. "It's Jim's. The Uber driver wouldn't bring the stuff inside. I had to go out and get it. In the blizzard. About froze to death." I poke my lip out and look up at the camera. "It was awful, Jake."

"That son-of-a-bitch."

I bat my lashes at him. "What are you going to do?"

There's a beat of silence as the rustle of fabric brushes over the phone. He must be getting dressed. "I'll tell you what I'm going to do," he growls. My blood heats at the imminent promise of torture he'll deliver to defend my honor. "I'm going to leave that motherfucker a bad review."

Wait.

What?

"A bad review?"

"That's right."

"Okay, stop with the Batman voice. Now you just sound ridiculous. We're coming up." I hang up before my desire for him ebbs even more.

Jim, who has been listening to only one side of the conversation, fights his laughter as he joins me. "Sounds like the weather isn't the only thing you're not used to. City boys are a lot different."

"I know, right? Whatever happened to the kind of good ol' chivalry where a man beat the shit out of another man? Don't they know it's way hotter than fighting someone with lawyers or...bad reviews?" I have to choke the last word out.

His strong laughter fills the room. "I've no doubt Jake would handle business physically if it came down to that." He brushes his shoulder against mine and winks. "Don't be too hard on him. It isn't his fault he's a city slicker. I'm sure he more than makes up for it in other departments."

Is he talking about...

No.

He's not.

There is nothing suggestive about what he says. He probably means he's intelligent. Powerful. Rich...

"You're right. I mean, he does have a Rolex."

"One of those real fancy watches?"

"Yep. I think the cheapest ones are like twenty grand. So I'm sure his cost well over a hundred."

"For a watch?"

"Mmhm."

"Does he know that it just...tells time?"

I look up at him and smile. "Jim. I think we're soul mates. Excuse me."

He chuckles, but it dies when I face the corner and start humming. I can feel him looking. Like they all look. Not that I care.

"That was...strange," he says, once we make it to Jake's floor.

"I am a strange girl, Jim."

I look up and Jake is standing in the doorway to greet us. Wearing a white Henley. And jeans. And he's barefoot. And I just died and went to heaven.

His smile is wide. Eyes fixated on me. And I'm positive he's about to say something sexy and sweet and swoony. Like maybe I'm his perfect kind of strange.

"Batshit crazy is more like it."

Or not.

CHAPTER EIGHTEEN

J ake and Jim have been in Jake's office for forever.
I've eaten my pancake breakfast platter.
Took a shower.
Dug through Miss Sims's wardrobe.
Found nothing as awesome as that Chanel pants suit.
Put the pants suit back on.
Straightened the guest bathroom.
Made Jake's bed.
Run out of lives on *Toy Blast*.
Texted Emily to send me another life.
Stupidly sent her a selfie of me wearing Chanel.
Now I'm waiting for her response.
I get the middle finger emoji.
And no life for *Toy Blast*.
So, so jealous.

I glance at the clock and realize "forever" has only been a few hours. It feels like longer because, though he's only feet from me, I can't see Jake. And I miss him. I miss his face. Mouth. Lips. Humor. I even miss his anger. And when I think about him, I get the sensation that I'm high.

Not high on pot, though. The few times I've done that, I just thought about stupid things like how numbers tasted. And whether it was the *s* or the *c* that was silent in the word *scent*. By the way, I still haven't figured that out.

Yeah. This definitely doesn't feel like I'm high on pot. It's more like I'm high on meth.

Not that I've done meth. But I hear it heightens your senses. Causes you to run really fast. Makes you never want to sleep again.

Maybe that's vampire venom....

Whatever.

Bottom line?

I'm falling for Jake Swagger.

He dominates my mind, my body and my heart.

My blood tickles when I think about him.

My nipples harden with every sore step I take.

My pulse speeds at the smell of him that's everywhere.

Last night, I was convinced I was falling in love. Today, I've decided to reevaluate the situation, considering I'm not under the influence of a post coital, mind numbing orgasm. And because I'm bored and have ten minutes until I generate a life on *Toy Blast*.

So, is it lust or is it love?

Lust is where it's at. Lust intensifies the moment. Amplifies the experience. Creates a sexual attraction that leads to a sexual encounter that leaves you walking funny while simultaneously anticipating the next time he bottoms out inside you. But lust is also something you can walk away from. Something you can smile about if you want to remember. Or something you can choose to forget.

Love?

Give your heart to someone and you'll regret it. Be it today, tomorrow or one hundred years from now, you will one day feel the downside. Nothing that great comes without repercussions. Which is exactly why love is so powerful.

If I had a choice, I'd choose lust. Problem is, it's not that easy. This isn't multiple choice. I don't get to choose anything. My heart gets that honor. And that stupid bitch has done nothing but make bad decisions since she tried to burst out of my chest at the sight of Eddie Smith stripping down to a cape and a pair of Ninja Turtle underwear during my sixth birthday party.

If only my heart were as smart as my vagina.

To hell with my heart.

My mind is made up.

It is lust that I feel.
Lust doesn't result in loss.
Only rewards.
There is no reward when it comes to love.
Love will cripple you.
Then again, fucking Jake Swagger will also cripple you.
So really...what the hell do I know?

CHAPTER NINETEEN

It's one o'clock in the afternoon before Jake and Jim finally emerge from the office.

They're laughing.

I'm hungry again.

I'm also entranced by the deep rumble of Jake's magnificent laugh. And the ripple of muscles beneath his shirt as he shakes Jim's hand. And the way his jeans hug him in all the right places. And how I want to lick all those right places.

Someone whistles. Snaps. "Hello...Penelope...." I jerk my eyes up to Jake's. Funny how my brain just stops functioning when I look at his crotch.

"Hello, Jake." I look for Jim but he's not here. And the idea that we're alone—again—excites the hell out of me.

"Where's your head at, gorgeous?"

I can't believe he just called me gorgeous. Sober. With his cock still in his pants.

I'm getting to him.

"My head is...everywhere. Are y'all finished? Did you do it? Are the Canton's rich as fuck? Are you the proud owner of some special contraption that waters crops?"

Jake's arms flail in the air. He kicks a leg out. Makes a strange face. Cuts his eyes from me, to his right, then back to me. It's quite entertaining and really confusing. Then he whisper-shouts at me and I get it. "Shut the fuck up! He's still here."

"Hell, I didn't know!" I whisper-shout back.

A door opens behind me and Jake shoots me a quick glare of warning before he plasters on his signature, Swagger smile. I roll my eyes, but soon my smile matches Jake's as Jim walks up.

While they discuss a few details about some shit I'm not interested in, I take Jake's cell out of his hand to order some more Uber Eats. This app is awesome. And they'll go anywhere. Even halfway across town to get some of that pizza I had the first night I was here.

I've just placed the order when Jake tosses an arm casually over my shoulders to get my attention. I slip his phone in his back pocket and my arm around his waist as I pretend to care about what he says rather than obsess over the pizza that will be here in thirty minutes. "The AFA has lifted the flight ban, so Jim will be returning home this afternoon."

Though I do not care, I respond with the appropriate frown to express my disappointment. "Well, it was great meeting you, Jim."

"The pleasure was all mine, Penelope." Jim takes my hand and kisses it almost reverently. "Until next time."

Jake walks him to the door and I can't stop my eyes from drifting to Jake's perfect ass as he walks away. But it has nothing on the smile he wears when he returns.

"Someone is happy. I assume the meeting went well?"

He nods, his eyes raking over me. "Very, very well."

"Mmm...."

His hands snake around my waist and he pulls me to him. "You're coming with me to Kansas."

I attempt a laugh, but it's more of a breath as I study his lips. Full. Smooth. Kissable. "So demanding, Mr. Swagger."

"That I am, Miss Hart. We leave the day after tomorrow."

He's so close. Smells so good. The struggle to find my breath is real. When I finally do, I can't help but tease him. "What makes you so sure I'll go? Maybe I have plans."

"You don't have plans," he says, his lips skimming my jaw.

I arch my neck to give him better access. "I might."

"Is that so?" He works his way to my earlobe and drags it between his teeth. "Like what?"

My thighs clench. The soreness there causes a shiver to run up my spine at the reminder of last night. "Maybe I have a date."

He stills. "A date?"

Hmm...this could be fun.

"Yeah. A date. You know...dinner. Wine. Candles...*sex*...."

"Penelope," he growls, the sound coming from deep in his chest.

"Does the idea of me having sex with another man bother you, Mr. Swagger?"

"Yes."

I grin against his jaw before placing my lips there. "I've been thinking of starting an escort service back home. Kind of like the one you use. I think I'd make a good Miss Sims. Don't you?"

I think he tries to say my name again, but it just comes out as a deep rumble. And I'm beginning to think Jake doesn't like me throwing the Miss Sims thing in his face. I want to apologize. Tell him I was only kidding. But before I can, everything just becomes...chaos.

Jake's mouth devours mine as he slips both his hands inside my pants and pushes them over my hips. I fist the hair at the nape of his neck. He grabs my waist and lifts me in the air. Our kiss never breaks as I kick my feet free of my pants then wrap my legs around his hips.

He carries me the short distance to his office. My back is against the wall. Chest arching into his. Needing to feel more of him, I let go of his hair long enough to unzip my top. Then I'm pressing against him again. My nipples hard beneath my bra. Breast achy. Desperate for his touch.

He pulls away to unbutton his jeans and I have to lock my arms and legs to keep from falling. My mouth trails along his jaw. Neck. Shoulder. He releases my waist and pulls a condom from his pocket. His words and the gravel in his voice making me whimper and moan when he speaks in short sentences.

"...Driving me goddamn crazy...a fucking date...trying to make me jealous...fucking succeeding...fucking hell, these panties are soaked."

His knuckle skims over the wet material. The touch ignites me. I throw my head back. Eyes closed. Lips parted. Nails digging. Hip lifting and thrusting against his hand.

"This sweet wet pussy is wet for me, Penelope."

I mewl an unintelligible response.

He pushes my panties to the side and drags a finger across my slit. "These pretty pink swollen lips are swollen from me."

I arch my back into his touch and he sinks one long digit all the way inside me. He fucks me hard with his finger. His knuckles slapping against my wet heat with every thrust.

"You're sore because of me. Because when I fuck you, I can't get enough."

Have mercy.

"Do you want me to fuck you with my cock the way I'm fucking you with my finger?"

I nod and whimper and beg and may die if he doesn't deliver.

"I'm going to sink this big motherfucker inside your tender little cunt and pound into you until you beg me to stop."

Shit. Okay. Now I'm afraid I'll die if he does deliver.

My body tenses and I open my eyes—blinking a few times to focus my vision. He looks so hungry. So feral. So raw and untamed. "Jake...I...."

"You what?" He pumps his finger harder inside me. "You don't want me to fuck you?"

What kind of question is that?

"I do, I just...."

My voice trails off when he pushes that finger he was just fucking me with inside his mouth. His eyes flutter shut and he releases a low hum as he slowly drags the digit from between his lips.

Holy hell that's hot.

He kisses me again. I'm sure to distract me from the head of that *big motherfucker* pressing against my opening. Thankfully, it works and I relax around him. He swallows my moans. Thumbs my clit when I whimper. Backs out when I tense. Pushes in when I arch against him.

His hips lift in a slow, rhythmic motion until he's stretched me enough I'm past any discomfort, tingling with need for more and drenching him with my arousal. "I'm going to fuck you hard now, Penelope." His promise is said with conviction so serious, I'm forced to meet his gaze. There's a depth there unlike any I've ever seen. "I want to keep you sore. So you don't forget whose pussy this is."

"YesJakeplease." Is now a word. And it's all I can say as he powers into me. Fucking me without restraint. Drilling me as he sucks my nipples through my bra. Slides his hands up my sides and curls them around the back of my shoulders. Pulls me down as he thrusts up.

His cock slides over the satiny spot that is the window to all my pleasure. His moves are so quick. So deep. So savage that I have no reprieve from the constant pleasure each stroke brings. And there's no mistaking that this pussy is, indeed, his pussy.

Within moments, a warmth spreads down my spine. Settles in my hips a moment before shooting straight to my core. I shatter around him in a release that takes my breath, stops my heart and washes away any doubt I felt earlier about letting him take me this hard, and all fear of what physical state it might leave me in.

Because the way Jake Swagger makes me come, is totally fucking worth it.

CHAPTER TWENTY

I've never had an angry fuck before now.

But I like it.

I'm still against the wall. He's still inside me. I'm sure that big rocket of his found its release, but I can't for the life of me remember when it happened or what happened. I was too busy trying to stay away from the light during my own orgasm.

I don't think I've ever been closer to Jesus.

I peel my arms from around his neck and my legs slide down his body until I'm standing on my own two feet. Though I feel like I'm floating from the sight of him studying my face as he sweeps his fingertips across my forehead. Brushes my hair behind my ear. Drags his thumb across my temple.

The moment shatters when the phone on his desk begins to ring. He doesn't seem to notice at first. Or maybe he just doesn't care. But then the phone in his back pocket dings with a notification and his eyes fall shut. He takes a deep breath and I do the same.

"That's probably Uber Eats," I whisper.

He cracks one eye open and smirks at me. "Again?"

"Yeah. I'm hungry. I ordered it from your phone. Is that okay?'

His eyes roll. "Of course." The phone on his desk rings again. "I have to get that," he mutters, his tone apologetic.

"Okay. I'll go get Uber Eats."

"Want me to have Vance bring it up?"

I shake my head. "No. I'll go get it. I could use some air." I grin. "Plus, if it's that same little shit from earlier, I'm going to let him know my big bad husband is going to leave him a bad review."

Jake's brow furrows. The phone continues to ring, but both of us ignore it. "Husband?"

"Mmhm. The Uber driver thinks I'm your wife. He even called me *Mrs. Swagger.*"

He throws his head back on a laugh. When he meets my eyes, they're sparkling with humor. "Well, Swaggers are known for their promptness. So you better get down there, *wife*. We have a reputation to protect." He winks playfully. Unbeknownst to him, I'm already planning our wedding. Naming our kids. Picturing the two of us chasing them through the park where we can live without fear of them stepping in a pile of dog shit.

His lips pucker and he leans in to place a wet kiss on my mouth as he buttons his pants. He steps away and grabs the annoying fucking phone on his desk. When he answers, his voice is controlled. Tone cool and business like. It takes me a little longer to get my shit together and find my clothes.

After I've located all of them and am dressed, I step out of the apart-ment—a dreamy smile playing on my lips that still tingle from his kiss. The elevator finally arrives and I float inside and press my nose to the corner.

I hum my song and grin. I feel happy. Tingly.

Who the fuck am I kidding?

I'm so in love.

The elevator slows to a stop sooner than expected. I shrug it off, figuring the ride felt quicker than normal because I was distracted. Or perhaps because I've gotten used to the travel. But when I open my eyes and step out of the corner, the lighting looks different. It's a muted yellow instead of a soft white.

And the doors aren't opening.

And I hear the faint sound of a power grid shutting down.

And the doors aren't opening.

And the little digital number box on the panel next to the door doesn't have any digital numbers showing.

And the doors aren't opening.

And there's a buzz and a click and a red light flashes in the corner.

And the doors aren't opening.

The room spins. I can feel the walls closing in. I can hear the creaks and groans and the snap of wires. I'm pretty sure I'm falling. But I'm not sure how I'm still standing up if I am falling.

I think I'm going to vomit.

I vomit.

Someone is talking. I can hear voices coming from somewhere. Maybe outside the elevator? Have I stopped on another floor?

Assaulted with the knowledge that I'm still hovering in the air and will plunge to my death any second, I become seized with panic.

I scream for the voice to help me. I bang my fists on the doors that aren't opening. My stomach lurches. My vision clouds. I feel like my throat is closing.

The voice comes from a speaker inside the elevator. I catch bits and pieces of what it's saying. Something about staying calm. Electricity went out. Generator problems. I scream at someone—anyone—to get me the hell out of here. Try to pry open the doors. Punch all the buttons. Where is the phone? There should be a phone. I don't have my phone. I'm going to die.

I vomit.

"Da-da-da-da...da-da-da-da..." Someone is singing the hook to my favorite song. I nod my head in tune for a moment while I try to breathe through the dry heaves now that my stomach is empty.

When I find my voice, I sing along with them. "Da-da-da-da..." On my knees. "Da-da-da-da..." Forehead to the wall. "Da-da-da-da..." I will the room to stop spinning. "Da-da-da-da..." Will my mind to not focus on the falling.

Falling....

Falling....

Falling....

"Penelope!"

Jake?

"Penelope!"

Not Jake.

The elevator jolts.

Fuzzy, black dots cloud my vision.

I'm vomiting again.

"Penelope, baby, give me your hand."

I'm so scared. But I swear that voice is real.

"Open your eyes, Penelope."

I can't open my eyes. So I sing.

"Da-da-da-da...."

"Penelope!"

"Da-da-da-da...."

"Please, sweetheart. Please, listen to me."

Jake?

"For fuck's sake, Penelope! Look at me!"

That's Jake.

"Jake?"

"Penelope! Baby, I'm right here!"

"Jake?" I open my eyes but only the wall stares back at me. "Jake!" I look to my left. My right. "Jake!"

"Turn around, Penelope." The calmness in his tone helps to quell my panic.

"Jake..."

"I'm here, baby. Just turn around."

I look behind me. Then I follow his voice up. And I see him. The first thing I notice is his eyes. They're soft. Determined. Full of...something.

"I'm sorry, Jake."

"Penelope, take my hand."

Fresh tears fill my eyes. "I threw up in your elevator. Don't be mad at me."

"Baby..." he breathes out. The sound is a mixture of relief and pity. "I'm not mad at you. Come here and take my hand." It's then I notice his head and shoulders are squeezed between the gap in the doors. His arms stretched out toward me. The elevator must have stopped between floors.

Stopped....

Hovering....

Falling....

"Penelope." His voice is firm but not angry. Just enough to keep my attention. "I want you to stand up and—"

"No. No. No." I shake my head. "I can't. I can't. It'll fall."

"It won't fall. I'm not going to let you fall. But I need you to stand up. Come on, baby...There you go...Good girl...Now, one step—"

"Jake—" my voice cracks on a sob. My vision fogs with more tears. "I can't."

"Yes, you can. One step...That's it...One more...Almost here...Just take my hand..."

I stretch up on my toes to reach for his hand. I'm afraid I'm too short. He's too far away. I'm going to fall.

Crash.

Die.

A hand circles my wrist. Then my other wrist. My feet leave the floor. The top part of my body is dragged through the opening. I'm lifted under my arms. Folded into Jake's arms. He sits on the floor in the hallway and leans against the wall next to the elevator.

"Good girl. Good girl. Good girl," he chants, over and over as he holds me to him and pets my hair. Peppers my head with kisses. He's controlled, but I can hear the relief in his voice. I remember the panic that tinged it only moments ago. Remember the panic I felt when I thought I would die. When I thought his voice wasn't real.

But it was real.

He's here.

I'm here.

I'm alive.

I'm alive.

CHAPTER TWENTY-ONE

T he elevator had stopped somewhere between the seventeenth and eighteenth floors. After the understanding that I was safe and alive began to sink in, I started to process another truth. I'd panicked in front of Jake. He'd seen me at my most vulnerable. And that made me feel...weak.

Still, I allowed him to carry me up fourteen flights of stairs, as if it was his duty. I'd protested, but he'd ignored me.

When I told him I was fine, that I could walk, he would simply respond with, "Hush."

When I couldn't stop my body from trembling, he would hold me tighter, kiss my hair and say, "I've got you, baby. You're safe."

When my tears leaked from my eyes and wet his neck, he would beg me, "Please don't cry, sweetheart."

And with every step. Every word. Every temple kiss, backrub, soothing sound and squeeze, I found that my weakness had its perks. But the downside was greater. My embarrassment. The shame.... How could I ever face him? He'd called me perfect only moments before I stepped on that elevator.

What would he think of me now?

He sets me on the couch and kneels in front of me. My chin in his fingers, he tilts my head so he can look at me. Before he can ask, I answer the question written all over his face and in his eyes.

"I'm fine."

"Don't lie to me, Penelope."

"I'm not. I'm okay, Jake. Really. I'm just tired. And sore. And my throat hurts."

He pushes my hair out of my face. "Your screams...."

"Yeah. I know. Sorry about that. I panicked."

"Don't apologize. I just figured that's why your throat is sore."

I shake my head and look away from him. "My throat hurts from throwing up."

"Don't be embarrassed by that, baby. It doesn't matter."

"I can smell it on me, Jake," I snap, swiping the tears from my cheeks. I'm not angry at him. I'm just...well I'm fucking embarrassed. "I'm pretty sure it's in my hair." My eyes widen as I scan his T-shirt. His neck. "God, I hope I didn't get it on you."

"You worry about all the wrong things," he mumbles, mostly to himself. "Tell me what hurts so I can fix it. What else besides your throat?"

His eyes travel over me. Looking for physical signs of injury. I close my eyes and try to keep the blood from rushing to my cheeks. I've humiliated myself enough for one day. Or one lifetime. As exhausted as I feel, I shouldn't care. But I do.

"Hey. Look at me."

I open my eyes and he's nothing but a blur. I'm an ugly crier. That's usually enough to keep my emotions in check. But my emotions are in turmoil right now. And I can't fight them no matter how hard I try.

I move to stand and he backs out of my way. I want a shower. A bed. A redo of today. I walk away from him but only make it a few steps when I feel his hand on my elbow. I stop, but don't turn to face him.

"You're tired because you've had hardly any sleep since you've been in Chicago. Your throat hurts because you were sick. You're sore because of me."

Humor. Where the fuck are you? Please come back to me. You're around for Cocky That Guy. Jerk That Guy. Sexy That Guy. Why abandon me with Nice That Guy? He's the only one I can't handle without you.

For fuck's sake. I'm having a conversation with my sense of humor.

"I just want to take a shower." I pull away and he releases me. I'm relieved. Yet I feel cold without his touch. I don't want to be away from him. But I can't look at him right now, either. Not like this. Not when I feel like this.

I walk to the guest bathroom in a zombie-like trance. Inside the shower, I plant my hands on the wall and stand under the hot spray—willing it release all the tension in my body. Wash away the morning. The panic that still simmers beneath the surface.

Sometime later, I'm still just standing there when a cool blast of wind hits my naked, wet skin seconds before large hands flatten against my back. I jump beneath the touch.

"You're okay. It's just me." Jake's thick tone instantly relieves some of the tension. Perhaps because I'm not facing him. I don't have to look him in the eye—see the pity there. The remorse. Or—God forbid—the disgust.

His thumbs knead the flesh on either side of my spine in a firm, circular motion. The result makes my knees wobble. "Feel good?"

Shivers ripple through me and I nod, unable to find my voice. His thumbs work their way up my back to my shoulders to focus on my neck at the base of my skull. After several minutes of his caresses, it's a struggle just to hold myself up. "Lean back against me, baby."

I stagger back until my head is on his shoulder. My back against his chest. His thick cock nestled between the cheeks of my ass. The water sluices over my breasts and causes an erotic sting in my nipples that shoots straight to my core.

His mouth finds the curve of my neck and he places soft, lingering, wet kisses there. I release a long, low sigh and his cock hardens against me. I wait for him to slide his hands to my breasts. Or down my stomach to my swollen clit. Or reach between us and stroke himself. Doing what he does best, which will help me forget everything. But he just continues to massage my neck and shoulders—his touch highly intimate and erotic in its own way, but not sexual or demanding.

He washes my hair. Massages my scalp. Spins me to face him. I keep my eyes closed as he soaps my body and cleans me from my head to my navel with his bare hands. I stand still and silent. Eventually, I lift my lashes just a fraction to peek at him. And I'm more than a little awestruck by the magnificence of Jake Swagger. Of his body that's chiseled perfection. His masculine facial features that are devilishly handsome.

That feeling that is becoming too familiar rocks through me when his eyes meet mine. They are as soft with kindness as they are fiery with lust.

I need to fill the silence with something. But all I can manage is his name. "Jake..."

"Shhh." He straightens and cups my face with his hands. "Let me do this. Let me take care of you."

I swallow hard. Blink away tears. Nod. Let him kiss my head. My eyes. Cheeks. Nose. Chin.

Son of a bitch why does that make me want to cry harder?

He kneels in front of me to wash my legs. Soaping his hands and rubbing the lather into my hips before making his way all the way down my legs in firm, circular strokes. When he makes his way back up my legs, his touch is more sensual. I never knew the spot behind my knee was such an erogenous place until the slow drag of his fingers there leave me trembling.

"Turn around, Penelope." His dark voice and even darker stare has me forgetting about everything but doing as I'm told.

This.

This is what he and I know.

It's safe.

It's distracting.

It's...normal for us.

"Bend over. Hands on either side of the bathtub."

My eyes fall closed and a noise I've never heard myself make escapes me. I try my best to forget that he's kneeling behind me. But it's impossible to do when I feel his lips skim my hip in feathery kisses moments before he breathes across my skin, "Spread your legs. I want to see your pussy."

"...Jake..." The cry is guttural. And I don't know if I'm trying to tell him I'm embarrassed by his words, or if I'm simply calling out to him because he's all-consuming.

I have that feeling.

The warm one.

The Pop Rocks are in my veins.

There's a flutter in my belly.

A heaviness in my chest.

And these things don't stem from a throbbing, sexual need for him to be inside me. These feelings come from somewhere even deeper. There's something about this humiliating, titillating, provocative moment that makes my body, mind and voice sing his name over and over.

"Hush, baby. Trust me. I got you."

There are those words again. The ones from the elevator. The ones he whispered when he saved me. The ones from last night. The ones that made me fall asleep with the realization that what's happening between us isn't just some fictional story I'm writing. This is real. What I feel is real. I *do* trust him. And with trust comes love. With love comes pain. And I know it's love because despite the fear of risking it all, I want to give myself over to him.

I cannot believe I'm having an epiphany while I'm bent over in the shower, my ass in Jake's face, legs spread so he can see all of me.

I guess that's what it takes for a girl like me who hides behind her humor and lives in an imaginary world to escape reality and all the heartache that comes with it. Because humiliation, uncertainty and vulnerability are feelings that can't be ignored. And those are the feelings I feel in this moment.

Jake's hands slide up the back of my thighs and cups my ass. "I should've done this last night." He spreads me open and his breath fans over me. "This morning. Every time you gave yourself to me, I should've been right here. On my knees. Worshiping what brings me the best goddamn pleasure I've ever felt."

Then his mouth is on me. Kissing my pussy. His tongue and lips like velvet on the sensitive, swollen flesh. It feels exquisite. Just like the massage. More cherishing than carnal despite where his mouth is.

This is nothing like last time. This isn't foreplay. This isn't him trying to make me come hard by sucking on my clit or fucking me with his tongue. This is him doing as he said—worshiping what he ravaged. Soothing what he hurt. Doing what he can to put back together the pieces of me that shattered in that elevator.

Everything inside me unravels. A sob escapes from deep in my chest. I don't know what's water and what's tears. I'm a boneless, exhausted mess. Completely numb aside from the low, steady hum that swims through my veins and sounds in my ears.

He shuts off the water and helps me straighten before turning me to face him. I want to look at him. To see if his eyes reflect a hint of what I'm feeling. But I can't lift my lids. "Wrap your arms around my neck, sweetheart."

By the time his demand breaks through the fog and registers with my mind, he's already placed my arms around his neck and effortlessly lifted me so my legs are around his waist and my head is on his shoulder.

I shiver when the air whips around my wet skin as he carries me out of the bathroom. I burrow deeper into him and he responds by tightening his grip. He stops walking. I feel his shoulder flex beneath my head as me reaches for something.

I moan against his neck as heat surrounds me. The towel is soft and warm and feels perfect against my achy, overly sensitive skin. I might not have just come from a session in a playroom, or been flogged or belted or shackled or clamped, but I'm pretty sure what I'm feeling is similar to the after effects of subspace.

He dries me like I'm his.

Like he has every right to wipe away the water from some places, and gently pat dry those that are much more tender.

Like he knows the weight of my hair. And what it takes to rid the water from my ringlets.

Like I'm his treasure to touch. To kiss. To call beautiful.

Like I was meant to wear the T-shirt he slips over my head—his T-shirt.

Like his bed was made just for me.

His body molded to perfectly fold around mine.

His lips created to worship my temple.

And then sometime later. Maybe minutes, maybe hours, he speaks words to me I'm not meant to hear. They're meant to fall on deaf ears. They're meant to be said to a woman who is asleep. But they're said in a whispered tone laced with such conviction and sincerity, that even if I couldn't hear it with my ears, I'd hear it in my soul. Because that's where I feel him most. Where I know him best. And his words are delivered in true Jake Swagger form.

"For fuck's sake, Penelope Hart...you're making me fall in love with you."

CHAPTER TWENTY-TWO

"You do realize that's thirty-two flights of fucking stairs, right?" Jake's voice echoes through the empty stairwell as he leans on the wall, dressed in jeans and a Henley, with one perfect eyebrow—that he swears he doesn't wax—arched in question.

"I do. Which is why we're leaving thirty minutes early. So either get to stepping, or be an asshole and take the elevator. But if it gets stuck, don't expect me to save you." I start down the stairs alone.

Before I hit the first landing, I hear his loud sigh followed by his heavy footsteps behind me. "Fine. And when you give out halfway there, because you will, don't expect me to carry your ass the rest of the way."

"You'll carry me, if I ask you to."

"No the fuck I won't."

I throw a look at him over my shoulder, surprised to see he's only two steps behind me. "Yes, you will."

"Penelope..." His growl is a warning.

To prove my point, I pretend to stumble. With lightning reflexes, he reaches out to steady me. "Watch it, baby."

Where's that growl at now?

I want to smirk, but I'm too busy melting on the inside. Just like I've been melting for the past two days.

Ever since the elevator crisis, Jake has been overly cautious. Treating me like a precious gem. Doting on me. Waiting on me hand and foot. I'm not sure if it's because I scared him, or because he's falling in love with me —his words. Not mine.

He doesn't know that I heard him that night. I have no intention of telling him. But even if he hadn't said it, I'd have known by the way he treated me.

After the incident, I'd slept nearly the entire day. When I woke, it was dark out. Jake was still in bed with me—wrapped around me as if he feared I'd take off without him knowing. He'd woken the moment I stirred. Kissed my head. Asked how I was feeling. Made me dinner and brought it to me.

The next morning, I woke up alone in bed. A feeling of sadness and loneliness washed over me. It quickly faded when I found him in the chair across the room. Typing away on his laptop. Dressed in gym shorts and nothing else. His hair slicked with sweat from his morning workout.

I went to him. Needing his comfort like I needed to breathe. When I crawled from bed, he folded me in his arms. And he held me. Rubbed my back. Then carried me to the shower. The fact that he waited to shower until I woke up wasn't lost on me. And, for some reason, I'd cried at that —my tears disguised by the spray of water.

We spent the day watching T.V. He even let me choose the movie. I, being the hopeless romantic cliché that I am, chose The Notebook. I cried during all of the sweeter scenes. Jake rolled his eyes. But he never complained.

Well...except for the part where the hero asks the heroine over and over and over, *"What do you want?"*

Jake had grunted his signature, "For fuck's sake," and shook his head.

Later that evening, he spent some time in his office. And he didn't seem the least bit bothered when I joined him. I sat across from his desk and read while he worked.

Cam showed up at some point and even then Jake didn't dismiss me. He simply tucked a blanket around my naked legs—I'd worn nothing but his T-shirts since he first dressed me in one—kissed my hair and let me stay while they worked. Cam looked at us like we were crazy. But something in Jake's gaze kept him from making one of his usual jabs.

By the time we went to bed last night, I was over the trauma. I felt like me—a very loved, very wanted, me. Falling asleep in Jake's arms was better than fucking him. And I couldn't imagine what it would be like when I went home and had to sleep alone. Or who might warm Jake's bed when I wasn't there to do it. The thought was so unsettling, I refused to dwell any longer. I was going to keep the faith—still am.

Jake loves me.

I mean, how can he not?

And with love comes happily ever after. Hearts and flowers and Pop Rocks and river dancing every day.

I come to another door and the big sign labeled *16* above it makes me groan. "Jake..." I whine, huffing and puffing dramatically as I lean my back against the door. "I'm tired."

"Tough shit."

"Carry me."

"Hell no." He steps around me and pushes through the door.

"Come on," I beg, following behind him. "Consider it your daily workout."

"I've already done my morning workout, Penelope. While you sat on the weight bench and watched me."

True. He'd left me a note by the alarm clock that blared in my ear at six freaking thirty this morning, telling me he was in his gym. Curious, because until that moment, I didn't even know he had a gym, I went looking for it.

It looked like a smaller version of the YMCA. Minus the scent of feet. With a view of Chicago. It even had three flat screen T.V.'s and a refrigerator. But it was the sight of Jake all hot and sweaty and fine as hell that forced me to sit to keep my knees from buckling.

"If I had known we were going to take the stairs, I might've forgone the six mile, morning run."

"Did you really think I'd get back in that death trap?"

He doesn't even blink. "Yes."

"Well, that's just...I don't like using the word stupid, but that's just stupid."

"Insult me if you want, but do it while you walk or else we're going to be late."

"Ugh. Fine." To distract myself from the million miles we have to go, I take a quick selfie, send it to Emily and imagine her reaction when she sees that I'm wearing Chanel—again. The oversized, cream colored sweater stops just above my knees. I'm also wearing some super thick, double knit brown leggings. And a pair of brown knee boots that are insulated. Oh, and they're made by Louis Vuitton.

She's going to be so jealous.

The idea gives me a boost of energy and I'm not even winded when we finally reach the lobby. Alfred is there to greet us with a smile and an apology for what happened with the elevator. I give him a hug because I'm a hugger. He returns it and I grin when I feel Jake's eyes on us. Before he can say anything though, his phone rings.

Ross ushers us to the car and even winks at me before he shuts the door. Jake doesn't notice. He's too busy talking about numbers and percentages and boring shit. So I play Toy Blast while he works the entire ride to the airstrip where a plane waits for us.

I was expecting something that looked like a crop duster. This damn thing looks like a mini Air Force One. There are couches. Captain's chairs that recline. A bedroom. Shower. Bathroom. Bar. A flight attendant who is too damn pretty to be smiling at Jake like that.

Layla, as her nametag reads, smooths her hands over her neatly pressed dress that's entirely too short. I look at Jake to see if he's checking out her legs. He's looking at me—his phone still glued to his ear. An amused smirk on his lips.

When she notices him on the phone, she turns to me. "May I get you anything, Miss Sims?"

My eyes roll.

Jake sputters a laugh and quickly ends his call.

Layla looks confused.

"My name is Penelope."

"My apologies, Miss Penelope." She looks contrite. But I'm too annoyed to care.

"It's just Penelope," I snap.

"Of course, Penelope. Can I get you anything?"

"We'll both have a vodka. Make hers a double."

Layla nods and quickly disappears. I move to the seat farthest from him.

"Penelope..." he breathes, humor evident in his voice. "Don't be upset. It was an honest mistake."

"I'm not upset." *Liar.*

I fumble with my seatbelt that is way fancier than a normal airplane seatbelt. I'm so focused on figuring it out, I don't notice he's left his seat until he's standing in front of me. He brushes my hands away and fastens my seatbelt himself.

"Hey...," he says and tilts my chin up with his fingers. "I'm sorry, baby. Truly."

"Yeah? Well you don't look very sorry."

He does a better job of containing his smile. "You're nervous. And now I've upset you. I'll make it up to you later. I promise."

"Have you flown a lot of women on this plane?" I bristle at my own question.

He, of course, grins. "None as pretty as you."

"That Guy would've flown me on a jet he hadn't fucked any other woman on. He would say it was because I deserved something more. To him, I was worth more than all of them. He would've burned this plane to the ground and just bought another one."

"You are definitely worth more than any other woman I've flown on this plane. But you're not worth more than sixty million dollars, baby."

I'm river dancing on the inside because I'm worth more and prettier than the others. And Jake Swagger is worth *a lot*. On the outside, I look unimpressed as I glance around at the cabin and all its ridiculous luxury. "You paid sixty million dollars for this?"

He grins. "You're such an asshole."

Jake grabs the drinks Layla left for us and hands one to me. I throw it back—realizing a little late that it was a mistake. He pats my back until my choking fit passes, then returns to his seat.

I snap a selfie and send it to Emily before I settle back in my chair and let the warmth from the alcohol swim through me. It's still too early in the morning for me. I'm tired. And before we leave the ground, I feel myself drifting—smiling at Emily's signature, middle finger emoji response.

Still jealous.

CHAPTER TWENTY-THREE

"**D**id you Bill Cosby me?"

I try to jerk my wrist free of Jake's hand but he doesn't let me go. He just looks up at me from beneath his lashes as he continues to kiss my fingers. Nip the tips of them with his teeth. Make me melt into a pile of goo on the backseat of this fancy car that's being driven by someone I don't even know.

"What?"

"Did you drug me?"

"No, Penelope. I didn't drug you."

"Then explain how I managed to sleep so hard the entire flight?"

He shrugs. "I guess you were tired."

"I wasn't that tired."

"Then I guess you have a low tolerance for alcohol. Which, now that I think about it, you do have a very low tolerance for liquor. I should've considered that. Forgive me?"

I pretend to be annoyed and glare at him. "How can you expect me to forgive you when you just keep fucking up? This is the second time you've apologized to me today. I'm starting to see a pattern. You know, this is how all relationships that end with the man killing the woman, start. With him constantly being mean, then apologizing and expecting to be forgiven immediately."

He smiles against my fingers. "So you think we're in a relationship?"

I snort. "Um. No. Duh. Geeze. Whatever."

Fuck!

"I'm teasing you, gorgeous. I didn't know a double shot of vodka would knock you out completely. If I had, I promise I would've used it long before now."

I smack his arm with the back of my hand. He grins and I can't help but grin myself. "Well, don't let it happen again."

"Noted."

"Good. Now feed me."

He leans over and gives me a kiss that I feel in my toes. Then, smiles and winks and says in his best southern drawl, "Yes, ma'am."

———

THE DINER JAKE took me to might've looked like something straight off the set of *The Texas Chainsaw Massacre,* but the food was the best I've ever eaten. And I've never been more thankful for stretchy pants than I am in this moment.

"Can we take a nap now?" I ask, yawning loudly as I rub my stomach.

Jake smirks. "No. We're meeting Jim and his daughters at the plant where they build the irrigation system."

"Why?" I frown, realizing I know very little about this trip. He asked me to go, I said yes. The end.

I'm so easy.

"Because I haven't seen it yet. And his employees are now my employees. So I'd like to meet them."

I yawn again. "But I'm so tired...."

"I'd take you back to the hotel so you could sleep if I could, gorgeous. But I have a full agenda today. And the Cantons like you. This will go much smoother if you're there." He sweeps my hair off my face and I rub my cheek on his thigh like a cat.

"To hell with the Cantons. I'd let you put it in my butt if you took me back to the hotel."

A throat clears from the front of the car and I stiffen. Jake dips his head and drops his voice. I know what he's going to say before he says it. "This car doesn't come equipped with a privacy partition, sweetheart. So you may want to keep your dirty thoughts to yourself."

I bolt upright in the seat and meet the eyes of the driver in the rearview mirror. All the blood in my body rushes to my face. "I'm so sorry."

The driver, professional as ever, focuses his attention back on the road. "No apology necessary, Miss." He swallows hard and shifts with unease before addressing Jake. "Mr. Swagger?" He pauses to clear his throat—his unease obvious. "Are we sticking to the schedule?"

Jake doesn't even look up—his concentration on his phone. "Yes. We need to be at the manufacturing plant by three."

The driver nods and mutters a, "Yes sir."

And though Jake seems oblivious, I don't miss the driver's smirk when I mumble a comeback.

"Wasn't gonna let you put it in my butt, anyway."

―――――

"I APPRECIATE each of you and what you've done for this company. I look forward to a future with you. To working alongside you as together, we introduce the world to the greatest change the agriculture community has seen since the tractor. Thank you."

And the crowd cheers.

I'd bore you with all the other bullshit he said, but there's really nothing exciting about a fucking sprinkler system. I don't care how you spin it. I mean, sure these people were engaged—hanging on Jake's every word. But they know shit about farming that I don't. And he really does look good standing up there all handsome and powerful, trying to be casual in his jeans and shirt as if he doesn't run the world.

I wonder if Jake is part of the Illuminati....

Amber nudges me with her shoulder and smiles. "They loved him."

I look back up to where Jake is shaking hands with everyone. "Yeah. It's easy to love him."

"I think I might love him."

"Couldn't blame you if you did."

"So do you?"

"Do I what?"

"Love him?"

I nod slowly. "I think I do."

She cuts her eyes at me. "Think? Girl you better know. Because there is no doubt that he's in love with you."

"I'm not so sure."

"Um. I am. The way he looks at you? Smiles at you? *Touches* you? Either you're blind or just really stupid if you don't see it. The two of you are like something out of a romance novel. You're the heroine and he's...I'd say hero, but that doesn't do him justice."

I stare at Jake from across the room. As if he can sense my gaze, he looks up—his eyes immediately meeting mine. Like he knew where I was all along. I give him a small wave and feel all the muscles in my back relax when he winks at me.

"You're right, Amber. He's more than a hero."

"So what do you call the man who is just...everything?"

"I used to call him That Guy."

"That Guy...oh, that's good. So what do you call him now?"

"I'm thinking something along the lines of future baby daddy. Love of my life. Reason for existence. Soulmate...." I purse my lips and tilt my head as I study him. "You think that's too extreme?"

At that moment, Jake picks up a baby.

I don't even know where the baby came from.

Didn't even know one was here.

But he has a baby.

In his arms.

And he...

Have mercy.

He kisses the baby.

Amber's dreamy sigh matches my own. "Extreme? Do I think it's extreme to want a guy like that to be your soulmate?" From the corner of my eye, I see her shake her head. "Nope. Not even a little bit."

"I think I'm going to tell him I love him."

"If you don't. I will."

I frown and turn to face her. "Why would you tell him I love him? That's...that's personal."

She rolls her eyes. "I'm not going to tell him you love him, dumbass. I'm going to tell him *I* do."

I'm not sure if she's joking or not. I can't read her. To be safe, I start plotting my revenge—you know...just in case she's serious. There's just one thing I have to know first. So in the most nonchalant voice I can manage, I ask, "On a scale from one to ten, how hard is it to find a fresh pile of dog shit in Topeka?"

CHAPTER TWENTY-FOUR

I watched Jake hug old people, pet dogs and kiss babies for as long as I could until the fear that my ovaries would explode consumed me. So I wandered outside. It was there, on the back dock of the ware-house, that I found a group of employees in an intense game of poker.

Unable to resist, I joined.

And thanks to my skills and ability to bluff like a pro, I'm one of the last two standing.

"I'll see your...." I pick up my opponent's watch and hold it toward the light. "...Timex, and raise you one Louis Vuitton boot." Sliding my seat—a five-gallon bucket—away from the table, I pull off the boot and toss it in the pile.

Jasper, a guy in his late twenties whose been at Canton Industries since he was fifteen, takes a drag from his cigarette, thumps it then shoots me an incredulous glare. "What the fuck am I gonna do with one boot?"

"Sell it to a pirate. I don't know. And I don't care. But it's worth a helluva lot more than that raggedy ass shit you've been throwing in the pot." Everyone around us laughs. It seems Jasper is one of those who can dish it out but can't take it. And he met his match when he met me—about twenty hands ago.

"How the hell do I even call that?" He picks up the boot and examines it. "How much does this thing cost?"

There are only a couple women still out here. Neither of them, like me, have a clue. But they, also like me, know enough to know that it's expensive. They're arguing that point while I try to decide what possessions of Jasper's might be equivalent to one boot.

"Your hat."

Jasper stiffens. "What did you say?"

"Your hat." I motion with my finger toward the hat he keeps twisting on his head. The one that's old and worn. That I'm sure has little value to anyone but him. "Throw your hat in if you want to call."

He shakes his head. "No. This is my lucky hat."

"Yeah? And how has that worked out for you?" I point to my stack of winnings that consist of money, a few keychains, a couple knives, a ton of pens, a rubber ball, a box of rubber bands and a rubber chicken—most of which belonged to him. "Throw in the hat or fold."

He narrows his eyes on me. "Throw in the other boot and I'll consider it."

"This boot is worth a lot of money."

"No. The *pair* of boots is worth a lot of money. One boot ain't worth shit." He points to his hat. "This hat? Is worth more than money."

I nod slowly. "Fair enough." I pull off my other boot and toss it on the table. "Well, there's my five hundred dollars."

"Um, I just Googled it," one of the women says. "Try two thousand dollars."

Everyone starts murmuring that it's not an equal bet. That Jasper is a piece of shit for trying to bet an old hat against a pair of designer boots.

I believe it's safe to say I'm the crowd favorite.

"You hear that?" Jasper waves toward the crowd circled around us. "I have to work with these assholes every day. This is a lose-lose for me. If I win, I'll be shamed for taking a lady's boots. If I lose, I'll never hear the end of how I lost everything to my boss's girlfriend."

I shrug and take a pull from my beer. "So fold."

"Not a chance in hell. I want to renegotiate."

"I'm listening."

"Keep your boots. They're probably fake anyway."

I shake my head. "Jake bought them. Trust me. They're not fake."

Suggestive murmurs and teasing sounds from the crowd. My cheeks flush and I roll my eyes at them—grinning ear to ear.

"Like I was saying, you keep your boots. I keep my hat. Winner takes the pot. And the loser..." He leans in and points toward the open field that stretches as far as the eye can see. His eyes twinkle and he grins. "Streaks across the field."

The crowd erupts in laughter. Some tell Jasper he's crazy. Some say they're going to video him streaking. One says Mr. Swagger is going to kill Jasper if he finds out. And that one is met with a response.

"Why would I kill Jasper?" I whip my head around to find Jake emerging from the shadows—an amused expression on his face. A possessive look in his eyes. "He's not the one betting something that doesn't belong to him."

Everyone falls silent as he approaches. I make a mental note to talk to him about when it is and when it isn't appropriate to show up unannounced around his employees. Nobody wants to hang out with their boss. But of course he wouldn't know that. He doesn't have a boss.

"W-what are you talking about, Jake?" I try to sound tough. I don't.

He places his hands on either side of the table, boxing me in. "I'm talking about you running across a field. Naked." He leans in and drops his voice so only I can hear. "Your body belongs to me, baby. And I'm not in the mood to share."

He pulls back and I swallow hard. It takes everything inside me not to wrap myself around him and dry hump his hip in front of God and his employees.

I shake away the thought.

This is a poker game.

Not a brothel.

We can fuck later.

Right now, I have a hand to win.

Jake's eyes drop to the cards in my hand. "May I?"

"No. You may not."

Jake ignores me and plucks my cards from my hand. Straightening, he examines them. I cast a quick glance to Jasper and find him fighting a smile. I give him the finger, and turn back to Jake whose expression remains stoic—thank fuck.

Jake slides my cards into a single stack and hands them back to me, face down. I snatch them from his fingers and spin on my bucket to face Jasper. "Winner takes the pot. Loser streaks. Is that the deal?"

Jasper nods.

From behind me, I hear a very deep and very final, "No."

I take a breath and look up and over my shoulder at Jake. "I'm not going to lose, Jake."

"You might."

"I won't. Trust me."

"No." His tone is dismissive and he speaks to Jasper over my head. "Winner gets the pot. You lose, you streak. She loses...I streak."

Nobody seems to care anymore that their boss is here. They're too busy losing their shit. Taking side bets. Getting their camera phones ready. I mean, I'm a little disappointed in the lack of faith these people have in me. Not that I can blame them for their enthusiasm. Hell, for the first time ever, I actually *want* to lose.

Jasper and Jake shake hands.

The moment Jasper pulls back, he flips his cards up on the table. He's all smiles. On his feet. Doing the robot. Pointing at his King high flush and demanding that I, *beat that shit*, and telling Jake, *take it off*.

I let him rejoice a few more seconds before I crush his dreams.

"I win," I state, matter-of-fact.

Jasper stills.

Pales.

Stutters. "W-w-what?"

I lay my cards down on the table, face up so everyone can see. I may not get to see Jake run across a field naked, but victory is still pretty fucking sweet. Besides, I can see him naked later.

Now I'm all smiles. On my feet. Telling Jasper to eat shit. Watching as he regretfully starts stripping. Reveling in the sound of Jake's laughter. At the sight of him bonding with his employees. And of course, I'm performing my own dance.

River dance, finger snap, finger guns...pointed at my *Ace* high flush.

———

"I CAN'T BELIEVE I LOST." Jasper gives me a onceover. "To a girl." He glances over at Jake and gives him a onceover. "My boss's girl."

My inner feminist kicks in and I point to his crotch. "I can't believe you can hide your entire pecker with those tiny little hands."

Once again, the crowd roars. Even Jake laughs. And Jasper, being a good sport, grins and removes his hands—holding them in the air, allowing his cock to hang freely.

Well...not really *hang*.

But before anyone can comment on that, he bolts across the open field. His bare ass is illuminated by the huge spotlights on the corner of the building. It would be lit up with the flash from his fellow employee's phones if it weren't for Jake's insistence that everyone be a good sport and not record this moment.

"Well, that's one sight I could've retired without seeing," Jim says, shaking his head as we all watch Jasper run back toward us—stopping every few feet to shake his dick. "I think these people are going to like you, Jake." Jim turns to Jake and gives him a nod. "I feel good about leaving them in your hands."

Jake's smile is humble. "Thank you for that."

"Come on, Mr. Swagger!" Jasper approaches us, trying to catch his breath. "The weather feels nice on the ol' balls. You should try it."

"No."

Jasper grins. "How about a hug, then?"

"No."

"Handshake?"

"No."

"What about you, Penelope?" He holds his arms open and shakes his dick at me. "Hug?"

Jake tosses him his clothes. "I like you, Jasper. Don't fuck it up."

The crowd—Jake's employees, every day average people—laugh good naturedly at Jake's words. If it weren't for the powerful way he carried himself, he could almost pass as one of them. It makes them feel good that he acts as their equal. He's not just some suit. He's not the richest man they'll likely ever meet. He's not even their boss. In this moment, he's just Jake.

As we say our goodbyes, I stand next to Jake—bag of winnings in one hand, his hand in my other—until the only people left are us and Jim, who has just invited us to have dinner with him and his daughters.

I'm famished—as usual—so I'm quick to agree. But Jake cuts me off.

"I actually have plans for us tonight, Jim. But we appreciate the invite."

Plans?

Jake has plans?

I didn't know about any plans.

I'm in shock as I hug Jim goodbye. Walk to the car. Let Jake usher me inside. It's not until we're driving away that I ask what I'm dying to know. "We have plans?"

"Yes. I'm taking you out on a date. Dinner...wine...candles...*sex*."

I throw my head back and laugh. "Are you serious?"

"I am."

"You call that a date?"

"I do."

I shake my head. "You're so lame. That date sounds terrible."

He lifts a brow. "What part?"

"Well...just the candlelit dinner part. With wine. I'm not much of a wine drinker. And I don't like fancy restaurants with candles. It's not me. To be honest? I wasn't aware places like that actually existed, outside of movies and books."

"They exist. But you're right. It's not you." His eyes darken and his fingers brush across my temple. "You deserve something much more special than that."

"I do?"

"Yes, Penelope. You most certainly do."

Heart flutter.

Belly flip.

Pop rocks.

Clit tingle.

"So where are we going?"

"To do something you love."

"How do you know I love it? Did I tell you?"

He grins. "No. But trust me. You'll love it."

I have to bite my lip to keep from telling him I love him. Instead, I just smile and curl into his side. I lean my head back so I can look into his eyes. So he'll know that what I say is true. And genuine. "If I forget to tell you later...."

"Yeah, yeah, yeah, Pretty Woman." He rolls his eyes. "You had a good time tonight."

CHAPTER TWENTY-FIVE

I'm so in love.

We're on our way back to the hotel and I'm seriously considering letting Jake put it in my butt. I mean, if he wants to. Because after the night we had...how can I not?

He said I'd love it.

I did.

Why?

Because this motherfucker took me river dancing.

Yes.

He.

Did.

He booked a class. With a professional river dancer. And I, along with ten others, earned a certificate for completing the intermediate level of dance at *Acreas Irish Dance Academy*.

But did the night stop there?

Nope.

Our next stop was dinner. But not just any dinner. It was a dinner and improv show. Where we had to act out scenes from different eras as we ate...you're not going to believe this...chicken wings.

Then we went to a little bar that had Christmas lights strung across the ceiling and concrete floors and a really old juke box and they only served beer. Not any of that fancy beer either. The good stuff—Budweiser.

And we shot pool.

And played darts.

And had there had been anyone else in there, we might have gotten into a bar fight with them.

It was perfect.

Jake Swagger is perfect.

Tonight?

Perfect.

And the night is still young.

We arrive at our hotel and Jake is in full *That Guy* mode—powerful. A little arrogant. He walks with his chin up. Back straight. Aware of everything around him. Politely ignoring the stares. Offering a courteous head nod at the appropriate times. Growing a little taller whenever he's addressed as, Mr. Swagger.

Welcome, Mr. Swagger.

We're pleased you're here, Mr. Swagger.

The stairs are this way, Mr. Swagger.

Eighteen flights of stairs later—which I didn't even ask him to carry me up because I swear I floated the entire time—and we're in our room that looks like the Penthouse Suite at Caesar's Palace in Las Vegas. Not that I've ever been, but I've seen *The Hangover*. The only thing this hotel room lacks is Mike Tyson on the piano and a tiger in the bathroom.

I didn't even know Topeka, Kansas offered rooms this luxurious. Although I wouldn't doubt it if Jake called ahead and had them build it just for him.

When the door to our suite closes behind the annoying guy who followed us around the miniature mansion to see if everything suited our needs, I turn on Jake and bat my lashes at him. "Are we alone now, *Mr. Swagger?*"

His eyes caress me from head to toe.

I take a step toward him and place my hand on his chest. With a gentle push, I urge him backwards. When his knees hit the bed, he sits.

"Would you like to fuck me, *Mr. Swagger?*"

Eyeing my breasts that are now at eye level, he licks his bottom lip then pulls it between his teeth.

I drop to my knees and boldly feel him through his pants before lowering his zipper. I free him and breathe in his clean, masculine scent that's all him and a touch of his cologne. His cock hardens by the second.

Growing thicker. Longer. Bigger until that flesh covered school bus of his is only a hairsbreadth from my lips.

"Can I suck your cock, *Mr. Swagger?*"

He groans. "Don't say cock, Penelope."

I kiss the tip of him. His entire body jerks and I look up from beneath my lashes feeling pretty damn smug. "Would you rather I use the appropriate medical term, *Mr. Swagger?*"

"Don't you fucking dare."

"Pe—"

Say penis.

Do it.

Right now.

Notice how your lips part and your mouth opens on the *peeee?*

Well that's the exact moment Jake's dick found its way between my lips.

I'm left with no choice but to open my mouth. It's either that or risk him knocking out my front teeth with that big cock canon of his.

I moan around him.

Take him a little deeper.

Remember I have a terrible gag reflex.

Pull back so I can work the head of him with my tongue. Lips. Hand. And judging by his grunts and groans, I must be doing something right.

Some girls can suck cock all day. They just *love* it. All those heroines in romance novels? Oh, they make it sound like sucking dick is the greatest thing in the world.

I'm not one of those girls.

As heady as it is to have him in my mouth, I much prefer being selfish and having his mouth on me. So, as graceful as I can manage, I crawl into his lap and straddle his thighs. I link my hands behind his neck and rub myself against his shaft. It feels so good, I'm sure that I can come just like this. So sure that for a moment, I'm so concentrated on making myself feel good, I forget where I am. The sounds I make. That he's watching.

"Damn girl..." he murmurs, sliding his hands beneath my sweater and palming both my breasts. His words—there's something about them. The way he calls me *girl.* It makes me feel...filthy. And I like filthy.

I lift my head to find his eyes on me. Wild with fire and passion. "Talk to me, Jake."

"You like when I talk to you?"

"Yes." I grind my hips a little harder against him. "Fuck yes. Talk dirty to me. Make me feel dirty. Please. Just...I mean...Like, don't call me names or slap me in the face or anything. You can slap my ass, though. If you want. I don't know. Tell me what to do. I'm so stupid. I should shut up."

"Hush, Penelope, unless you want your mouth filled again."

I whimper. Nod. Do everything I can to tell him that's the tone, words and filth I want him to use without actually talking. Because he told me not to. And I want to be a good fake sub and listen.

"Stand up."

It takes me a second to comply, but eventually I manage to scramble off his lap and stand in front of him. He doesn't touch me but the sight of his hands so close—lying motionless on his thighs—has my hips bucking toward him on their own accord.

"Strip for me."

I blink.

"Um. Do what?"

"Strip for me, Penelope. I want to see you naked."

I can do that.

Surely.

I take a step back from him and pull my sweater over my head. His eyes stay on mine instead of falling to my black lacy bra—one of those that are cut so low, the tops of my areolas are visible. I look down to see if something is wrong. See if I can find a reason behind him not looking. I find none.

I shrug it off and hook my thumbs into the waistband of my leggings. Only when they're to my knees do I realize I forgot to take my boots off. So I attempt to use the toe of one boot on the heel of the other to take it off. When that doesn't work, I hop around on one foot. Seventeen hours later, I've managed to remove the bastards from my feet.

Then I stand before him.

Bra.

Panties.

Goosebumps...everywhere.

"You are a fine sight, Miss Hart." Jake takes a few seconds longer to drink me in, then stands.

He towers over me.

I look up at him.

We're not touching.

And the lack of contact makes the promise of what's to come even more exciting.

"I don't want to rush this." His fingers graze my temple and for a second, I think he's talking about something else—that maybe he doesn't want to rush *this* as in *us*. Together. This thing, whatever it may be, between us that's been building since the first time he found me in his apartment. But then he clarifies what he means, and though my body heats at the idea, my heart falls a little.

"I want to take my time with you tonight. Touch you everywhere. Kiss you where I touch. Make love to you for hours until you can't think...."

Can't walk...

"...Can't remember anything but how it feels when I'm inside you."

Pretty sure I won't ever forget if he fucks me for hours....

He takes a step back so he has a full view of me. "Take your panties off."

Oh have mercy he said panties.

I do as he says. I even manage to do it with grace. May even look sexy.

His eyes are on my sex. "Is your pussy wet for me, Penelope?"

"It could be wetter," I say, hoping he understands that I'm actually suggesting he put his mouth on it.

He smirks, telling me he gets it. "Now the bra."

I frown. "I really, really suck at doing that. It's super unsexy, too. Like I have to pull it over my head because it hurts my shoulders to—"

I stop speaking when he reaches behind me and releases the clasp with just a flick of his fingers—his eyes never leaving mine. His fingers not touching my skin.

Fuck he's good.

I roll my shoulders and the material falls away. I'm naked. He's not. I'm about to tell him so when he says, "Undress me."

Undressing Jake Swagger is like unwrapping the Christmas present you've waited all year for. One that you've already unwrapped and rewrapped so you know what's inside. But it doesn't make unwrapping it a second time and playing with it any less exciting.

Also, like a Christmas present, I take my time at first—removing his shirt slowly. But it doesn't take me long to grow impatient and soon I'm ripping his clothes off in a rush to get to the parts I can play with.

Gloriously naked, Jake stands before me. He's all chiseled perfection and tanned flesh over rock hard muscle. My mouth waters. Fingers explore. Mouth kisses until he groans his impatience, wraps his hands around my waist and pulls me to him.

Heat.

THAT GUY • 199

Lips.
Tongue.
Hands.
Moans.
Love.
My heart feels his touch as much as my body. In the way he caresses. Possesses. Kisses. Worships every bared inch available to him as we stand. And when he can't reach other parts of me in this position, he lifts me, spins me, lays me down and touches me everywhere else.

He kisses my toes.

My knees.

Hip bones.

The line of my ribcage that's exposed every time I pull in a deep, shuddering breath.

Then he looks at me—dark. Feral. Hungry. *In love.* Just long enough to tell me, "Come as much as you want," before spreading my legs and burying his face in my pussy.

Like I could hold back.

He does that figure eight move with his tongue until my back arches from the bed as he fucks me with his finger. Then his mouth settles on my come button.

Yes.

I said come button.

Because when he sucks hard and flicks his tongue rapidly across my clit, aka come button, guess what.

I come.

He eases the pressure. Slows his pace until I float back from whatever galaxy he just sent me to. When I'm no longer a shivering, moaning mess, he repeats what he just did.

Figure eight.

Suck.

Tongue flick.

Finger pump.

And I come.

After I've joined the living, he restarts the process. I'm not sure I can handle it. Not the orgasm, of course. I mean, I'll take those as long as he wants to give them. I'm talking about the emptiness I feel without him inside me. So I beg.

"Please, Jake. Fuck me. Fill me. I need to feel you."

"And I need to taste you."

It's all he says before he brings me to another orgasm—this one taking a little longer now that my clit is nearly numb.

Then, finally, I feel him—all of him. *Just* him. No condom. No barrier. He slides into my wet heat, skin on skin and stretches me until he's buried deep and all the fires that had died to embers only moments ago ignite into an inferno.

The things he says as he makes love to me....

"You're so goddamn beautiful."

"You feel like fucking satin."

"Your pussy is perfect."

"You, Penelope Hart, are perfect."

The way he touches me...

Thumb brushing my temple.

Fingers digging into my hips.

Hips rolling to meet mine.

Lips kissing my lips.

My jaw.

The tip of my nose.

The way he looks at me...

Like I'm precious.

I'm pretty.

I'm his.

Like he knows I love him.

Like he knows that I know he loves me too.

All these things are what make this moment as terrifying as it is special. Because I'm not sure where we go from here. What we are beyond...this.

Two people making love in a way two people shouldn't, unless they're ready to commit to something greater. But can he commit? Will he? Or will I be forced to give him an ultimatum? To demand that he tell me how he feels so that we can take the next step, or I walk away because I can't be with him if there's only this.

"Stop thinking, Penelope." Jake's demand is delivered with a swivel of his hips that has me temporarily forgetting who the fuck I am. When I remember, he pushes my knee toward my head and I let out a low moan. But I'm still thinking. And I'm pretty sure he knows what I'm thinking. And for some reason, I want him to know that I'm not going to just let this go. That we're going talk about all this shit that's not being said.

My eyes flutter open and I meet his hooded gaze that is centered on me. I glance at his parted lips for a second before finding his eyes once again. His look begs me to forget. And I will—for now. But first, I tell him the same words Scarlet said in *Gone with the Wind*—sure that he won't get the reference, but will understand the meaning.

"Tomorrow. I'll think about that tomorrow. Okay?"

He smirks. Fucks me harder. And just before the pleasure consumes me and expels me from reality once again, he responds with the Jake Swagger version of Rhett Butler's infamous one-liner: "Frankly, my dear, I don't give a fuck."

CHAPTER TWENTY-SIX

The sound I make when Jake pulls out of me is a long, guttural song best described as a whimper-meow-snort-moan-moo-hiss.

I expect Jake to laugh. Chuckle. Smirk. Moo. Something. Instead he says, "I'll make it better, baby."

He sweeps my hair off my neck, fists it and tugs gently to reposition my head so he has better access to my shoulder. Then he trails kisses over the exposed skin all the way to my ear.

"Bath or shower?"

I grunt.

This time, he does chuckle. "My choice then?"

Grunt.

"Bath it is." He stands and reaches for me, then pulls me from the bed and into his arms. He walks with me wrapped around him like a monkey. I inhale his scent. Soap. Clean. Masculine. Rich. *Gah, Penelope. Could you be any more shallow?* Probably not. But rich has a smell. And it's Jake Swagger.

I open my eyes and the side of his strong neck stares back at me. A single, thick vein pulses beneath his skin. Stubble darkens his flawless flesh. I have the urge to stick my tongue out and lick it. When I do, I find my tongue is too short and I'm too lazy to get closer.

I have to pee.

The urge is so sudden and so strong, I clench everything to keep from giving him a golden shower. Jake tightens his hold in response. Which only adds to the pressure on my bladder.

And if he presses any tighter....

Oh dear Lord, please don't let me pee on this man.

Jake kisses my brow and the tiny hairs on his chin tickle my nose. He's in a giving mood because he skims his lips over my temple. Those hairs still tickling. Now I want to sneeze.

And if I sneeze....

Oh dear Lord, please don't let me sneeze and pee on this man.

We're climbing stairs now. I forgot this suite had a second level. It houses the master suite. And adjoining the master suite is the master bath.

Which is where he's taking me.

Because I stupidly let him choose a bath over a shower.

And the only bath is upstairs.

And with every step, my bladder feels like it's being tossed around like a hacky sack.

I think he's doing this shit on purpose.

And if he doesn't stop....

Lord. It's me again. Please teleport us to the closest toilet so I don't pee on this man.

"What are you praying about?"

Why can't I do anything right?

My eyes close and I say nothing.

There is no damn way it takes this long to get to a damn bathtub.

Jake slows his stride. "Talk to me, gorgeous."

"I'm about to pee all over you if you don't get me to the bathroom."

He stills for just a split second before picking up his pace. "For fuck's sake, Penelope. You could've just told me that instead of praying about it."

"Yeah? Well it wasn't something I wanted to admit."

"Well a golden shower is something I don't want."

"Then I suggest you—"

My words are cut off when he unceremoniously drops me on the toilet. The movement is more than my bladder can handle and I'm peeing the moment my ass cheeks hit the porcelain. When he straightens, I lift my eyes and one of his eyebrows sits halfway up his forehead.

"What? I told you I had to pee."

Hmm...I wonder if that's why my orgasm was so intense?

I believe it was Christian Grey who taught us that coming on a full bladder was better than coming on an empty one. Damn if he wasn't right.

Thank you, E.L. James. I am forever in your debt.

I'm still peeing. Jake has left me alone and shut the door behind him. This bathroom, like the one at his apartment, has a toilet that's separate from the rest of the bathroom. It even has a magazine rack. And an iPad. Which is fucking nuts because people like me might be tempted to steal it. But even with all its amenities, the small space is a little claustrophobic. And I'm curious about what Jake's doing.

I stretch my fingers and can just reach the door handle. I pull it open to find him standing with his hands on his hips, naked, looking down at the tub as it fills with water. My eyes zone in on the dark hair that makes a trail down his V.

I want to lick his abs.

His cock.

His fucking kneecaps if that's what turns him on.

"You don't think it's weird to pee with the door open?" he asks, a smirk on his chiseled, handsome, wonderfully fuckable face.

"Do you?"

"No. But women usually do. Then again, you're pretty unusual."

"I am that."

"How are you still peeing?"

I shrug. "Must have an enlarged bladder."

He groans. "Don't say enlarged bladder, Penelope."

"It's the appropriate medical term, Jake."

He levels me with a look. Miraculously, I stop peeing.

"What if I have a kidney stone?" No sooner does the thought cross my mind and I'm pulling the iPad out of the little magazine rack next to the toilet and typing my symptoms into the search engine.

"You don't have a kidney stone."

"Dr. Google says I have a kidney stone."

"Dr. Swagger says you had three glasses of champagne in the car before you took a really big cock that distracted you from everything other than the best orgasm of your life, which left you weak and resulted in the sudden awareness that you had to pee due to..." he snaps then shoots me with his finger guns, "...three glasses of champagne. Not a fucking kidney stone."

I just stare. And blink. Once. Twice.

Yeah. That makes more sense.

Of course I'm not going to tell him that. Instead, I kick the door shut because I want to read up more on the causes of my diagnosis—*bladder hypertrophy.* And because peeing is one thing, but a real lady doesn't wipe in the presence of others.

When I'm finished and have convinced myself that, despite what Dr. Google says, I'm *not* experiencing the final stages of renal failure, I move to stand. I end up sitting back down and having to attempt it again, then again, before I'm steady on my feet.

I'm contemplating whether to put my foot on the toilet to get a better look at the damage to my vagina, then asking Dr. Google what he thinks when the door opens.

Jake eyes me. Clearly amused. "What are you doing?"

"Well, I'll tell you what I'm glad I wasn't doing, considering you just barged in here without knocking."

I'm being serious. But he's fighting a smile. Eventually, he gives in and it spreads across his face. "Come on, pretty girl. Your bath is ready." He takes my hand and I float behind him. He could be leading me to the edge of a cliff. Off the side of a bridge. Into Hell's fire and I'm pretty sure I'd willingly go. All because he called me pretty.

I'm such a sucker.

And he's added another "must have" to *That Guy's* list.

The lights are dim. Soft music plays—barely audible over the hum of the Jacuzzi jets. Candles line the edge of the tub. I breathe deep, inhaling the lavender-scented bath oil and a quiet peace settles in my soul.

There are few times in my life when I've had no desire to speak. This is one of them. I want nothing, not even the sound of my voice, not even the sound of his, to threaten the tranquility of this moment.

But then he speaks.

I answer.

And the moment becomes even more perfect.

"You're beautiful when you're happy."

"I'm always happy."

"You're always beautiful."

I swoon so hard I'm sure the floor would meet my face if Jake's hands weren't settled on my hips. Big hands that slide up my sides. Masculine hands splay across my stomach. Greedy hands palm my naked breasts as if not doing so would be a sin.

Jake places my hand in his and lifts it to his mouth. He kisses the tip of every finger. Burning me with those gray-green-blue eyes as he leads me to the one spot on the tub that isn't decorated with candles.

The water is hot, but not unbearably so. I try to stifle a whimper as I submerge myself into the heavily oiled bath, and find it impossible. My lower lip quivers slightly and I breathe out a half sob/half moan.

Even with my eyes closed, I'm aware of Jake standing next to me. I want to look, but looking is what got me here in the first place. The last thing I need is for my greedy vagina to override my brain once again.

Jake's big body folds around mine. My hands rest on his powerful thighs as he settles behind me and leans me back against him. He dips a sponge into the water then holds it over my breasts and squeezes it—wetting my chest before caressing the skin there.

After he's done this several times and I'm borderline comatose, he threads his fingers through my hair and massages my scalp. I breathe through my nose. Inhaling the scent of lavender into my lungs and feeling its soothing effect spread through my body.

I don't even realize I've drifted off to sleep until I'm startled awake by those fingers that are no longer on my scalp, but instead skimming the tender lips of my pussy.

"Relax," he soothes, dragging his nose along my hairline. "I love the way you smell."

Did he say love?

He said love.

This is the second time.

I said I'd wait until tomorrow.

But I can't help it.

I have to ask.

"I'm making you fall in love with me, aren't I?"

Jake Swagger doesn't scare easy. Nor does he stop the pad of his finger from moving up and down my slit. But he is easily amused. The low, deep rumble of laughter against my back proves it. "How sore is your pussy?"

Really?

"Talk about ruining a moment..."

"I didn't realize we were having a moment. Answer my question."

"What question?" I ask only because I like the way my spine tingles when he says, "Pussy."

He must know. He does that low laugh again. Then he slides his finger between my lips and pushes the tip inside me. I'm swollen and tender and wet and not just from the water. Lips at my ear, he whispers the question again. "How sore is your pussy, Penelope?"

I want to say something sexy. Or maybe something that will get me some sweet attention like my whimper-meow-snort-moan-moo-hiss got me this candle lit bath. But that hardening redwood tree at the small of my back dissuades me.

"It's sore."

"Hmm." He hums against my ear. "Deliciously sore?"

"What? No. There's no such thing as deliciously sore when you're referring to a completely destroyed pussy."

He groans and rocks his hips against me. "Don't say pussy, Penelope."

"That's what you said when I called it a vagina."

"Well, hearing you say pussy makes me want to lift your pretty little ass on my lap and sink my cock into your sweet, swollen cunt."

"My sweet, swollen, *destroyed* cunt."

"For fuck's sake, woman."

"What? All I said was—"

"Don't. Stop talking. Just be quiet and be still and I'll try to make this as painless as possible."

He lifts me onto his thighs and I panic a little—grabbing the sides of the tub and trying to pull out of his embrace while mumbling a shaky, "No, Jake. Stop. I can't."

"Easy, baby." His words are so soft. Laced with a tenderness and a hint of regret. "I'm not trying to fuck you." He kisses that same path from my shoulder to my neck that he tends to do a lot. And just like every other time, it melts me. "I only want to finish what I started."

What the hell does that mean?

I figure it out when he grabs the sponge and slides it over my sex that is now only partially underwater. And he...

Wow.

Yeah.

Most heroes treat their heroines to a warm towel after sex. Or a T-shirt. Or they leave them sticky so they'll smell like them. Which is just fucking gross.

But Jake Swagger?

He's an overachiever.

I got a bath. Candles. Scalp massage. And a friggin' vaginal cleansing. He's cleaning me in the most delicious, intimate way. Granted it's probably more out of guilt for ravaging my pussy rather than the desire to be sweet.

"Why are you doing this?"

"Doing what?"

I sweep my hand around the room then down my body. "This."

"Taking care of you?"

My heart skips and I can't speak. So I simply nod.

"I'm doing this," he mirrors my hand sweep motion, "because I told you I'd take care of you. I'm a big man who's not gentle during sex. Never have been. I should've taken it slow with you. Been easy. Denied you even when you begged. But there's something about your wicked little body that makes me lose control."

He holds the sponge over my sex and squeezes it. The water feels like satin as it cascades over my bare slit and his lips are just as soft when he trails them from my neck to shoulder.

"I love how you take all of me. How you scream my name when you come. How sweet you taste. I can't resist you. I always expect you to deny me, but you never do. You let me take what I want. Trust I'll make it good for you. This is me not breaking that trust."

Oh my God that is just...beautiful.

And of course I have to say something to fuck it up.

"I forgot to ask, but now that I'm thinking about it, you don't have any diseases, do you? Because you didn't wear a condom. And if I start itching in places I shouldn't itch...well...I mean, that's going to break my trust."

He chuckles. "You really know how to ruin a moment."

I spin to face him—sloshing water over the side of the bathtub but too excited to care. "We were having a moment?"

"Not one I care to remember now that you've talked about itching. And to answer your question, no. I don't have any diseases." He must think I'm about to say something else stupid because he quickly changes the subject. "How about a toast?"

He grabs two glasses from beside the bathtub, then hands me one with a wink. "Wine. Because I know how much you love it."

I roll my eyes. "You know I hate wine."

"Humor me."

I sniff it like I know what I'm doing. It smells good, but I wrinkle my nose just to be a jerk. "What are we toasting?"

"Whatever you want."

His eyes twinkle. I want to toast to love. To us. To marriage and kids and growing old together. But that seems a little heavy for this moment. Besides, I promised I'd wait and think about it tomorrow.

So I smile, lift my glass and toast the next best thing.

"To staying positive and testing negative."

CHAPTER TWENTY-SEVEN

"Aww...how sweet."

Jake grunts and I crack one eye open to see Cam sprawled across the foot of our bed smiling at us. I smile back because...well because I'm fucking happy. Like, I didn't even know happiness until I knew Jake Swagger—who sits up suddenly and looks over me to make sure I'm covered from Cam's view.

I warm all over.

"How the hell did you get in here?" Jake grumbles, falling back on his pillow as he tightens his hold on me.

"I have my ways."

"You mean you charmed the housekeeper into letting you in."

"That's exactly what I mean." Cam tickles my feet and I kick them away from him—planting my heel into Jake's shin.

"For fuck's sake...Cam go away so we can get up."

"You mean so Penelope can get up without me seeing her naked."

"That's exactly what I mean." Jake kicks his foot out but before it makes contact with Cam's crotch, he moves and strides out of the room—whistling some tune like he's the happiest person in the world.

He's not.

I am.

I actually feel sorry for everyone who woke up this morning and wasn't me.

Seriously. I feel sorry for you.

"Sorry, baby." Jake's lips on my naked shoulder have fireworks exploding in my chest. And groin area. I turn and snuggle into him. He buries his nose in my curls and inhales. "Your hair smells so good."

"You should smell my breath."

I feel his smile. "So no good morning kiss, I presume."

"Not a chance in hell. At least not until I brush my teeth."

He pats my ass. "Well go brush your teeth, gorgeous. I'll have Cam order room service."

I ease out of bed and pad to the bathroom. "What's he doing here anyway?" I call over my shoulder.

"We have a nine a.m. conference call with an overseas distributor."

"Couldn't he do that from Chicago?"

"He could. But Cam never does anything the easy way."

I pause my brushing when he walks into the bathroom. He strokes his morning wood and winks at me. Then he graces me with a view of his toned ass as he walks to the toilet.

He's peeing.

I'm brushing my teeth.

It should be weird, right?

It isn't.

"Is he your assistant?"

Jake snorts. "Ask him."

I make a mental note to do that then rinse my mouth. Wash my face. Wrap myself in the hotel's complimentary bathrobe that I think I'm going to steal.

When I turn, Jake is there. Framing my face with his hands. Kissing my head. My lips. He pulls away and I'm thankful he didn't try to stick his tongue down my throat. Because he hasn't brushed yet. And I have a weak stomach in the morning.

"Everyone decent?" Cam doesn't wait for an answer as he pushes his way into the bathroom. He's not bothered by Jake's nakedness, but he does look a little disappointed that I'm fully covered.

"I ordered breakfast. A little bit of everything. Wasn't sure what you liked."

"Thanks. Are you Jake's assistant?"

He throws Jake a look that suggests he'd kill him if there weren't any witnesses. Jake only laughs. Neither answer the question. It's completely forgotten as Cam announces the time and Jake curses beneath his breath and throws a towel around his waist.

With a final kiss—this one a little deeper because now Jake is minty fresh—I leave them to their call and go in search of breakfast. I follow the scent of bacon until I come to a dining room with a table big enough to seat eight. And every inch of it is covered in food.

I wonder how it got here so fast. But the thought is fleeting as I uncover steaming plates of pancakes. Bacon. Eggs. French toast. Sausage. Ham. I don't make it further than that. I don't bother with a plate either. I just eat straight from the platters.

As I eat, I plan how I'm going to tell Jake I love him. By the time I'm full, I decide I'm just going to blurt it out and see what happens. In my head, it goes down like this.

I tell Jake I love him.

He says it back.

We kiss.

He drops to one knee.

Gives me the ring he bought right after he first met me and knew that he couldn't live without me.

We skip a big wedding.

Drive to the courthouse.

Get married.

And become the envy of every human on the planet.

Perfect, right?

I'm anxious. And I have a reception to plan. So I make my way back upstairs and pray that the conference call is over.

Jake's voice can be heard the moment I reach the second floor landing. The sound of it—deep and rich with an undercurrent of authority—makes my heart pound faster. Steps feel lighter. Breath heavier.

The call ends just as I make it to the partially closed door. But when Cam says my name, I stop. I eavesdrop, like I know I shouldn't. But just like anyone in my situation would.

"And what about Penelope?"

Through the crack in the door, I see Jake's shoulders rise and fall with a shrug. "What about her?"

"You going to take her with you? To Africa?"

Jake snorts. "Penelope? In Africa? Fuck no. Can you imagine the destruction she could do to a place like that?"

Um. I could do Africa. I like lions and shit.

"Have you told her you're even going?"

"I mentioned it."

True.

Jake—ever the philanthropist—plans to take his fancy sprinkler system to Africa. Not to sell, but to give so that villages there can more effectively grow crops. He told me this while lying in bed last night. He also said it was something he planned for the future. I assumed months from now—maybe even years. But Cam speaks as if Jake's leaving a lot sooner than that.

"So when you mentioned it, did the two of you talk about what would happen when you're away? Or what will happen when you get back? Are you going to stay in touch?"

Jake lets out a laugh as he closes the file in his hand and tosses it on the bed next to Cam. "Who are you? My therapist?"

"I'm your best friend. And I won't sit back and watch you throw something good away because you're too fucking stubborn to acknowledge it's worth."

Fucking Cam. I love him.

"Look, I like Penelope. Hell, I may even care about her. But..."

There's this sinking feeling in my gut. This tightening in my chest. My knees are wobbly and my hands sweaty. I swallow the lump in my throat and wait for the rest of what Jake has to say—something that, whatever it is, gives him pause.

Jake's phone chimes with an email notification. Cam snatches it from him and holds it out of reach. "But..." he urges, demanding Jake give him an answer.

"For fuck's sake, Cam. I live in Chicago. She lives in Nowhere, Mississippi. It is what it is. I mean, we can stay in touch. She can visit whenever she wants. We can have a good time, then go back to our lives. No strings attached."

Cam scoffs. "Do you fucking hear yourself? No strings attached? Come the fuck on..."

"What? I'm not looking for a fairytale, Cam. And to be honest, I'm not so sure Penelope is either. Casual is good for us. Fucking perfect. Think about it. Who wouldn't want a relationship like that?"

Um.

Me.

CHAPTER TWENTY-EIGHT

Remember those five stages of grief my mother goes through when she calls me? Well, I think that shit is hereditary.

Step 1: Denial.

Jake never used the word *casual.* I, obviously, heard him wrong. Because if he thought of us as casual, he wouldn't have walked downstairs—where I'd escaped to after I heard what I clearly never heard—pinched my chin with his fingers. Lifted my head. Kissed my lips. Then mouthed, *beautiful.*

Other than the designer labels, there was nothing beautiful about my outfit—boots, jeans, scarf, awesome-ass long sleeved shirt with thumbholes. Or my messy-bun hair. And while my makeup was on point, I wouldn't call it beautiful.

But God I felt beautiful when he grabbed my hand. When he rubbed his thumb over my knuckles as we walked down eighteen flights of stairs. When he kept his hand on my thigh the entire ride to the airport. When he moved it only to hold my hand again as he pulled me from the car.

Led me to the plane.

Tucked his phone between his shoulder and cheek.

Strapped me in.

Grazed my temple with his finger.

Casual my ass....

Step 2: Anger.

Fuck Jake Swagger. Fuck him for thinking I can't handle Africa. Fuck him for referring to my hometown as Nowhere, Mississippi. Fuck him and his "no strings attached" comment. Fuck him for assuming I don't want a fairytale. And fuck him for ever mentioning the word *casual*.

Step 3: Bargaining.

God, please let this man love me. Take me. Marry me. And put his baby in me. Do that, and I promise I'll donate a bunch of his money to a charity once I gain access to his accounts. That's if he doesn't make me sign a prenup. So God, don't let him make me sign a prenup.

Step 4: Depression.

That's the stage I'm experiencing right now.

I glance up at Jake who sits like a king in the captain's chair of his sixty-million-dollar plane. He's dressed for business in his perfectly tailored dark gray suit. The only wrinkle on his body is the tiny one between his eyes—ever the CEO as he pounds furiously on the keys of his laptop.

The sight of him does crazy things to me. I feel like animals are doing shit in my belly. Butterflies flutter. Birds flap their wings. Fish swim. It's bottom lip-biting, grin-hiding good. Until, I remember what he said. Then it feels as if I've been stabbed in the heart by one of those big Texas Longhorns.

I can't be his Miss Sims. I can't be his Pretty Woman. I can't come to Chicago when it's convenient for him, let him make love to me, fall deeper in love with him, then wake up alone in his big bed with a stack of cash and a note next to me telling me he'll be in touch.

I move my eyes away from him and have to blink back tears. I take a couple deep breaths. Nothing helps. This emptiness...

Fuck.

I close my eyes against the pain. Will myself to move on to the next stage of grief—acceptance. But how can I accept this when my heart refuses to let go of the greatest love it's ever known? How can I move forward when the only future I want is sitting right across from me?

I ask myself these questions over and over as the plane lands. As we settle in the car waiting for us on the tarmac. As we drive through the busy city traffic. As Jake's hand stays firm in mine through the lobby of his apartment building and up stair after stair.

"Penelope? Did you hear me?"

I tilt my head to look up at Jake who has been on the phone since we landed. I'd tuned him out long ago. It was easy considering the thoughts in my head were screaming too loud for me to pay attention to anything else.

"Huh?"

"I said I have to go to the office. But I'll be back in a couple hours."

It's then I realize we're in his apartment. In the kitchen. I'm holding a glass of wine. And my calves burn like a bitch.

"Oh. Yeah. Sure. Okay."

He frowns. Takes a step toward me. Does that fucking thing with his fingers and my temple. "You okay, baby?"

I clear my throat and swallow my emotions. "Me? Yeah." I swat my hand in the air and force a smile. "I'm fine. Just tired from the flight. And the stairs."

His smirk is as cocky as it is relieved. "Think you'll ever ride in an elevator again?"

"One day. Maybe."

"You know, I could always buy a helicopter. There's a helipad on the roof." A look of dread crosses his face. "Even though I hate those fucking things."

"Then why would you buy one?"

He shoots me a look that suggests the answer is obvious. "For you, of course."

I melt like butter.

There goes all my "stages of grief" progress....

"You'd buy me a helicopter?"

"To keep from walking up all those stairs? Absolutely. Although, I'd have to find a song like your elevator song to keep me calm so I don't... what is it you say? *Lose my shit?*"

He winks.

I open my mouth to ask him to marry me.

His phone rings.

I hate that motherfucking phone.

"Yes, Sandra?"

My eyes narrow and I whisper shout, "Who the fuck is Sandra?"

"Assistant," he mouths.

I thought Cam was his assistant... Or maybe I just assumed that...?

He tugs my hair until my head falls back then dips to kiss the place where my neck meets my shoulder before he walks away, chatting with this *Sandra* about important things that require big words that I don't understand.

I will him to turn around. To ask me to go with him. To do something other than keep walking toward the door like I'm not even here. Because that sight—the one of him leaving—triggers something inside me. I don't like the empty feeling growing bigger and bigger as he gets further from me. Or that voice in my head asking if this is what it will always be like.

Him offering to buy me a helicopter.

Kissing my neck.

Making me swoon.

Then running off to his office.

Or Africa.

Expecting me to be here when he gets back.

Because that's what happens in a casual relationship.

But what about me? What about what I want? What about my life? My dreams? My home? I have a life too, you know? I do things. They might not be as important as saving the world with a sprinkler system and shit, but still.

Perhaps that's why I feel like I'm drowning. Because not once has he asked what I want. Every minute of every day we've spent together has been about him. His life. His career. Is my life that insignificant to him? Or does he just not give a damn?

"Jake?"

He pauses at the door. Tells *Sandra* to hold on a minute before tilting the phone away from his ear to address me. "Yeah, baby?"

Baby.

"Do you know who The Proclaimers are?"

"The band?"

I nod. "Yeah."

"I've heard of them."

"Well, you should listen to their Sunshine on Leith album. They have some songs I think you'd like. You know...for your helicopter fear."

"I'll do that."

He winks and his lips curve into a smile.

That smile...it's something to behold.

Something to remember.

To cherish.

But it's the sound of the door closing behind him, and the punch-in-the-gut feeling at my core, that brings me to this....

Step 5: Acceptance

Our story could've been a romance novel. I mean, we had the makings of something great—I found my *That Guy*. I fell in love. He did too....

We had the chemistry. The build-up. The sex. The sixty percent mark where we found out why Jake was a dick. Then he redeemed himself.

I had a damsel in distress moment.

He did all that sweet shit like the hair-tucking and the bath and the whispering of *shh, I got you.*

We danced. We dated. We laughed. We shared. We bonded.

I swooned. He smirked.

I fell. He caught.

I wore his shirt. He dressed me in it.

Yep. We had it all.

Almost.

Problem is, we're missing the best part...

The motherfucking happily ever after.

CHAPTER TWENTY-NINE

"**H**e's never coming for me! He's never going to call! He doesn't love me!" I fall across the bed next to Emily and bury my face in her shoulder. I need her to hold me. Instead, she pulls away and stands up.

"For crying out loud, Penelope. You've been home three hours. Chill out."

I know Emily is annoyed with me. Hell I'm annoyed with me. Running away without so much as a goodbye? That's typical heroine bullshit. And I pride myself on not being the typical heroine. But at the first chance I had, I ran. Now here I am—back home in Mississippi. Sad because I miss Jake. And angry because he hasn't come begging for me back yet.

What the hell is wrong with me?

Millions of women would kill to be casual with a man like Jake Swagger. Me? Noooo...I'm in *love*....

Why do I think my heart is so important? Who cares if it gets crushed? Jake is good looking. Great in bed. Rich. Smart. Fun. Sweet. How many people are married to men who aren't even half that?

Stupid heart.

But right now isn't about me. It's about Emily who needs to step up and be a best friend. If that means lying or doing something extreme to make me feel better, then that's exactly what she needs to do. But when I tell her this, she rolls her eyes.

"What do you want? Hmm? Me to fly to Chicago and set a bag of flaming dog shit on his porch?"

I don't even have to think about it. "Yes."

She leans against the dresser and narrows her gaze at me. Even after all these years, I still haven't gotten used to how creepy her crystal blue-gray eyes are when she squints like that. "You know what you are, Penelope? A hypocrite."

Shocked, I rise up to a sitting position. "Hyp-hypocrite? D-did you just call me a-a hypocrite?"

"That's exactly what I called you. And stop with the stuttering theatrics. There's nobody here but us." Bored, she takes a pull from her vape. She doesn't even vape. She's just doing it because it tastes like blueberries and she claims it helps curb her appetite. She also claims she needs to lose fifteen pounds. Which is ridiculous.

"How am I a hyp...hyp...I can't even say it." I cross my arms and look away from her.

She breathes out an exasperated—overly dramatic, if you ask me—breath, and pulls her long black hair over one shoulder. "You're mad at him for calling what the two of you had *casual,* but you never once told him you wanted more. You're mad because he didn't tell you he loved you. Even though you never told him. And you're mad he hasn't come after you. Yet you're the one who left without so much as a goodbye."

I know these things. These things are the truth. I know that too. Doesn't mean I want to hear it.

"Fine." I grab my keys and my phone and push past her.

"So you're going back?"

"No." I take the steps two at a time until I reach the garage.

"Then where are you going?"

I look up to find her leaning against the door of my apartment. Fighting a smile. Which solidifies my decision to do what I should've done when I first got home. "To find a new best friend."

————

I GLANCE over at the empty carton of Blue Bell Dutch Chocolate ice cream sitting on the coffee table and feel tears well in my eyes.

I ate my new best friend.

After I bought the ice cream, I came to my mom's house—which is literally in my front yard, since I live in an apartment above her work shed in the backyard. I planned to pout and sniffle until she asked what was wrong. Then I was going to tell her everything as she held me and stroked my hair. She'd say all the right things. We'd watch a chick flick. And my tear-soaked ice cream would be the result of someone else's heart breaking and not my own—because my sweet mother would assure me that Jake would indeed come.

Problem is, she wasn't home. So I was forced to eat ice cream soaked in my tears, shed over my own broken heart, all alone.

God I'm pathetic.

And what do pathetic people do? They get in their best fat clothes—a size 3xl T-shirt and threadbare stretchy pants—eat junk food and watch Pretty Woman, all alone, curled up on their mom's couch feeling sorry for themselves.

NINETY MINUTES later

"...SHE RESCUES HIM RIGHT BACK..."

"Oh, fuck off, Vivian. Nobody says that shit."

I throw a Funyun at the T.V. And when that doesn't make me feel better, I throw the entire bag.

"Whoa, kid. What did my T.V. ever do to you?"

My head jerks up from my crumb-covered pillow to find my Mom smiling down at me. All the anger and envy I'd built up toward Vivian and her ability to get Edward to chase her vanishes as a deep sadness sweeps over me. Tears flood my eyes and a choked sob escapes as I struggle to untangle my body from the covers and throw myself into my mother's arms.

"What's got you so upset, sweet girl?" I cry harder at the sound of her voice. It's controlled. Even. Soothing and soft, yet strong enough to penetrate my cluttered thoughts. She smells like cookies and apples and everything wonderful.

She smells like Mom.

"Jake wants casual and I want more and I left thinking he'd come for me and he hasn't."

I swear I hear her chuckle but when I pull back, I only see sympathy on her face. "Did you tell him how you felt?"

I just stare at her.

She sighs. Smiles. Smooths my hair out of my face and dusts the crumbs from my shirt. "Why don't you take a shower and I'll fry you something."

"I'm not hungry. I already filled up on Funyuns and beef jerky." I poke my lip out on a pout.

"And you smell like Funyuns and beef jerky. Which is why I suggested the shower."

Emily, who has been standing silent behind my mother, nods emphatically. She even goes so far as to scrunch her cute little button nose up and curl her lip in disgust.

I'm surprised Emily and Mom aren't happier that I'm back. We all know they couldn't make it without me. Who would Mom cook for? Who would make Emily laugh when all she's done lately is cry? They should be doing everything in their power to make me hate Jake—cursing him. Prank calling him. Threatening his life on social media. Or at the very least, starting a vicious rumor.

I think I need to find new people to comfort me. These two are only interested in pointing out my flaws. I mean, every girl with a broken heart deserves to fall apart. Especially the one who holds these two together. Why can't they just let me stink for a while?

"Fine. I'll shower."

"There's my girl," Mom says at the same moment Emily mutters, "Thank God."

I give her the evil eye as I pass. And just because she looks perfect and maintained good hygiene during her breakup, I can't refrain from breathing my hot, onion-jerky breath in her face.

INSTEAD OF A SHOWER, I took a bubble bath. But that sucked because all it did was remind me of Jake.

So I cried.

When I got out, I put on one of Jake's shirts and a pair of his underwear—yes, I stole a pair of his underwear. But that sucked because they smelled like Jake and reminded me that he wasn't here.

So I cried.

I found my Mom and Emily in the kitchen. Laughing. Frying dill pickles. Dressed in matching aprons. Flour on their noses and cheeks. Like a happy fucking family. And it made me realize that maybe I wasn't needed around here as much as I thought. I felt like a third wheel in my own mother's home. And that made my walking out on Jake an even harder pill to swallow.

So I cried.

Ugly cried.

That finally got me some attention and soon I had my head in Mom's lap and my feet in Emily's while we sat on the couch and watched Jeopardy and ate pickles and pie and didn't get a single question right.

"How we doin'?" Mom asks, her voice low as she rubs my hair.

Fresh tears form in my eyes. "I think I made a mistake." The truth of those words hit me dead in my chest. My stomach twists. Heart falls to my knees. "I'm so stupid."

"You're not stupid, honey."

I twist my body to face her. "Yes I am. He was so perfect, Mom. Sweet and kind and funny and good in bed—"

"And rich," Emily adds.

I nod. "And rich. Like, Christian Grey rich."

Mom chooses to ignore the shallow rich comment. "So why did you leave?"

"Because I overheard him tell his friend that we were just casual. And that it was perfect. And that he didn't want more."

"Did you talk to him about it?"

"No." I drop my eyes. "I just left."

"Penelope Lane...you sound like the typical heroine."

"I know!" I cry, throwing my hand over my eyes. "What do I do now? I can't just call him or go back. That would be weird. And it would mess up my dream for him to do a *That Guy* move and miss me so much he comes to get me."

Knowing how much I need this, everyone agrees. Even though I can see their need to tell me I'm being stupid in their eyes.

Mom stands and pulls me from the couch. "You and Emily go out. Have a few drinks and see if you can't get your mind off of him."

I swipe the tears from my cheeks and nod so hard my neck hurts. "Okay. That sounds fun."

I look to Emily who shrugs. "Sounds pretty typical heroine to me."

Whatever.

CHAPTER THIRTY

Hiccup.

Throat cleared.

Eyes closed.

Three count.

"*Des...per...ado...o...o...o...*"

I suck in a breath after my killer opening, ready to amaze these people with my angelic voice that will no doubt have the angels in heaven green with envy and dreading the day I join their choir. But just as I'm about to belt out the next line, I hear a grumbled phrase from the crowd that is all too familiar.

"Oh for fuck's sake..."

I scan the eight hundred square foot karaoke bar to find the source of the male voice who used Jake's signature line and interrupted my song. The nearly bald, red-faced, overall wearing big guy in the corner looks like the type to get pissed over just about anything. So, no surprise he's mad at me because I'm awesome.

I motion to the guy running the karaoke machine to stop the song. When the music dies, I turn back to the man. "Um. Excuse me, sir. But I'm kinda havin a bad day." Hiccup. "The man I love wants us to just be casual. So I'm a little sensitive right now and I'm gonna need you to not be a dick, 'kay?"

My speech earns me a room full of sympathetic faces, three shots of cheap whiskey and a round of applause encouraging me to finish the song. So I let everyone feel sorry for me. Drink the whiskey. And nod to the karaoke guy to restart Clint Black's rendition of *Desperado*.

Deep breath.

Hiccup.

Eyes closed.

Three count.

"Des...per..." Hiccup. *"Ado...o...o...o..."*

"My fuckin' ears are bleeding."

This motha...

"Sir!" Everyone flinches at the squeal of the mic when I rip it off the stand so I can face the douche canoe who clearly doesn't know a legend in the making when he hears one. "Would you kindly shut the hell up and let me have my moment?"

Hiccup.

"Sure, sugar. Have your moment. Just don't sing."

I glare at him. "Singing makes me feel better."

"Makes us feel worse." His weak-ass comeback earns a few chuckles from the crowd of thirteen. Laughing along with them, he turns to Emily who sits alone at the bar. "Has she always been this bad of a singer?"

"She has."

Fucking Emily.

Hiccup.

"Can a girl have a broken heart? Please? Can I just sing like shit and drink cheap whiskey," hiccup "and hiccup and not have to hear any of y'all's criticisms?"

"You can do anything you want on that stage, girl. As long as it ain't singing."

Another round of laughs.

Another hiccup.

Another raised glass to toast the suggestion of my silence. Even Emily lifts her Green Apple Smirnoff.

What is she? A sophomore in high school?

"So let me get this straight." Hiccup. "I can't sing...on karaoke night... to help deal with what is possibly the worst day of my life...but I can do anything else? I guess if I took my clothes off for your pervy ass that would be okay."

Red-faced-asshole lifts his glass. "Hell yeah it would!"

"That's not going to happen."

The bar falls silent.

Every head turns.

Panties disintegrate.

Men wither.

I hiccup.

Jake Swagger is here. In a suit. Staring at me so hard—so intensely—my knees go weak and I have to cling to the microphone stand to keep myself upright.

He came.

He came!

Fuck he looks good.

So damn good.

Play it cool.

Play it cool.

I cross my arms over my chest, lift my chin and square my shoulders as I try not to crumble at the sight of those gray-blue-green eyes that level me through the cloud of smoke separating us. "Can I help you?"

"Maybe. I'm looking for a girl."

I can't keep the hope out of my voice. "You are?"

"I am." *That damn smile of his...* "Her mother told me I could find her here."

Aww...thanks, Mom.

"Right. Um. Well. Maybe you should've tried calling her."

"I have."

"No you haven't," I deadpan.

"Yes. I have. Seems she forgot to pay her cellphone bill."

You gotta be shittin' me...

"No. I'm not *shittin'* you."

Thoughts! Be silent!

"Why are you lookin' for her?"

"Because she ran out on me earlier today without so much as a goodbye."

"Typical heroine." I shoot Emily a look of warning. "What? It's true."

I pull in a breath and stand a little taller as I address Jake once again. "Well you must've done something," hiccup, "for her to just up and leave like that."

"You're right. Perhaps it was because I offered to buy her a helicopter."

Some drunk chick gasps. His eyes swing to hers and he shrugs all sheepish and shit. "I know. Too much?"

"Hell naw it ain't too much. You can buy me a heli-chopter."

Everyone laughs. Even Jake chuckles. And I have to clear my throat to get the attention back on me. *This is the Penelope show, damnit.*

"I doubt it was that."

Hiccup.

"Well maybe it was because she eavesdropped on a conversation I had this morning with a friend of mine."

Oh shit.

"Someone should tell her how rude that is," the drunk chick offers.

Jake nods. "Oh, I agree. And if my memory serves me correctly...," he glares at me "someone already has."

Hiccup.

"Are you finished yet? If not, I'd like to get back to my song."

"For the love of God, keep talking." Red-faced-overalls-asshole lifts up his praying hands to Jake.

Whatever.

"So my friend asks what the deal is with this girl and me. And I tell him that our relationship is casual."

A few murmurs from the women in the room have me wanting to fist bump the air. Luckily, a hiccup distracts me.

Jake holds his hand up. "Hang on, ladies. There's more to the story. You see, the only reason I said that was because I thought that's what she wanted."

"It wasn't what she wanted," I snap, then quickly add, "Maybe. I'm guessing. I don't know. I mean, why would you think that?"

"Because she never said she wanted more."

I snort. "Oh. So you just *assumed* without even bothering to ask her?"

"Well this girl..." he breathes out a laugh and runs his hand through his hair. "This girl is known for speaking her mind. She'll say just about anything. I've never had to wonder what she was thinking. Because if it crossed her mind, it came out of her mouth. Even when she didn't intend for it to." He grins at me. "Sound familiar?"

The air between the two of us starts to suffocate me. I want to end this bullshit banter, jump off this crappy little stage and launch myself into Jake's arms. I want him to hold me and kiss me and tell me he loves me. But even though I understand why he said what he said, and even though he's here, a part of me still wonders if it's possible for this guy—my very own *That Guy*—to love...*me.*

"Why did you run, Penelope?"

The entire room holds their breath as they wait for my answer. I consider lying, but my walls are crumbling. I'm exhausted. And drunk. And stiff from trying to hold my posture.

I let my shoulders slump forward and hold onto the mic stand. "I can't do casual, Jake." A weight I didn't realize I was carrying lifts from my shoulders.

"So tell me what you want." He says it so simply. But it's not that simple.

"I don't know."

"Yes you do. What do you want, Penelope? What do you want...what do you want!?"

Okay. Now I see why he found that scene so annoying.

He asks me again and I lose my shit and half scream/half sob, "I want the song!"

His head tilts slightly as he studies me. "Your elevator song?"

Hiccup. Sniff. Snort. Deep breath. "Yes. I want a guy who will walk five hundred miles for me."

"I've walked five hundred miles five times over going up and down those fucking stairs with you."

Truth.

"Well, I also want a guy who will wake up with me every day. And some of those days may not be in his penthouse apartment overlooking Chicago. They might be in *Nowhere, Mississippi,* in a one-bedroom apartment, above a workshop, overlooking my mom's backyard."

He shrugs. "Done."

It can't be that easy.

"We live a thousand miles apart."

"We'll figure it out."

"I'm not always going to want to go to your business meetings to win you clients."

I'm grasping at straws here....

He smiles. "Then you can just go for the alcohol."

"You don't even know anything about me."

"I know everything about you. Background check, remember?"

Shit.

"I know nothing about you."

He lifts a brow.

Hiccup.

"What are you so scared of, Penelope?"

Fuck it.

"I don't want to love someone more than they love me."

"Not possible."

"I'm not easy to love, Jake."

His deep, rumble of laughter can be felt in my toes. Then, in a voice as equally sincere as his gaze, he tells me a truth that rocks my damn soul. "Loving you is the easiest thing I've ever done."

Oh. My. God.

Is this were a book, that would be the most highlighted line in it.

"I love you, Penelope Lane Hart. You're my *That Girl*."

I'm not sure how long I've been standing here swooning, just feeling my ovaries explode inside me and my heart swell to the point of bursting. But it's long enough for Jake to grow annoyed.

"For fuck's sake, Penelope. Are you going to say it back or not?"

"Oh. Yeah. Right. I lo—"

Hiccup.

"Shit. Let me start again." And as easy as I breathe, I tell him, "I love you too, Jake Swagger."

He smiles. Like God just granted him the greatest gift in the world. Well, I mean, he kinda did.

"Get your ass down here and kiss me."

I do. Nearly break my neck in the process, but he catches me. Because that's what he does.

Then he kisses me.

And it's just like all our kisses—hot, sweet, toe-curling perfection.

I've missed him.

I love him.

He knows it.

And guess what?

He loves me too.

Jake dips his head and places his mouth at my ear so he can be heard over the cheering bar crowd. "So what happened after he climbed up the tower and rescued her?"

This motherfucker...

I'm not Vivian. He's not Edward. This isn't Pretty Woman. This is a story about a writer who found her muse. Her *That Guy*. Who ended up falling in love. Running from love. And, of course, trusting that love would come chasing after her.

Totally cliché.

And every bit as real as any story can be.

But our story doesn't end with the words, *and they lived happily ever after.* And it sure as shit doesn't end with some lame ass line about how she rescues him right back. Matter of fact, there are no words at all. Because words can't express the love and shit we feel between us.

So I pull away and give my *That Guy* what he wants—the beginning of our future and the ending of this story in true Penelope fashion.

Finger snap.

Finger guns.

River dance.

EPILOGUE

Cam

L ove is an enigma.

You never know when. You never know who. You never know how.

It just happens.

Thank fuck it's never happened to me.

I can't imagine being the pussy-whipped, cloud-floating, emasculated, river dancing vagina Jake has become. Don't get me wrong, I'm happy he's happy. But I miss the days when he used to walk away when Penelope called. Or at the very least, cover his mouth in an attempt to shield me from the *you hang up first, no you hang up first* bullshit banter between the two of them. It gave me hope that my friend still had his balls.

But it's been three months since he confessed his love to his woman in a bar somewhere down in Mississippi. Now, he doesn't even try to be a man. And I'm pretty fucking sure if he does still have any balls, they're not hanging below his dick. They're tucked neatly inside Penelope's purse so she can take them out and squeeze them whenever she feels the need to remind him who's in charge.

Shit's gotten so bad that I look forward to the days when they fight.

Like today.

"For fuck's sake, Penelope. I said no."

In the quiet of the car, I can hear her response clearly through the phone.

"You have plenty of money. It's not like you're poor."

"No. I'm not poor. Because I go to work every day. And I do have plenty of money. But I won't if you keep trying to give it away."

"If I don't make good on my promise to God and he makes me die a horrible death, that's on you. Until then, me and my vagina will be in the guest room."

"Don't say vagina—" He stares down at his phone. "She fucking hung up on me."

"Imagine that."

"She claims she made a deal with God and now she has to give money to charity. *My* money. And she thinks everyone is a charity case. Right now, she's trying to give one of my Rolexes to Alfred. Do you have any idea how much I pay that old man? Trust me. He can buy his own fucking Rolex."

"So did she give him the Rolex?"

He sighs. "Probably. She's always doing crazy shit like this behind my back."

I laugh. As much as I'd hate to deal with a girl like Penelope on a regular basis, I can't deny that she's perfect for Jake. He needed someone to ground him. She needed someone to love her. The two of them could play the leading roles in one of those *Boy-meets-girl-love-at-first-sight-*romance-novel-turned-movie.

"Did I tell you that her and my grandfather went to play laser tag last week? Fucking laser tag. He's never done shit like that with me."

I look away. "I had no idea."

"You went too, didn't you?"

"Maybe..."

"You son of a bitch."

"What? It was Penelope's idea. And say what you want, but that girl is fun to hang out with. We would've invited you but you're too competitive. Nobody wants to play with a sore loser, Jake."

"You probably helped talk her into begging me to go to Africa too, didn't you?"

I shake my head. "Hell no. You were right. Penelope in Africa would be a complete clusterfuck."

"Good. Because she's not going. I put my foot down with that one."

I snort. "Yeah. Clearly you run shit."

The car comes to a stop in front of Jake's apartment all too soon. "And, just so you know, I'm not looking forward to entertaining myself while you spend the next five minutes fighting with Penelope. And then the next hour having make up sex. But we have business to handle this evening that can't wait. Or else I'd let you go in alone and find my own woman to piss off just so I could fuck her until she forgot why she was mad in the first place."

"We're not having make-up sex."

"That's what you always say."

"I mean it this time."

"Sure you do."

"I'm going to propose."

My hand stills on the door.

Wasn't expecting that.

Jake pulls something from his pocket. When he opens the velvet box in his hand, I have to squint against the light reflecting off the biggest goddamn rock I've ever seen. I lift a brow and meet his gaze. "You sure about this?"

"Never been more sure about anything in my life."

He doesn't look the least bit anxious. There's no room for uncertainty in his eyes because those motherfuckers are just *brimming* with love. And as much as it pains me to admit it, I couldn't be more proud of him.

I lean in to give him one of those one-armed man hugs. "Congratulations, man."

"You'll be my best man?"

I pull back and smirk at him. "Planning the wedding already, are we? What next? You going to ask me for a tampon or to braid your hair?"

"Fuck you." Grinning—like a man in love—he snaps the box closed and tucks it inside his jacket.

"Yeah. I'll be your best man. *If* she says yes."

"She'll say yes."

"You never know..."

"Cam." He levels me with a look. "We're talking about Penelope. She's been planning our wedding since she broke into my house. I'm surprised she hasn't proposed yet."

I'm still laughing at that when the door opens and Alfred greets us. My eyes fall to the Rolex on his wrist and I laugh harder. The noise attracts the attention of a woman as she walks out of the lobby. She bats her lashes and I give her a onceover.

She's everything I look for in a woman. Blonde. Tall. Sexy. Flirty. Confident. I give her my sideways smile the ladies call irresistible. When she licks her lips, I know I can have her if I want her. But the look of disapproval I get from Jake distracts me and before I can get her number, she's gone.

"What?"

"You need to settle down."

I stare at him. "Are you fucking with me right now?"

"No, Cam. I'm not. You're twenty-seven. It's time."

"And you're thirty." I clap him on the shoulder as we step inside the elevator. "Which means I have three years left of doing who and whatever I want before I offer my balls to a woman. The same woman. For the rest of my life."

He smiles. "When you find the right woman, it'll be worth it."

"You've been watching Oprah. Or Dr. Phil." When he doesn't confirm or deny, I narrow my eyes at him. "You have, haven't you?"

He mumbles something I can't understand.

"What was that?"

"I said, I don't watch that shit."

"Not even Ellen? Hell, I watch Ellen."

He shoots me a bewildered look.

I shrug. "She's funny."

"Who are you?"

"Your best man. If she says yes."

"Would you shut up? She'll say yes."

"Who'll say yes?"

We both turn to find Penelope standing outside the elevator door, arms loaded with, what appears to be, Jake's suits.

"Are those my clothes?"

"Say yes to what?"

"Penelope, are those my clothes?"

"Jake, who are you asking a question?"

"Are you kicking me out of my own house?"

"Are you asking me to marry you?"

"For fuck's sake..."

"Yes! Yes! I'll marry you!" Penelope drops the clothes and leaps into Jake's arms. If he was mad about her ruining his proposal, he's over it. Because he's kissing her back with just as much fervor and heat as she's giving. So much that I look away to give them some privacy.

And that's when I see her.

Waves of black hair. Porcelain skin. Petite. Curvy. Shy. And looking up at me beneath long, dark lashes are two crystal gray-blue eyes that have my cock pounding in my jeans as hard as my heart pounds in my chest.

She's everything I don't look for in a woman.

Everything perfect I've never noticed.

I don't know when I've ever seen someone that's captivated me as much as she has.

I don't know how she does it.

I don't know who she is.

This—whatever this is I feel—just...happened.

"Cam!" Penelope's squeal knocks me out of my temporary fog and I brace myself just in time to catch her when she wraps her arms around my neck. "I'm getting married! To Jake! I said yes!"

I force my eyes away from the vision who is—whoever she is—and smile down at Penelope. "Congratulations, babe."

She rambles on some more shit and my eyes wander back to the girl who's staring back at me as if she's scared I'm going to bite her.

God I want to bite her.

Taste her.

Whisk her away to a deserted island so I can strip her down. Fuck her senseless. And make her scream my name in pleasure over and over without anyone hearing her voice or seeing her body but me.

"...You'll be walking her down the aisle..."

Damn right I will.

"...You two will look perfect together..."

Fuck yes we will.

"...Our wedding is going to be fucking epic..."

Their wedding.

Penelope and Jake's.

Not mine.

What in the goddamn hell is wrong with me?

"Emily, don't be rude. Say hi to Cam."

Emily.

She cuts her eyes to Penelope before glancing back up at me. She doesn't move and I wonder if I look as possessive and feral on the outside as I feel on the inside.

I try to relax and get a grip on these emotions that Jake somehow rubbed off on me, but when she flushes a deep shade of pink, my cock stiffens further and I groan.

"Yep. This is going to work out perfectly," Penelope announces, snapping and shooting her finger guns before shuffling her feet in a river dance. "Cam, meet Emily. She's gonna be your *That Girl*."

I grin at Emily. It widens when she flushes darker. So I offer her a real smile just to see her reaction and I swear she whimpers. It strengthens my confidence and I summon my charm. Ignore my pounding heart. Take a step toward her. She looks like she wants to take a step back but holds her ground and lifts her chin to keep those magnificent eyes on mine.

It makes me like her even more.

I take another step.

"I hate to break it to you, P, but Emily isn't *That Girl*." I reach out and tuck a lock of Emily's hair behind her ear—noting the way goosebumps break out across her neck.

"Oh yeah?" Penelope is pissed. I can only smile. "And why the fuck is that, *Cam*?"

"Because *That Girl* can be anybody's girl." I lock my eyes with Emily's. "But this girl?"

I wink.

And if I wasn't sure before, I know the moment she melts before my eyes that my next words are nothing short of the fucking truth.

"She's...*My Girl*."

ABOUT THE AUTHOR

I always feel so stupid writing about myself in third person. I mean, this is my book. It's not like someone else is writing this shit. So instead of saying, *Kim Jones is blah, blah, blah,* I feel like I should tell you about myself. But how I view myself isn't how others view me. I mean, that is if they view me as anything less than awesome. Which some of them do. But they don't count, so whatever.

Any who, I'm not going to talk about myself and tell you I'm from a small town in Mississippi and that I love dogs and I drink too much and smoke too much and all that. You can just find me on social media and decide who I am for yourself.

Find me on Facebook: kim.j.jones.7

And on the Twitter: @authorkimjones

Stalk me here:
www.kimjonesbooks.com
kimjones204@gmail.com

ACKNOWLEDGMENTS

Some of these are the same in all of my books. Some different. I should make a better effort at acknowledging people. But really, who the hell reads this anyway?

Last, last, last book.

LAST, LAST BOOK.

LAST BOOK.

this book

To God for giving me the gift of life, writing and an eternal love.

Reggie: All those nights spent in bed alone will be worth it one day. I hope. — YEAH... STILL TRYING HUN... **8 MONTHS LATER...STILL A SHITTY WIFE.** *better get you a new sandwich maker.*

Amy Owens: ~~Don't replace me. I'm trying like hell to be a better best friend. It's just taking a little while.~~ I DEDICATED THIS BOOK TO YOU, SO I'M OFF THE HOOK. **I'M STILL A SHITTY FRIEND.** *You know, I haven't gotten any better.*

Parents: We're gonna get rich one day, I promise. — I KNOW, I KNOW. IT DIDN'T HAPPEN WITH THE LAST BOOK, BUT THIS MAY BE THE ONE.

YEAH...THAT ONE WASN'T "THE ONE" EITHER. BUT....THIS MAY BE IT! <— *that wasn't it. But this one, I'm sure of it!*

Sisters: You'll be rich, too. ~~Maybe.~~ DEFINITELY. **DON'T QUIT YOUR JOBS...***really. don't quit.*

Katy: Thank you for loving my ~~Cook Marty.~~ **JINX.** *~~Jake.~~* Your encouraging words help to breathe life into my characters. **STILL DO!** *Yep!!!*

Aunt Kat: I don't think I could've done this without your continued support. **I LOVE YOU!** *so, so much!!*

Uncle Don: I never would've mentioned Aunt Kat without mentioning you—after all, I am the favorite...author. WHO ARE WE KIDDING? I'M THE FAVORITE NIECE, TOO. **STILL THE FAVORITE**... *I know, I know. I'm not supposed to tell anyone. But who reads this anyway? I know I'm the favorite.*

Natasha: ~~You held my hand. Well, in spirit.~~ I'M NOT EVEN SURE YOU KNOW ABOUT THIS BOOK, BUT I'M KEEPING YOU HERE ANYWAY. ;) **I FINISHED THIS MOTHERFUCKER!!!! YAY!!!!!!!** *You didn't do shit on this book! What is wrong with you? If it tanks, it'll be all your fault.*

Josephine: You owe me ~~87 88 89~~ *90* drinks. BY THE WAY... NOW THAT YOU'RE ENGAGED, I'LL NEVER GET THE BASTARDS. **STILL AIN'T MARRIED....SMH. STILL AIN'T GOT NO DRANKS.** *Y'all should seriously get your shit together. No dranks. No wedding.*

Sali: My first ever audiobook listener. I love you. I HAVEN'T READ THIS ONE TO YOU YET. BUT I WILL. **I DIDN'T READ THIS ONE EITHER. MAN... I'M SLACKING!** *Um, I read part of this one. And you responded with the right words—"I love it!."*

HNDW: This may just be the one that gets that Bahama bottom rocker. KEEPING MY FINGERS CROSSED! **HELL, CROSS YA FUCKIN' TOES TOO. THIS SHIT AIN'T WORKIN'!** *We'd be better off selling 4 Barrel's body and getting the money to go to the Bahamas.*

Hang Le: The cover—perfection. ALWAYS!! **STILL AWESOME!** *Hang... I did this one all on my own. But you taught me well. So thank you for that!*

Amy Tannenbaum: ~~Um...hang on. I'm checking my voicemail. Get back with you soon.~~ THIS IS BOOK NUMBER 5 WITH YOU AND YOU STILL TREAT ME LIKE A REDHEADED STEP CHILD. BUT CONSIDERING I STILL HAVE NOTHING NICE TO SAY ABOUT YOU IN THE ACKNOWLEDGEMENTS SECTION OF MY BOOKS, I GUESS I'LL LET IT SLIDE. **YEAH... I GOT NOTHING.** *Wow. I literally can't think of a single thing. I mean, who doesn't invite their favorite person to their damn wedding?*

Chelle Bliss: My a big thanks goes to you. For helping me figure out this damn Mac. You rock. I STILL CAN'T FIGURE IT OUT. BUT YOU'RE ALWAYS THERE TO ANSWER MY CALL!! ACTUALLY, I'M TALKING TO YOU AS I WRITE THIS. **STILL STRUGGLIN' WITH THIS MAC. AND YOU STILL ANSWERIN' THE PHONE!** *My love for you is like a flower... one that blooms beautifully for you to pick and give to someone when you've done something shitty. okay. That made no sense. But know I love you.*

Paul Kirkley: YOU ARE TOO FINE. THANKS FOR BEING SEXY! **YOU DIDN'T MODEL ON THIS BOOK...BUT YOU STILL SEXY.** *Still fine.*

Todd Jones: YOU MAKE MY LIFE HAPPY. THANK YOU FOR BEING HERE. AND MIXING ME DRINKS, GETTING ME DRUNK AND WAY BEHIND ON MY WORK. IT'S BECAUSE OF YOU I'M UP ALL DAMN NIGHT DOING THIS. **LOOKY LOOKY TODDY PODDY! I MADE IT TO NUMBER 11! SUCK IT, BITCH.** *I've decided that I'm the reason you're awesome. And when you're not, that's on Regg.*

FORGY: THANKS FOR MAKING ME RE-WRITE THIS BASTARD AT 65K WORDS. :) LOVE YOU! *Forgy, I still love you. Even though you never call me.*

ROSE HUDSON: WHATEVER I SAY ISN'T GONNA BE AS AWESOME AS WHAT YOU SAY....SO JUST KNOW I LOVE YOU AND I THINK YOU'RE PERFECT! *Rose. Secret <insert secret three letter abbreviation> thanks for being everything awesome. And marlboros.*

JESSICA HAM: I LOVE YOUR FACE! I'D TOTALLY SHARE MY HUSBAND WITH YOU. ;) <— *Yep. Still would.*

SLOANE HOWELL: I'M MENTIONING YOU BECAUSE YOUR GROUP HAS LIKE 5K PEOPLE, AND I'M GONNA SHARE THIS SHIT SO THEY THINK WE'RE FRANDS AND HOPEFULLY THEY'LL BUY MY SHIT. CAUSE I'M ALL ABOUT DEM DOLLAS!!!!! AND 3 ICE CUBES. *Sloane, you're a good friend. That's the nicest thing I'll ever say to you and I only say it in hopes that no one ever reads this and tells you about it.*

HOUSE OF WHORES: KEEP BEING NASTY BITCHES!

OLIVIA BROWN: I CAN'T THANK YOU ENOUGH. SO I'LL JUST PUT YOU A LITTLE SOMETHING HERE. IT'S ALWAYS GOOD TO HAVE FRIENDS YOU CAN CALL ONLY WHEN YOU NEED SOMETHING. ;) *All you doing is building a house. See? I didn't even call you on this book!*

Colleen Hoover—thank you for reading my book even when I couldn't get past chapter 3 in yours. Once I shit in your toilet, I'll consider you a true friend.

I'M FORGETTING SOMEBODY. I JUST KNOW IT. SO THIS ONE IS FOR YOU! PLEASE WRITE YOUR NAME HERE:_____

ALSO BY KIM JONES

The Saving Dallas Series:
Saving Dallas
Making the Cut
Forever

Standalone MC novels:
Red
The Devil
Devil's Love

Sinner's Creed Series:
Sinner's Creed
Sinner's Revenge

The Whore Series:
Clubwhore
Patchwhore
Cutslut

Made in the USA
Columbia, SC
09 October 2024

43379284R00150